*It was all Parker could do to remember he shouldn't be kissing Tess Kendrick at all.*

He'd never intended to act on the pull he'd felt toward the woman playing utter havoc on his nervous system. When he'd reached for her, he honestly hadn't been thinking of how badly he'd wanted to do exactly what he was doing now. Yet one touch of her lips to his, one taste of her and his thoughts had moved straight from offering comfort to how incredible she felt beneath his hands.

She would feel even more amazing in his bed.

The thought made him groan. Or maybe it was the feel of her perfectly molded to the length of him that pulled the sound from his chest. All he knew for certain was that wanting her threatened to overtake his common sense. His job was to protect her.

From himself if necessary.

Dear Reader,

Have you ever wished you were rich and famous? Have you ever wished you were a celebrity? Or royalty? Have you ever considered how you would handle being followed by paparazzi, or having everything you say and do scrutinized by the public? I've been fascinated by royalty for as long as I can remember; by their sense of duty, their intrigues, their lives of privilege. (When I was ten, I desperately wanted to be a princess. After all, no princess I'd read about then *ever* had to do housework.) I'd just never truly considered the invasion of privacy certain people must deal with until I started writing about the Kendricks. I'd still like to be rich. I'd like us all to be. But I think there's a lot to be said for being anonymous enough that our mistakes don't make the evening news.

Here's to *your* wishes!

Christine

# FALLING FOR
# THE HEIRESS

## *CHRISTINE FLYNN*

**♥ *Silhouette*®**

# SPECIAL EDITION®

Published by Silhouette Books

**America's Publisher of Contemporary Romance**

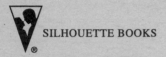 SILHOUETTE BOOKS

ISBN-13: 978-0-373-24816-2
ISBN-10:    0-373-24816-4

FALLING FOR THE HEIRESS

Visit Silhouette Books at www.eHarlequin.com

**Printed in U.S.A.**

**Books by Christine Flynn**

Silhouette Special Edition

*Logan's Bride #995
*The Rebel's Bride #1034
*The Black Sheep's Bride #1053
*Finally His Bride #1240
†The Housekeeper's Daughter #1612
†Hot August Nights #1618
†Her Prodigal Prince Charming #1624
§Trading Secrets #1678
§The Sugar House #1690
§Confessions of a Small-Town Girl #1701
‡The City Girl and the Country Doctor #1790
†Falling for the Heiress #1816

*The Whitaker Brides
†The Kendricks of Camelot
§Going Home
‡Talk of the Neighborhood

## CHRISTINE FLYNN

admits to being interested in just about everything, which is why she considers herself fortunate to have turned her interest in writing into a career. She feels that a writer gets to explore it all and, to her, exploring relationships—especially the intense, bittersweet or even lighthearted relationships between men and women—is fascinating.

For Tracy Horowitz,
my ever-so-organized cousin,
with thanks for a fabulous family reunion!
Just remember, what happens in Las Vegas,
stays in Las Vegas…

## Chapter One

Tess Kendrick balanced her three-year-old son on her hip and descended the steps from her grandmother's private jet. A hot summer breeze whipped the whine of aircraft engines around her, causing little Mikey to bury his head against her shoulder at the noise.

At the base of the stairs, a member of her grandmother's elite security service gave her a deferential nod while a uniformed steward quickly moved her luggage from the cargo bay to the trunk of a waiting black Lincoln SUV.

It had been over a year since the bottom had fallen from her world, a year since the scandal of her divorce had forced her into exile. Granted, that exile had been in a royal palace on the Mediterranean and her maternal grandmother, the queen of the tiny jewel-like kingdom of Luzandria, had been most gracious offering Tess and Mikey accommodation, but Tess couldn't continue to live in those gilded confines.

Isolation, homesickness and a desperate need to get on with her life had finally brought her back to Camelot, Virginia. The family estate outside the picturesque little town was where she had been born and raised. It was where her parents still lived, for part of the year, anyway. But most important of all, it was home.

"Do you require help with the child, ma'am?"

"Thank you, but I have him." She hoisted the towheaded boy clinging to her neck a little higher, adjusted the oversize bag hanging over her other shoulder. A massive case of nerves remained hidden by her soft smile. "And thank you for the escort. You've all been most kind."

The solemn soldier with the heavy French accent dipped his head in a deferential bow. "It was our pleasure to be of service, madam." He motioned her ahead of him. "I will see you to the car."

He hadn't smiled back. It was almost as if it were against the rules, the code or whatever it was the men trained to serve Her Majesty followed. Even as a child on summer visits to her grandmother with her siblings, it had seemed to Tess that smiles were allowed only by personnel in closest service to the royal family and their guests. Even then, any expression of friendliness had seemed subdued.

As much as she loved her grandmother, the formality of the palace was one of the reasons she'd become so restless to return. Though her basic nature yearned for less structure, she'd learned to live with propriety. Her energetic and endlessly curious little boy didn't need to suffer such constraints, though. His enthusiasm had been suppressed enough before they'd more or less been forced to leave the country. His father—her now ex-husband—had not only preferred that the child not be heard, most of the time he hadn't wanted him in his sight.

She hugged her precious son more tightly, her narrow

heels clicking on the tarmac as she moved quickly toward the waiting vehicle. Her prince had turned into a frog, her charmed life into a nightmare and her personal reputation had been totally destroyed in the process, but there wasn't a thing she could do to change that harrowing bit of history. She could only remind herself of the phoenix that rose from the ashes and hope that her singed wings would be strong enough to lift her back up. All she wanted was to forget the past few years, to buy a house and to go back to work on her project for the Kendrick Foundation.

If she'd had any idea how to restore her reputation, that would have been on her to-do list, too, but she couldn't figure out how to counter all the lies told about her without causing greater problems. The best she could do on that score was hope that people would remember her as they had known her, not as her ex and her silence had portrayed her to be, and that time would have healed the worst of the damage.

Certain time would never heal *some* wounds, she picked up her pace.

What people didn't know was that her marriage to Bradley Michael Ashworth III had disintegrated within the first year and that the fairy-tale life she'd appeared to be living had been a sham. Because she'd been raised to never say anything to anyone that might get passed on and wind up in print, she hadn't confided the difficulties in her marriage to any of her friends. Even her family didn't know how abusive the relationship had been. They knew only that Brad had promised a protracted and embarrassingly public divorce if she didn't take full blame for the demise of their marriage.

The divorce had been humiliatingly public anyway. But her family had no idea that had she not complied with Brad's wishes, he would have gone to the press with photographs he'd taken of her father with another woman. He'd even shown her some of the photos that would have sent the media into a frenzy scavenging for more dirt and completely broken her mother's heart.

The breeze loosened strands of her hair from the clip at her nape and blew them across her face. Smiling at her son as he pushed them back for her, she tried not to think of her father and reminded herself that the business with Brad was behind her. He now managed his family's property investments in Florida, so the chances of running into him were as remote as a sudden snowstorm in the Sahara. Same for most of the country-club set, which included his parents and other former friends. Most everyone she knew vacationed during the summer, so avoiding them shouldn't be a problem. Avoiding the public, however, was another matter entirely.

The steward from the plane hurried past, pushing Mikey's backpack and a half dozen suitcases on a rolling cart. As her escort joined him to load her luggage into the back of the SUV, her attention shifted to the six-feet three-inches of brawn and testosterone opening the back passenger door. Broad-shouldered, lean-hipped, he wore his dark suit and tie with an air of quiet power and watchful authority. Behind his dark sunglasses, she knew he was looking for potential trouble, which meant he was looking everywhere but at her.

He was her bodyguard from Bennington's, the exclusive security service her family had used for years. The female she'd requested—the former Secret Service agent who'd shadowed her through college—was on an assignment for the next two weeks. The no-nonsense mountain of muscle with the shaved head and the shoulders of a linebacker had been recommended by her brother, Cord.

She had never met Jeffrey Parker, but she recognized him from the photograph that had been e-mailed to her so she'd know he was indeed the man she'd hired and not an imposter bent on grabbing headlines or a slice of her family's fortune by holding her and her son for ransom. When she'd first seen his unsmiling image, he'd struck her as surprisingly handsome—in a formidably male, serious and decidedly ex-military sort of way. Now, other than to think him even more imposing than she'd anticipated, she was simply grateful for his presence. She and her siblings had been followed by paparazzi off and on all their lives. But she'd never been hounded as mercilessly by them as she had before she'd left last year. In that time, she had learned to truly appreciate a good bodyguard's ability to evade and avoid.

Cord had assured her that the man he'd referred to as "Bull" was the best.

He moved behind her as she reached the car, blocking her from view as she slid inside and lowered Mikey into the child seat he'd had installed. It seemed he'd no sooner closed her door behind her than he opened the door opposite and reached in to assist with her son.

His big frame filled the space as she reached to secure Mikey's shoulder straps. Her bodyguard had aimed for the same strap, too. With her hand suddenly trapped beneath his, her glance shot up.

His dark sunglasses had been pushed back so he could see inside the vehicle. The information sheet she'd been sent on him had indicated that his eyes were blue. There had been nothing in that dry recitation of facts, however, to describe the depth of that startling, clear color or to prepare her for their unnerving intensity as they easily held her own.

"We can do this," she assured him.

"I'll do it, ma'am."

"Really, we're fine…."

"We're not going anywhere until I know myself that the child is secured. You said you wanted your arrival to be as unobtrusive as possible. The sooner you let me do my job, the quicker I can get you out of here."

He hadn't moved his hand. Since it appeared he had no intention of moving at all, at least not until she did, she slipped her fingers from beneath his and edged herself back.

She hadn't been able to go anywhere before she'd left without a camera following her. That was why she had specifically requested that he make her arrival as efficient and discreet as possible. That he was only doing what she'd asked of him, however, did nothing to explain the wholly unexpected and unfamiliar jolt of heat she'd felt at the contact of his very capable-looking hands.

More than willing to blame that disconcerting reaction on her already jumpy nerves, she watched him smile at her wide-eyed son.

"How does that feel, buddy?" he asked. "Too tight?"

Eyeing him cautiously, Mikey shook his head.

The man looked capable of snapping body parts, but his smile just then seemed incredibly kind. The unexpected expression did interesting things to the aristocratic lines of his face, made them more arresting, more compelling. Though his hair was shaved so close it was impossible to tell its color, the heavy slashes of his eyebrows were dark, his lashes sooty and thick. The lines at the corners of his eyes crinkled, taking the coolness from that intense blue and allowing her son to see something that somehow invited a hesitant smile back.

Mikey rarely warmed to strangers. Especially large strangers like the guards around the palace who had ignored him, anyway.

Clips clicked into place. A quick check of the restraints' fit against Mikey's shoulders and the man's smile vanished. Within seconds, he'd backed out the door, shoved in the suitcases that wouldn't fit in back and closed the door with a thud.

Getting her out of public view and her son secured clearly had been his first priority. Only after he'd settled his big frame behind the wheel did he bother with the preliminaries.

He glanced into the rearview mirror. "I'm Jeff Parker, Miss Kendrick. But 'Parker' works just fine. My instructions say you want to go directly to your family's estate. Is that still your plan?"

Pure professionalism had replaced the unexpected bit of warmth she'd seen when he'd smiled at her son. Thinking that her brother was right, that the man could, indeed, appear pretty intimidating, she offered a determined smile of her own. "Do you know how to get there?"

Assuring her that he did, Parker turned his attention to the runway attendant waving them toward the gate. He not only had directions to the estate just outside the little town of Camelot, he had pulled as much information as he could find about Theresa Amelia Kendrick, once Theresa Amelia Kendrick Ashworth, off the Internet and from Bennington's files. He always made it a point to know who he was protecting. Just as he made it a point to research his surroundings.

His client's landing at the small regional airport near Camelot had caused none of the hassles that would have been created landing at Richmond International thirty miles away. Without masses of people watching runways from panoramic terminal windows, the arrival of a private jet went virtually unnoticed. Private jets and small craft were all that ever landed there. The royal-blue crest of Luzandria plastered on the jet's tail didn't do much for anonymity, however. Nearly everyone in America knew Luzandria was the country Katherine Kendrick would have someday ruled had she not given up her crown to marry then-Senator William Kendrick years ago. But the plane wouldn't be there long enough to attract much attention. It was already being refueled and readied for its turnaround back to Europe.

The member of the security team who'd handed over the Kendrick woman to him had told him that the jet flew with two full crews. That meant no layover was required for the inbound pilot and copilot to rest. The plane would be gone before anyone who noticed it could do much more than speculate about which member of the Kendrick family had arrived or departed. As quickly as the transfer from plane to SUV had been made, Parker felt certain his client's identity remained secure.

With his initial objective accomplished, he left the small airport by a back access road and glanced into the rearview mirror.

Tess Kendrick was stroking her son's pale hair, murmuring something to him that had the child giving her a tired nod.

She was taller than he'd thought she'd be. Thinner, too, in a willowy, waiflike sort of way, and even more striking than she'd appeared in photographs. Mostly she looked more delicate to him than he had expected. More…fragile, somehow. But he knew looks could be deceiving, especially among the rich and pampered. And pampered she clearly was. With shades of gold and platinum woven through her sable hair, her French manicure and the white, undoubtedly designer pantsuit that seemed totally impractical for a transatlantic flight with a small child, she practically screamed high-maintenance. And quiet sensuality.

She'd secured her shimmering hair back from the classic lines of her face, exposing the delicate lobes of her ears, the long line of her neck. The low cut of her jacket ended at the buttons between her breasts. An arrow of bare skin adorned with varying lengths of gold chains beckoned between the lapels. The longest of those shiny strands rested against a hint of cleavage.

Ignoring the tightening sensation low in his groin, he jerked his glance back to the road. He would admit that she was incredibly easy on the eyes, and the heat he'd felt at the contact of her impossibly soft skin when he'd found her hand beneath his had definitely caught him off guard, but he dismissed his body's primitive response as nothing more than a normal red-blooded male's reaction to a beautiful woman. A spoiled, childish woman ten years younger than his own hardened thirty-six years, he reminded himself.

Other than for her physical appeal, he wasn't impressed with his new client at all.

From what he'd heard, her bewildered husband had been as shocked as the rest of the world when she'd suddenly asked him for a divorce, taken his son and left the country. Bradley-Something-Ashworth-the-Whatever apparently hadn't had a clue there'd been any sort of problem. Even her friends—women she'd known since before college—had indicated nothing more substantive than that she hadn't seemed as happy as she once had. For her part, Tess had publicly refused to say why she'd wanted out. The press had found no clues in the couples' no-fault divorce petition, either. She'd left all the explanations up to her ex.

In his review of old news videos a few days ago, Parker had watched her yacht-club-type husband reluctantly confess to a barrage of reporters outside a courthouse that she had finally told him marriage bored her and that she didn't think she could ever be happy with just one man.

A guy had to feel for any man who'd married a woman like that.

Parker had a healthy respect for the state of matrimony—for everyone but himself. He was wedded to his work, and what he did for a living wasn't a job for a married man. Especially a married man with kids. It was his unfaltering belief that kids deserved to have their dad around, and he never knew where he'd find himself next. But the woman now resting her hand on her son's knee while she gazed out the tinted window beside her had made a promise when she'd married. A promise she'd broken because she'd been *bored,* he reminded himself with a mental shake of his head. Taking a guy's son and leaving him to deal with the public humiliation of her decision on his own was pretty low in his book, too.

The GPS on the dashboard gave a low ding, pulling his attention to the navigation system directing him to a turn up ahead. It wasn't his job to like her, he reminded himself. His job until the bodyguard she'd requested became available was to act as her driver and to protect her and her son from any of the public or paparazzi who might attempt to encroach upon her privacy. In his spare time, he would stay in touch by computer and cell phone with the tactical team he'd been promoted to oversee.

With everything else he had to do, he wouldn't have taken this additional assignment at all had her brother, Cord, not had her ask for him. He liked Cord, though. The man was a good client. He'd been his bodyguard on a few decidedly wild gambling jaunts to Las Vegas and Monte Carlo and one memorable trip to Cannes. He'd gotten to know the internationally infamous playboy over hands of poker in various hotel suites when Cord hadn't felt like hitting the clubs or playing high-stakes games with the other whales. He had even once provided protection for his ladylike sister, Ashley, and for Madison, the woman Cord had just married.

Having watched out for the other women in his client's life and being nothing if not loyal to those loyal to him, he would have felt a certain obligation to protect the man's kid sister even if his boss hadn't pretty much insisted that he take the assignment. The Kendricks were some of the firm's oldest and best customers. Since declining wouldn't have been the politically correct thing to do, that left him to do his regular job and keep up with the logistics for security surrounding an upcoming judicial conference in his downtime.

The drive from the little airport took less than ten minutes. Miles of open fields planted with peanuts and corn led to land that had been left forested to seclude the mansions and more modest residences of the local gentry. Like many of those homes, the Kendrick estate wasn't visible at all from the two-lane country road. A double iron gate suspended between stone pillars blocked the driveway itself.

Parker pulled to a stop beside the pillar concealing the entry keypad.

Tess leaned forward. "Twenty-four, sixteen, fifty-seven."

Aware of her settling back to cross her long legs, he punched in the security code, waited for the gates to swing open and pulled onto the long drive. The late-afternoon sun slanted through the trees lining the way, their leaves joined at the tops like the arches of a cathedral. With his window still down, he felt the change in the air, the coolness of the shadows, heard the distant whinny of a horse. The manse itself, all three gabled and mullioned stories of it, came into view as the road curved to the left.

The trees opened to a sweep of manicured lawns, a bubbling fountain in front of a wide portico and a view of enough windows to keep a Manhattan window-washer busy for the rest of his life.

A man didn't do what Parker did for a living without being exposed to a certain amount of extravagance. He'd protected clientele on yachts, in the world's finest hotels, on estates that rambled on forever. What impressed him about them all was the amount of staff it took, invisible for the most part, to keep the places running.

He fully expected to see staff now as he pulled beneath the portico, climbed from the driver's seat and opened the back door for his passengers.

The mansion's massive double doors stayed closed as he leaned forward to take the now-sleeping child from the woman who'd already unfastened and lifted him from the child seat.

"I'll carry him and his backpack," she said, "if you'll get the rest of the luggage. Here's my key." With the boy's head resting on her shoulder, she dangled a small gem-encrusted key ring toward him. "It's the silver one."

Thinking it odd that she didn't expect a butler or maid to unlock the door for her, he ignored her intention to slide out on her own and cupped her elbow as she rose. The slenderness of supple muscle beneath white silk barely registered before she thanked him, headed for the back of the vehicle and stood there waiting for him to lift the tailgate.

Her little boy hadn't moved. The child lay limply against her, drooling on the shoulder of her jacket. Fine blond lashes formed crescents against his pink cheeks.

Struck by how oblivious she was to the drool and still expecting someone to show up and help, he handed her a bright blue Harry Potter backpack and started hauling out enough designer luggage to stock a small boutique. Not quite sure how to tell her that playing butler wasn't part of the service, he grabbed four of the suitcases—one under each arm and one in each hand—and followed her up the rounded and sweeping stairs to the massive double doors.

Using the key she'd given him, he opened one door, picked up the luggage again and followed her inside.

"Just leave the bags here in the foyer," she said, "and come with me, please."

Her voice was hushed in deference to the sleeping child.

She clearly didn't want to disturb him. Or wait for Parker's response. The tap of her heels echoed on white marble as she crossed the edge of the malachite-and-onyx sunburst tiled into the floor and passed the circular table in the middle of it holding an empty urn.

In the dim light, his glance left her back to skim the curved arms of double staircases, the crystal chandelier centered two stories above the table and the various and vast rooms visible through the open doorways.

Dustcovers concealed much of the furniture. Lamps were dark. The drapes were all closed. Yet what he noticed most was the heavy stillness that indicated an empty house.

With the sudden and unwelcome feeling that this particular assignment might not be as straightforward as he'd thought, he followed her toward a narrow butler's door camouflaged by the paneling beneath one staircase and into a long equally dim hall.

They were clearly in the servants' wing. The white hallway and the utilitarian rooms off it had an infinitely more practical feel to them than the areas furnished with the velvet side chairs he'd noticed in the formal dining room or the ornate bombé chest in the foyer.

After passing two rooms with twin beds, she opened one that held a neatly made double bed and a dresser at one end and a desk and small seating area at the other. Lowering her son to the mauve tweed sofa, she pulled a brightly knit afghan off its back and settled it over him. Her motions seemed almost unconscious as she pulled off his shoes, tucked the afghan over his feet when he stirred, then gently touched his head as if to reassure him before slipping back into the hall.

Considering how totally unmaternal Parker would have expected her to be, her easy affection for her son surprised him. Or maybe, he thought, it was protectiveness he sensed in her. Whatever it was, he found himself far more interested in why her smile seemed so uneasy when she moved past him and into the huge—and deserted—kitchen.

He was wondering where the devil everyone was when she flipped on the overhead lights and illuminated a room filled with what looked like miles of counters and glass-fronted white birch cabinetry. Stacks of dishes gleamed through the glass panes. Copper pots glinted from the rack high above a white-tiled center island the size of a boardroom conference table.

"You can stay in the room where I put Mikey. It belongs to the head housekeeper," she said, her expression polite, her voice still low. "Rose is with my parents in the Hamptons for the summer. The rest of the staff is on vacation, too. Except for the stable master and his wife. They live above the stables. And the groundskeeper is in the cottage near the lake. Rose's room has its own bath, and you're welcome to use the pool and the exercise room downstairs if you'd like."

Tess watched a frown pinch the dark slashes of Parker's eyebrows as he glanced from her to the office alcove and the window above a table in the far corner where the staff took their meals. The man was difficult to read, a trait his profession seemed to demand, but he appeared far more interested in what surrounded him than in his personal accommodations.

In the space of seconds, it seemed to Tess that her paid protector had absorbed who was on the property, managed to take in the details of his immediate surroundings and just as thoroughly searched her. He'd no sooner noted the utility room leading to the back door than his scrutiny moved from the top of her head to the toes of her pumps. She could swear he'd missed nothing in between.

Had it not been for her brother's recommendation, she would have felt far more uncomfortable than she already did at that unapologetic appraisal. Those arresting features gave away nothing of his impressions.

Feeling totally disadvantaged, nerves ruined the cultured poise she constantly strove to achieve. That poise seemed to come as naturally as breathing to her mom and her older sister, but neither of them had been cursed with the inner energy she constantly battled to tame. Even fighting fatigue from a week's worth of sleepless nights stressing over her trip home, it was either pace or fidget. Since pacing seemed more dignified, she turned away to do just that. All that mute and massive muscle unnerved her, too.

"I assume you've done your homework," she began, hating the position she was in, knowing no other way to address it. "So I imagine you're aware of what was being said about me before I left."

She turned back, met his too-blue eyes. He stood ramrod-straight in the arch of the hallway, one hand clasping the opposite wrist. "The majority of it," he conceded.

Not caring to imagine what he thought of all that dirt, she tipped her chin, only to immediately check the motion. She couldn't allow herself to get defensive with him. She needed him on her side. More important than that, she desperately needed an ally.

It seemed a true indication of how much she'd lost that she'd had to hire one.

At the dispiriting thought, she resumed her pacing. "You've worked for my brother," she reminded him, arms crossed as she made her way up one side of the island, "so you know that people distort things to serve their own purpose. And you know that the press has a definite tendency to exaggerate." Among other transgressions, real and imagined, her brother had been sued for support for a child that wasn't his and blamed for a nightclub brawl that started after he'd left. If she remembered correctly, Parker had been with him that particular night. "I hope you've kept that in mind with anything you've heard or read about me.

"I also hope my brother is right about you," she continued before he could ask why she hadn't defended herself if what he'd heard wasn't true. "Cord said I could trust you. I don't know anyone outside my family that I can trust anymore," she stressed softly, "so I had to rely on his judgment. That's why I asked for you. That and a comment he made about you being up for just about anything."

She turned again to face the man filling the space with his powerful presence, saw the faint lift of one dark eyebrow.

"I didn't want to indicate my plans over the phone or the Internet, but aside from you being my driver and keeping me clear of paparazzi, there are some other things I need you to do for me. I hope you won't mind."

Parker had spent years learning to anticipate people and situations. Little caught him unprepared. Since he inevitably prepared for the worst, even less surprised him. He had not, however, expected the open candor of the woman giving him a cautious, almost hopeful smile or the isolation he sensed about her as she stood waiting for him to confirm or deny what her brother had claimed. He recognized that sense of separation, that sense of no longer being a part of the whole, only because in the past year he'd felt it so much himself.

Dismissing that unwanted thought, not appreciating the reminder, he studied her even more closely.

"You can believe your brother. You and your plans are secure with me." He was nothing if not honorable. "But he may have misled you on just what I'd be willing to do." He rarely objected to having a good time, situation permitting. He had the feeling Cord's little sister wasn't looking for a good poker game, though, or an escort to the local clubs. He hadn't read a single report about her doing the party circuit or getting wild and crazy in some trendy hot spot. "I play by the book, Miss Kendrick. I might bend rules, but I won't break the law."

Her lovely eyes widened. "I'd never ask you to do that. What I want is perfectly legal."

"Then what is it exactly that you want me to do?"

"Just set up some appointments." She replied quickly, as if she wanted her request to sound as if it were nothing of any import at all. "And run errands. And maybe watch Mikey for me. But only for a few minutes at a time," she hurried to explain, "and only if absolutely necessary."

Parker stifled a mental groan. He was a bodyguard. Not a personal slave. He most definitely was not a babysitter.

"Due respect, Miss Kendrick, but my duties are laid out in your family's contract with Bennington's. I'll provide surveillance, protection and evacuation if the latter is necessary. But if you need a personal assistant, you'll have to hire one. Same goes for a nanny."

His glance shot over the hair she'd smoothed back into place, over her perfectly made-up face, down the buttoned silk jacket that allowed that tantalizing glimpse of soft-looking skin between her breasts.

He would be willing to bet his tickets to the next New England Patriots game that Tess Kendrick was accustomed to getting everything she wanted. And to getting rid of whatever she did not, he reminded himself, thinking of how she'd shed a husband. If she was even half as spoiled as he'd read, he figured he was about to face major attitude.

Yet, rather than offense, all he saw enter her expression was something that looked almost like an apology.

"That's my problem," she murmured, pacing again. "Even

if I knew who to hire…who I could trust," she emphasized, "I don't want more people around. The fewer people who know I'm here, the less the chance of the press finding out that I'm back. It's taken forever for all talk and speculation to die down, and if they find out I'm here, it'll just start up again."

Something pleading crossed the delicate lines of her face. "All I'm asking is for help buying a house. I need you to make appointments under another name," she explained, because her own would be too easily recognized, "then maybe act as if you're the one buying when we look at the properties. When I find something that will work for Mikey and me, I'll turn it over to our lawyers and they can take it from there. And a car," she said, faint lines of concentration forming in her brow as she checked off items on her mental list. "I need to buy a car, too. I lost mine in the divorce."

She'd lost everything, actually, except for some personal items, her clothes and Mikey's things, most of which were stored in her parents' attic. She didn't mention that, though. Partly because she desperately wanted to forget the past few years. Mostly because the big man silently considering her wouldn't be interested in her need to rebuild a life for herself and her son. Or in how ill-equipped she felt to be doing it on her own.

"What about your brothers?"

"Gabe doesn't have any spare time. Buying a car is the kind of thing he'd staff out anyway."

Her oldest brother was governor of the state. Yet, more than the demands of the job on his time kept her from seeking his help. He and his press people hadn't been too happy with her for what the publicity surrounding her divorce had done to his family-values platform. Under the circumstances, asking a favor of him would take more nerve than she wanted to spare right now.

She could only conquer one mountain of ashes at a time.

"Cord knows real estate. And he's into cars. What about him?"

"He and his wife are in the Florida Keys. Sailing," she added, to prove just how inaccessible he was for the tasks. "I'd ask Ashley to help me look for a house, but she lives an hour away and is really busy with her kids. The two of us together would attract too much attention anyway."

Two Kendrick sisters together truly would be like waving a red flag at the press. Even if that hadn't been the case, Tess wanted to avoid Ashley right now. Long before her ex-husband had started pointing out how miserably Tess had failed to live up to her older sister's accomplishments, Tess had been aware of how Ashley had always done everything so well, so flawlessly. At least it had seemed so to the little sister who'd followed in her footsteps.

Because of Tess's place in the hierarchy as the baby of the family, she'd had none of the first-son or -daughter pressure to perform thrust upon her. For as far back as she could remember, everyone had insisted on watching out for her, doing for her, and nothing had been expected of her other than to maintain the integrity of the family name.

Image and integrity were paramount to their parents. The actions of one Kendrick inevitably affected them all. Having a brother who'd possessed an unfortunate tendency to draw embarrassing headlines had proved that often enough.

She hated that the one big choice she'd made on her own had turned out to be an error in judgment that had not only screwed up her own life but done an even more spectacular job than her once-prodigal brother of tainting the family's good name.

"What I want won't take long," she promised, trying desperately to push past feelings of failure and helplessness. "I need to be in my new home before my parents return." They would arrive right after Labor Day. That gave her roughly six weeks.

Skepticism slashed his broad brow.

"Do you know how long it can take to buy and move into a house?"

"Actually, no," she admitted. She hadn't a clue. She'd never had to deal with that particular detail before. "But I can't let it take long. It will be too uncomfortable living here with Mom and Dad." Her voice dropped. "Especially with my father. If I have to, I'll rent or lease something until I find what I want. I'd rather not move Mikey around that much, but I'll do it if I have to."

Thoughts of her father put a new face on her pacing. She wasn't ready to be around William Kendrick yet. She hadn't dealt well at all with the pictures Brad had shown her.

She didn't know which had the firmer hold—the disappointment she felt in her dad or her anger over his betrayal of her mom. Both were there, demanding to be dealt with. She just didn't know how. With no one to confide in, all she could do was jam down the emotions the same way she had the anxiety of everything else she'd had to cope with and force that energy into moving past her...past.

Parker remained discouragingly silent.

"I'll pay you whatever you ask."

It wasn't what she'd requested of him that kept Parker quiet. It was the tension in her body as she spoke and the faint anxiety running just beneath the surface of her practiced composure. Knowing how upset the senior Kendrick had been over Cord's indiscretions on occasion, he didn't doubt for a moment that the famously powerful head of the Kendricks' massive corporate and philanthropic holdings had been less than pleased with the unflattering publicity his daughter had brought. Yet, when she'd mentioned her father, he'd seen more than the embarrassment or discomfort he would have expected. He'd seen hurt.

He didn't want the bit of empathy that hit him just then. It was simply there as he pushed his hands into the pockets of his slacks, buying himself time as he considered what she wanted. He knew what it was to have lost the approval of a parent. Since he'd left the Marines five years ago, his own father had barely spoken to him. But then, his father was a three-star general and the military was, always had been and always would be his life. The only time the man had ever had time for him was when Parker had been in the military himself.

Frowning at the thought, he dismissed the old resentment that came with the memory as irrelevant. He didn't appreciate her reminding him of it. He didn't appreciate the way she'd distracted him either. It wasn't like him to get sidetracked. Yet, in less than a minute, the woman who'd gone still waiting for him to respond had reminded him of the isolation he'd felt since he'd lost his sister and the father neither one of them had ever really had.

He'd just reminded himself that neither had a thing to do with the requests she'd just made when the pounding of footsteps on the veranda outside had him jerking toward the back door an instant before it flew open.

## Chapter Two

The rattle of a key in the lock preceded the thud of the utility room door hitting the wall and the sharp bang of the screen door behind it.

Before Tess could begin to imagine who would be in such a hurry to get in, she found her view of the doorway entirely blocked by her bodyguard. It barely occurred to her that the man's silence and speed were more unnerving than the commotion when a startled feminine yelp joined the thump of something hitting the floor.

With his broad back to her, Parker signaled for her to stay put. Ignoring him, Tess glanced around his side to see an apple roll through the doorway.

Ina Yeager, her mom's dark-haired, late-thirty-something maid, had gone as still as Lot's wife. Her right hand lay splayed over her chest. In her left arm she clutched the bag of groceries she hadn't dropped as if it might somehow shield her lean frame from the unexpected presence that had nearly stopped her heart.

Tess quickly stepped around the small mountain in navy worsted. "It's all right. Both of you. Ina, this is Mr. Parker. He's my driver and bodyguard," she explained, terribly conscious of him herself. "He'll be staying for a couple of weeks.

"Parker," she continued, expecting him to stand down now that he knew he didn't have to whisk her to safety. The man was only doing what he'd been trained to do, but at some point she obviously needed to explain to him that she was as safe here as she was anywhere. It was beyond the estate she was concerned about. "Ina is one of mom's housekeeping staff." With a smile for the woman with the deep dimples and long French braid, she snatched the still-rolling apple off the floor. "Her husband is the stable master."

Seeing Tess reach for a head of lettuce and a red onion that had also rolled from the dropped sack, the clearly rattled maid bent to pick up the vegetables herself.

"I'm so sorry, Tess," she began, adding the onion to her bag. "I didn't think you'd be here. In the kitchen, I mean. Eddy went out front to help with your luggage," she told her, speaking of her husband. "I thought you'd be in the foyer directing him where to put it."

"He can just leave it there."

"I'll tell him."

Ina glanced up as she spoke, taking in Parker's big, shiny black shoes, his long, powerful legs, his impossibly broad shoulders. Stopping short of the strong line of his jaw, she grabbed the only remaining item—a bunch of bananas—and looked to Tess with another apology.

"Your mother called to tell me you and your son will be staying here for a while and asked me to stock the refrigerator. I'd meant to be here before you arrived and have every-

thing put away. I bought enough for your dinner and breakfast, and there's scones for tea, if you'd like."

The squeak of her tennis shoes sounded like chattering
mice as she hurried to set the vegetables by the sink and grab
a bowl from a cabinet. "I remembered some of your preferences but not all," she rushed on, filling an Italian ceramic
bowl with the fruit before unloading milk, butter, bread and
eggs. "If you'll give me your menu for the week, I'll go back
to the market tomorrow."

The woman easily ten years her senior looked terribly
self-conscious as she moved between the pantry and the
built-in refrigerator. Tess figured part of the reason for that
awkwardness stemmed from being out of uniform. Members
of the estate's staff, everyone from the butler to the cook,
maids and gardeners, wore their respective uniforms when
on duty. Rarely did any employee appear in or around the
main house dressed in anything else. Wearing a cotton shirt
and denim capris, Ina seemed painfully conscious of her casual attire. From her furtive glances toward the splendid
specimen of masculinity in his uniform of tailored suit and
tie, she seemed just as aware of Parker silently watching her
every move.

Or so Tess was thinking before she realized that some of
those darting glances were aimed at her. She was the daughter
who had caused so much gossip and speculation among her
parents' staff. She didn't doubt for a moment that the maid
was more than a little curious about her and her return.

She could only imagine the rumors that had flowed among
the staff. At least right now, talk would be kept to a minimum.
With most of the staff gone, there were blessedly few people
to generate it.

"I'll prepare your meals for you since Olivia is with your
parents. Will you be staying in your old bedroom?"

"Mikey and I both will." *But I'll take care of it,* she would have said, except Ina was already talking.

"Then I'll freshen it up as soon as I'm finished here." With a quick and diplomatic glance toward where Tess's body-guard remained, wrist clasped, waiting for her to conclude, she dropped her voice and hurried on. "Which room do you want Mr. Parker in? There's only one extra in the servants' quarters, but it's not very big."

Ina apparently couldn't picture him in a twin bed, either.

"I've already shown him which room he can use. I think Rose's is best." It was the largest. The room that belonged to the head housekeeper was also the only one in the servants' quarters with a double bed.

Considering his sizable frame, even that would be small.

If Ina had any reservations about putting another employee in her immediate boss's space, she dutifully kept them to herself. "I'll put fresh towels in his bathroom."

"Just tell me where they are. I'll take care of it."

Ina opened her mouth, closed it again. The faint frown creasing her brow made it look as if she couldn't possibly have heard correctly. "I need to freshen all the rooms. Nothing has been done in here since your parents left last month. I need to vacuum, dust. You'll want fresh flowers…."

Tess was already shaking her head. "Don't worry about any of it. You don't need to use your vacation time to wait on me. Go on with whatever plans you have and just pretend we aren't even here. And please," she requested, old anxieties never far from the surface, "don't mention to anyone that I've returned. No one off the property, I mean. You didn't say anything to anyone at the market, did you?"

"Not a word," Ina replied, looking puzzled. "Your mother already asked for our discretion about your presence. I passed on her request to Eddy and to Jackson," she said, speaking of the groundskeeper. Puzzlement shifted to consternation. "But she specifically asked that I be available to you and her grandson...."

"And I'm asking that you forget we're here."

The woman clearly didn't want to upset her employer. Tess didn't want to cause problems for Ina either, but having staff wait on her in any way was not part of the plan she'd devised for herself to get on with her life. She had gone from being the protected baby of the family to the wife of a man who'd turned out to be a master at control and manipulation. She'd spent years having people take over, take care of and take charge and done next to nothing to stop the slow erosion of her personal freedom.

It had taken years, the past few in particular, but she had finally realized how much independence all that acquiescence had cost her. It was time she learned to take care of herself and her son on her own.

Preparing to do just that, she gamely offered the only reason she could think of that might override her mother's orders and ease Ina's mind.

"I just need time alone. Just me and my son. If I do find I need your help, I'll call you. I'll explain to my mother if she says anything," she promised. "All right?"

Ina looked doubtful. "If you're sure..."

"I'm positive. Really. Enjoy your time off."

It was hard to tell which had the firmer hold on the maid at that moment—skepticism at leaving her employer's daughter to fend for herself or gratitude that her vacation wouldn't be further interrupted. She glanced uncertainly around the kitchen, looking as if she wanted to be positive there wasn't something else she should do. Apparently she found nothing.

"Well," she murmured, "it would be nice to finish redoing

our son's room. He joined the Navy when he graduated from high school a couple of months ago, so I'm turning it into a sewing room. With your mother's permission, of course."

"Of course."

"You'll call if you need anything at all?"

Tess mentally crossed her fingers. "I will."

"Well, if that's the case, I guess I'll go tell Eddy just to leave your luggage in the foyer." She hesitated. "We can carry it up if you'd like."

"It's fine, Ina. Really. Just tell me where I'll find clean towels for Mr. Parker's bathroom."

The clearly baffled maid showed her a large linen closet inside an even larger laundry room, then disappeared through the door that led to the family breakfast room, which led to the formal dining room and into the foyer. As far back as Tess was in the house, it was impossible for her to hear movements or conversation in those areas, but within a minute she saw both Ina and her rangy husband walk beneath the kitchen windows and cross the cobblestones between the house and the garage on their way back to the stables.

"Can you trust her?"

Tess turned from the window to open one of the drawers beneath a long expanse of counter.

"I hope so. Probably," she amended, closing that drawer with the clatter of cutlery to open the next one. "Ina has been with the family for at least ten years. I've never heard of her saying anything she shouldn't." Unlike certain people who used to work for me, she thought. "My mother tends to inspire loyalty better than I do."

She looked distracted to Parker as she closed that drawer and opened another. She also sounded like a woman who had been betrayed somehow, he thought, only to remind himself again that her personal business was none of his. Not unless it impacted his ability to do his job. He was more interested at the moment in what she was doing, anyway.

She'd turned to the upper cabinets behind her, going through them much as she had the drawers. The way she moved about the room made him think she was looking for something in particular. Or maybe trying to acquaint herself with an unfamiliar space.

"So," she prefaced, "are you going to help me?"

Parker's sense of practicality jerked into place. He was already committed to being her driver and bodyguard. Considering that he'd be driving her wherever she wanted to go, he wouldn't spend any more time looking at houses with her than he would otherwise. Making a few phone calls wouldn't take that much time either.

"I don't babysit."

Her fingers tightened around the knob of a cabinet as she looked toward him. "That means you'll help me with the house?"

"I'll make calls," he agreed.

"And the car?"

One of the things he had in common with her brother was that they both appreciated pretty much anything with wheels and an engine. Helping her buy a car wouldn't exactly be a hardship.

"Tell me what you want and I'll help you get it."

For a moment she looked hesitant, as if she was afraid to believe he'd agreed so easily.

"Thank you," she murmured, sounding as relieved as she looked. "Thank you very much."

As if she knew he could see how desperately she'd hoped for his help and how grateful she was for it, she looked away. Preoccupation settled over her again as she continued her search. But it was only when she set a pot on the stove on the island and disappeared into the deep, shelf-lined pantry that he realized what she was doing. It also seemed a good bet from the consternation in her pretty profile that she wasn't all that certain how to do it.

The way she studied the cooking directions on a box of dried linguine made it look as if the process was a total mystery to her.

He was now confused himself. "Do you mind if I ask why you didn't let your help cook for you?"

"Because it's time I learned how to do it myself." The delicate arches of her eyebrows drew inward. "What do you suppose goes into marinara sauce? It's Mikey's favorite." She clutched the box as she searched the fairly well-stocked shelves, the desperation he'd glimpsed in her overridden by purpose. "If I can figure it out, that's what we'll have."

He offered the obvious. "You need tomatoes."

She reached for a can. "Like these?"

Taking a step forward, he scanned the label. "Those have chilies in them. You want plain."

"Thanks," she murmured, continuing her search. "It's only five miles into Camelot. You'll probably be safer trying one of the restaurants there, but you're welcome to join us if you're up for an experiment." She picked up another can. "These?"

Parker wasn't sure which threw him more just then—her easy invitation for him to join her and her son or her obviously newborn attempt at self-sufficiency. Wondering what he'd gotten himself into, knowing it was too late to get out of it, he gave her a cautious nod.

"Have you ever cooked anything before?"

"I've never had to learn," she admitted. "When I was growing up, Mom always had a cook. In college and after I married, I lived where there were good restaurants, takeout or staff. It wasn't anything I was interested in pursuing."

*Until now,* she might have said.

Parker didn't ask why she'd chosen to develop the interest on his watch. Her totally matter-of-fact reply resurrected the unflattering impression he had of her before he'd met her—that she was an indulged and discontented socialite who handled boredom however she chose.

Wondering if it was boredom pushing her now and afraid to wonder what else she didn't know how to do, he stepped back to resume his stance at the end of the island. She was already down a personal assistant and a nanny. No way in Hades would he be her cook.

"You can probably find a recipe in a cookbook," he informed her, thinking now as good a time as any to get on with what he'd been hired to do. "In the meantime, I'd like to do a security check of the outside of the house. Where's the main security alarm located?"

Pure apology entered her tone. "I'm sorry. I was only thinking about feeding Mikey," she replied, setting her ingredients by the pot. "I meant to tell you not to worry about us while we're here. It's only when we're in public that you need to watch out for us."

"So you have security on-site?"

"There's the alarm," she offered, thinking back to when she'd lived there. "It goes to a security service in Camelot. Or maybe," she said, reconsidering, "it goes right to the police."

As if calculating how long it would take for a patrol car to arrive from five miles away, Parker narrowed his eyes toward the window. "Any regular security patrols? Any dogs?"

"I don't know about patrols." She'd been aware of people in the background of her life as she'd grown up there, but she had no idea who her parents might have contracted with locally since she'd married and moved out. "Mom and Dad have an Irish setter, but Cooper is with them." The dog she'd grown up with was gone now. But the thought of how much she still missed that old setter was pushed aside when she remembered another resident canine, "Eddy and Ina have a German shepherd."

"If they do, it isn't a guard dog. It was nowhere in sight when we drove in."

"Maybe he was out by the lake."

"This place is how many acres?"

"Twenty-five or so."

"And how many rooms in the house?"

"Including bathrooms and the rooms back here?" She shrugged. "Maybe thirty-five."

"That's a lot of space to be alone in," he informed her flatly. "I know you don't want anyone to find out you're here, but if someone does, it won't be long before the press and the paparazzi show up. There could be breaches."

As anxious as she had been to return, Tess had considered only how safe she'd always felt in and around Camelot. But with his cool, detached conclusion, Parker had just forced her to remember that there had been occasions when the estate's privacy had indeed been breached. She discounted the time paparazzi had scaled the walls to take pictures of her wedding and the enterprising photographer who'd rented a hot-air balloon to fly over Ashley's sweet-sixteen party simply because the events were the sort that attracted such intrusions.

There had been unexpected invasions, though, like the time her brother Gabe had been photographed by the lake inches from a kiss with the head housekeeper's daughter. He and Addie were married now, but the press had had a field day with that one.

Like nearly every security person she'd ever encountered, Parker's expression remained as matter-of-fact as his voice. "I just want to make sure you're as secure as you think you are."

He was doing what he was trained to do, what she'd paid him to do. Yet she didn't care at all for the way he'd just robbed her of what little bit of security she'd finally felt.

Suddenly feeling vulnerable, she lifted her hand toward the hallway.

"The security system is behind one of the panels in the furnace room. The stairs to the basement are at the end of the hall."

"And the monitor for the front gate and perimeter cameras?"

"By the computer. Over there," she said, nodding toward the alcove by the utility room.

"Is that the only one?"

"The stable master has a monitor, too. There's one there because someone always has to be here with the horses."

He moved to the alcove where the head housekeeper apparently attended the duties of the household. Above the desk that held a state-of-the-art computer, a built-in television screen displayed rotating views from the various security cameras situated around the property. Integrated into the wall beside it was an intercom connected, presumably, to the front gate and possibly to the stables.

A shot of a lake came into view on the screen, followed by a view of tennis courts, expanses of lawns and gardens, horses grazing, a Roman pool. Then came a series of shots showing nothing but stone walls and foliage. Those were of the property's perimeter, she told him.

"There's no one on the property other than Ina, Eddy and...what's the groundskeeper's name?"

"Jackson. And no. There's no one."

"I need to know what they look like in case they show up on the monitors."

"I'll call down and ask Ina to introduce you."

Parker watched her move past him to pick up the phone on the desk. As she did, the softness of her perfume, something subtle, warm and as elusive as the woman herself, drifted in her wake.

He had first become aware of that disturbing scent when they'd both reached to strap her son into his seat in the car. He'd thought then that the tightening low in his gut had been caused by the purely feminine softness of her skin brushing his. He knew now that he didn't have to touch her for that unsettling sensation to take hold.

He needed to move.

"She'll meet you by the hedge arch," she said, giving him the excuse he needed to head for the door. "Just follow the stones across the lawn."

"I'll check out the interior when I get back."

Tess started to tell him he didn't need to worry about the inside of the house, only to remember that she'd never been alone in the big and rambling mansion before. When she'd lived there, even with both parents gone for a weekend and all her siblings having moved out, the cook, the head housekeeper, at least one maid and her dad's butler had been in their respective quarters.

Tonight it would just be her and her son—and the nononsense bodyguard who walked out the door as if desperate for fresh air.

Tess leaned past the computer, watching his powerful strides carry him across the expansive deck and along the stone path by the flower beds.

It wasn't air he was after, she thought. He'd just wanted to use his cell phone.

\* \* \*

"I'm sort of in the middle of nowhere at the moment. But it won't be a problem to keep up from here."

Parker held the small cell phone to his ear as he angled for the gap in the hedges some twenty yards ahead. The logistics of juggling two jobs at once came easily to him. The admission that Tess Kendrick had a definite effect on him did not.

"The best thing to do is send them to the FedEx office in Camelot, Virginia," he continued, grateful for the diversion from her. "I'll pick them up there. Give me a couple of days to compare them to the diagrams we already have and I'll get back to you."

On the other end of the line, his counterpart at the U.S. Marshal's service told him he'd have the blueprints they'd been waiting for by noon. Those blueprints of a hotel they were securing for a high-risk conference would indicate everything from the public and restricted areas to ductwork, access ports, elevator shafts and any other place someone bent on mayhem or sending a message might hide in, slither through or plant devices of varying degrees of destruction.

After a quick briefing on the status of surveillance equipment being installed at the hotel and an even quicker "Thanks," Parker flipped the phone closed and dropped it into his jacket pocket.

In the past year he'd coordinated security for rock concerts in Central Park, Los Angeles and London. He'd worked with the security teams for the Oscars. He would begin consultant work on the Emmys and a film festival in Cannes within the next month. Presently he was coordinating individual protection and exit strategies with the Marshal's Service and existing hotel security for a judicial conference in Minneapolis next month. Because judges could be targets for retaliation from those who didn't agree with their sentences or judgments, the government spared no expense on protection.

Considering how seriously he took his obligations, Parker spared nothing of his expertise. That expertise was considerable and current. He'd been Special Ops in the Marines and still remained on call as part of a special training group. He loved the tactical end of the business. Unlike his father, he just didn't want the military to be his whole life.

He could easily live without the mayhem he'd encountered—and caused—in clandestine operations in certain Third World countries. But his heart and soul would always crave a challenge. That was why he hadn't thought twice about taking the job with Bennington's at its headquarters in Baltimore. Or about taking the promotion he'd been offered a couple of years later to coordinate the firm's high-profile tactical projects. When he'd first signed on with the company, the novelty of the job, the varied and exotic locations and the firm's exclusive clientele had been enough to keep him intrigued. Yet it hadn't been long before he'd begun to miss using his psychological and technical skills. He missed strategizing. Mostly he missed the challenges that came with the bigger projects.

The whinny of horses drifted on the early-evening breeze. Up ahead, emerging through the break in the high hedge, Ina waved to him.

Seeing the maid Tess had dismissed reminded him that, for all practical purposes, he was her only employee. That alone warned him that challenges on this particular job wouldn't be in short supply.

His client's unanticipated decision to attempt self-sufficiency was no longer on his mind when he returned to the house a half an hour later. Now that he had a general idea of the property's layout, he remained totally preoccupied with his visual inspection of the back of the house as he approached it. The bad news was the number of balconies and French doors overlooking the admittedly beautiful grounds. Every one was a potential photography or entry point. The good news was that anyone trying to get up or down from them would probably break a body part if they fell.

He walked in the back entrance, catching the screen door before it banged shut so he wouldn't make noise if the boy was still asleep. Even before he'd cleared the utility room, with its walls of cabinets, he could see Tess at the island in the big kitchen.

She'd raided the cook's stash of cookbooks from the open bookcase in the hallway. The sizable collection sat in stacks on either side of where she leaned with her forearms on the white tile studying one of them.

She looked up when he stopped in the doorway. The overhead lights caught shades of pale gold in the depths of the hair clasped at her nape. Pushing back the strands that had escaped in the breeze at the airport, she straightened.

It was then he noticed that she'd kicked off her heels. Bright coral toenails peeked from beneath the hem of her slim white slacks. The gold chains she'd worn sat in a gleaming pool near a stack of three blue pottery plates topped by silverware wrapped in cloth napkins.

"Is everything okay?" she asked.

"Seems to be. Ed said there are no alarms on the perimeter of the property because of the wildlife, but the intrusion alarm for the main house and the garage goes off in his quarters and at the security company. He thinks it can take anywhere from two to ten minutes for the Camelot police to get here, depending on where their patrol cars are."

"Did he say something to make you think we'd need the police?"

"If you mean has he seen paparazzi hanging around, no. Everything's been quiet here this summer."

Her slender shoulders lowered with the breath she quietly exhaled.

"Mind if I look around inside now?"

Knowing the layout of the interior was essential to his work. He especially wanted to know the location of doors or any other possible points of access or egress. He wasn't aware of any threats against any of the Kendricks, and according to Bennington's files there had been no incidents involving kidnapping for ransom, revenge or recognition for someone seeking their fifteen minutes of fame. But as with others with wealth, high-profile or celebrity status, kidnapping was always a possibility. The children were especially vulnerable.

"I need to know where you and your boy will be sleeping, too," he told her, watching the toes of one foot disappear into a three-inch-high pump.

She slipped on the other, reaching back to tug the back strap over her heel as her glance darted toward the back hallway.

"Do you mind if we wait a while? I need to stay here until Mikey wakes up. He won't remember this house and he'll be scared if I'm not here." Her concern shifted uncertainly to the cookbook. "I need to figure out how to get this going, too. He's going to be hungry."

Parker had been gone half an hour. "You haven't found a recipe?"

"I've found several. They just all seem…complicated."

One of the cookbooks she'd selected bore the title *The Chef's' Book of Sauces, from Artichoke to Zabaglione.* Another, *Creative Italian Cuisine. The Art of Pasta* sat atop *Mastering Mediterranean Cooking.*

What she needed was Cooking 101.

He nodded to the book open in front of her. "May I see that?"

She handed it to him. The page she'd been so diligently studying held a recipe for Bolognese sauce and the marinara she'd been looking for.

He indicated the latter. "What's wrong with this one?"

Her expression mirrored his. "I'm not exactly sure how to 'sauté' or 'reduce.'"

He hadn't really noticed the faint shadows beneath her eyes before now or how tired she looked beneath her faintly frustrated smile. But then, he hadn't wanted to acknowledge much of anything about her that didn't directly affect the reason he was there. He considered himself a fair man, though, and to be fair, he had to admit that she didn't seem much like the woman he'd expected. She was young, to be certain, and there was no mistaking that she knew privilege. Yet she hadn't once acted spoiled, selfish, difficult or demanding. A little needy maybe, though he couldn't put his finger on exactly what it was about her that made him think so. But so far she didn't appear to be anything like the diva the press had portrayed.

With hints of her fatigue staring him in the face, impressed by how intent she seemed to disregard it, he felt his priorities take a subtle shift. It was nearly two o'clock in the morning in the country she'd just left. The woman was probably dead on her feet.

Telling himself he was only taking pity on the boy, he ignored his earlier insistence that he wouldn't be her cook and handed her back the book.

"They aren't that complicated," he told her, slipping off his tie. "But you shouldn't practice on an unsuspecting child. I'll make it."

Tess blinked in disbelief. "I can't ask you do that."

"You didn't ask."

"What I mean is that you don't have to do it. I can manage this."

His response was the challenging arch of one dark eyebrow as he shrugged off his jacket,

"Well, I can if you'll tell me how," she qualified.

"It'll be faster to just do it myself." The jacket was dropped over the back of a chair at the staff's table. "The pot by the stove will work for the pasta," he said, rolling up the sleeves of his starched white shirt. "But I'll need a small one for the sauce. Mind if I look in the pantry?" he asked, already heading for it. "All I need is garlic, olive oil, salt and basil. Fresh is best if there's any growing outside, but dried will do."

Tess opened her mouth, closed it again. She didn't know if her bodyguard wanted to speed up the dinner project so she could show him around as soon as Mikey woke up or if he thought her incapable of the task herself. The latter thought stung, especially since she already had the feeling he thought of her as either naive, young, helpless or some unflattering combination of all three. But whatever his rationale, she couldn't allow him or anyone else to defeat her purpose.

The man was accustomed to taking charge. He'd already found the olive oil and had removed a bottle of something green and flaky from a shelf when she stepped into the pantry herself.

She'd been around big men before. A couple of her grandmother's sentries had been built like tanks, and her own brothers were over six feet. But Parker's body seemed to dwarf hers, and she wasn't a short woman by any means. Barefoot, she stood an easy five foot seven inches. In heels, five ten. Even at that, she barely reached his broad shoulders.

Terribly conscious of the scents of clean soap and warm male, she took the ingredients from him.

"You don't need to do this," she repeated more firmly. "But I would appreciate it if you would tell me how."

She stood too close to look up without bending back her neck. Ahead, all she could see was the solid expanse of his chest. A woman would feel very safe held there.

The unexpected thought brought a flush of heat, caused her to turn away. "Please."

Her request seemed to give him pause. Probably, she suspected, because he was accustomed to bulldozing ahead once he'd decided on a course of action and wasn't used to anyone slowing him down.

She rather envied him that.

He finally muttered, "Fine," as she set the ingredients by the tomatoes and pasta she'd left on the island. "Take off your jacket and get yourself an apron."

"I'll leave my jacket on."

"You don't want to ruin what you're wearing."

A white silk Armani wasn't the most practical thing to wear for her first cooking lesson. She would, however, have to make do. She didn't want to leave to change clothes. "It's okay."

Parker frowned at her slender back. Okay? he thought, absently watching her go through the drawers again. Okay because she could afford to stain two-thousand-dollar suits? Or okay because she was inherently stubborn and accustomed to getting her own way?

"Tomato sauce stains," he warned.

An odd note of awkwardness slipped into her voice. "I don't have anything on under it," she explained, coming up with a white chef's apron. "No blouse, I mean."

His glance darted to the V of flesh exposed between her

lapels as she held the white cotton apron by its inch-wide strings.

That was more information than he needed.

"Here." Feeling chastised, he jerked his glance to what she held. He did not need to be imagining her standing there in a skimpy lace bra. "Turn around."

Dutifully she did as he asked.

"Lift your hair."

She did that, too, gathering the thick mane below the intricate clip already restraining it.

His fingers felt clumsy as he tied the strings behind her neck—quickly so he couldn't think too much about the appealing curve of her shoulder, the baby-fine hairs below her nape. Her skin felt like warm satin to him, the brush of her hair against the back of his hand like strands of silk.

Her scent assaulted his remaining senses.

The tightness low in his gut seemed to make its way to his voice.

"The first thing you do is mince a clove of garlic."

She dropped her hair as she turned. Stepping back, she met his oddly guarded eyes. "I don't think Mikey will like garlic."

"You can't make a proper marinara without it."

"Then, show me how to make an improper one."

Tess could practically feel his eyes boring into her back as she hurried to gather a pen and notepad from the desk. "I need to write this down," she explained. "I want to be able to do it again."

She had the distinct impression that he was mentally shaking his head at her. At that moment, she really didn't care. She would not have considered an ex-Marine who looked capable of bench-pressing her mom's Mercedes to know his way around the kitchen. Since he did, she intended to take full advantage of his knowledge.

She also wanted to know how he'd acquired it.

"Where did you learn how to cook?"

"From my mom."

"Is she a chef?"

"She's first violin with the Philadelphia Symphony. You need to put a few tablespoons of olive oil in this," he said, clearly changing the subject as he set a pot on the eight-burner stove in the middle of the island. "If we were doing this right, you'd put the garlic in next, then open the tomatoes and add them. Since we're not, just add the tomatoes to the oil."

"How much?"

"The whole can."

"Oil, I mean."

"A few tablespoons," he repeated. "It's a matter of taste. A little more or less won't hurt."

"Give me exact."

With a pen poised above a notepad, she looked much as he imagined a young student might waiting for a teacher to proceed. Yet it wasn't her expectation that struck him as he found measuring spoons for her and she dutifully wrote out his instructions before adding the ingredients precisely as he instructed. It was how young she looked each time she glanced up to make sure she'd done the step correctly or to ask what came next, how very innocent and how incredibly, unbelievably tempting.

The texture of her skin all but invited a man's touch. Her lush lips fairly begged to be kissed. And a man would have to be dead not to notice the appealing concern in her lovely dark eyes when an uncertain, "Mommy?" had her abandoning everything to turn to the hallway.

"I'm right here," she called. "Will that be all right?" she asked with a quick glance back at the pot.

He'd no sooner told her he would watch it than she headed for the sleepy-looking child who'd wandered toward the sound of her voice.

She scooped him up and turned, smiling, with him in her arms.

Parker had known beautiful women. They'd been arm candy for rich clients or the men's daughters, wives or mistresses. He'd guarded female rock stars and models and on occasion found himself in the unenviable position of having to decline advances he wouldn't have minded pursuing, on a purely recreational basis, had company policy not frowned on fraternization.

But recalling company policy wasn't necessary as he deliberately dismissed the sharp physical pull he felt toward Tess. It wasn't even necessary to remind himself that she was Cord Kendrick's little sister and that the only reason he'd recommended Parker was because he knew he could trust him.

Shifting his attention to the boy as she set him down and took his hand, all Parker had to do was remind himself that she had robbed the child of a relationship with his natural father.

That alone was enough to dampen the heat.

The little boy with the button nose and big brown eyes stared at him uneasily. A tuft of his cornsilk hair stuck up in back.

His mom smoothed it down.

Snagging his slacks above his knees, Parker crouched down to bring himself more or less to the child's level.

"Great shirt," he said, smiling at the logo above the tiny pocket. "Do you play soccer?"

Smashed against his mom's leg, Mikey nodded. "I have a ball."

"You do?"

Fine blond hair brushed his eyebrows as he gave a vigorous nod.

"You'll have to show it to me sometime."

Without moving from where his arm wrapped his mom's leg, he tipped back his head and looked up at her. "Do I have my soccer ball?"

"It's not unpacked yet."

"Can I show it to him when it is?"

"If Mr. Parker wants to see it."

Parker gave the boy a wink.

Mikey grinned.

Planting his hands on his knees, Parker rose to tower over them both.

"That can simmer for a while," he said, nodding toward her creation. With the little boy looking a little less wary of him, Parker pulled his professionalism back into place. "Where do you plan to eat?"

"It's so nice outside, I thought we'd eat out there. Unless you'd prefer the dining room," she offered, much as she might to a guest.

He was not a guest. He was her employee. "I'll eat at the staff table." Distance seemed prudent. So did boundaries. "Why don't you show me around the house now?"

The unexpected ease Tess had started to feel with him vanished like smoke in a stiff wind. She had just been quite pointedly reminded that there were certain distances to maintain. Certain protocols to follow. She had thought they would eat together simply because it was only the three of them and it hadn't seemed right that he should eat alone. Especially since he'd shown her how to prepare the meal.

The reserve he had just pulled into place brought a tug of embarrassment. The way his manner changed so quickly almost made it seem as if he thought she'd been coming on to him. She wasn't sure she'd know how to come on to a guy even if she wanted to. Despite what Brad had told the world about her supposed inability to settle for one man, she was nowhere near as experienced as he'd portrayed her to be. Certainly not as experienced as the press had assumed in its relentless attempt to discover her non-existent lovers.

It hadn't helped that one enterprising reporter claimed to have unearthed two of them, then gone on to explain that they had refused to go public out of respect for how special the relationships had been. It had been the sort of tabloid treachery that couldn't be refuted without adding fuel to the fire but fed the gossip and scandal just the same.

Hating where her thoughts had gone, she straightened her shoulders, smiled politely and took her son by the hand. Re-energized, Mikey could inadvertently do serious damage to her mother's Mings. The large, ornate vases flanking the foyer staircases had survived for over four hundred years. Not only her mother but museum directors and antique dealers all over the country would weep to discover that in his first couple of hours in the house a three-year-old whirlwind had caused a crack or a chip, much less destroyed one.

She really needed her own place.

Doing her best imitation of her sister's cool poise, she moved through the swinging door leading to the family dining room. Mikey trotted along beside her, looking around to check out the man following them. She felt like a tour guide as she called off the names of the still and silent rooms they entered and left. The music salon, the living room that was seldom lived in at all and used mostly for entertaining, the library, her father's study, her mother's office. The sunroom. The atrium. The family room. The game room. And that was before Parker helped her carry up the luggage he'd brought in along with the bags Eddy had left beside them and they went through the two wings of bedroom suites upstairs

Parker said little as he lifted back drapes, checked out windows and doors and looked up at the ceiling in search of heaven only knew what. She had no idea how his mind worked. She knew only that it was with some relief that he disappeared to retrieve his own luggage from the SUV while she and Mikey dined on the first meal she'd ever made.

The fact that it was good—very good—filled her with a definite sort of relief.

At least her son wouldn't starve.

She would have thanked Parker for that. She didn't see him, though, until after she had dumped their dishes in the sink, too tired to tackle them that night, and he knocked on her bedroom door.

## Chapter Three

Tess was now officially exhausted. She'd lost nearly an entire night's sleep to stress before she'd left Luzandria and she hadn't slept on the plane at all. Having crossed multiple time zones, she wasn't even sure how many hours she'd gone without rest. It didn't matter. She was just hoping that Mikey's hour-long nap before dinner wouldn't keep him up past a bedtime story when her search for his pajamas was interrupted by three short raps on the door.

Leaving her son and the open suitcases on the daybed in her sitting room, she hurried past the king bed that had replaced her old twin, tossed a throw pillow from the floor onto the piles of powder-blue and cream pillows already covering it and pulled open the door.

Parker filled her doorway. Even with his white shirt open at the collar and his sleeves rolled to just below his elbows, he looked much as he had when she'd seen him a while ago. Just as staid. Just as professional.

He held something small and black out to her.

"Use this if you need me at night. Just flip back this guard, punch this key and I'll be here."

She took what looked like a small pager.

"The doors are all locked and the alarm set. I'll be in my room," he continued, glancing to where Mikey peeked around the corner. A smile tugged at the sensual line of his mouth as he winked at her son. That smile and the ease in it was gone by the time he looked back to her. "I think that's everything," he concluded, "so I'll say good night."

Her hand shot out as he started to turn. "Wait," she said, pulling back before she could overstep the employee-employer line and grab his muscular forearm. "Thank you for helping me tonight. With dinner," she murmured, because she didn't want him to think she hadn't appreciated what he'd done. He hadn't had to offer the assist.

Though his smile had died, she offered a weary one of her own. "And thanks for this." She held up the device that would keep her linked to him while she slept. Peace of mind in the palm of her hand. "Rest well."

For a moment he simply looked at her. Then, incredibly, she saw his facade crack. That fissure was pathetically slight. Yet, as his glance slowly skimmed her tired features, it was enough to allow a bit of warmth back into the cool blue of his eyes. "You rest well, too," he said, sounding as if he knew how badly she needed sleep. With a nod he added, "See you in the morning," and left her staring at his back.

The burgundy carpet with its Persian runner absorbed the sound of his footfall as he walked down the hall, past her brothers' and sister's old rooms, and headed down the curving stairs. Moments later the crystal chandelier lighting the foyer, the stairway and the first few yards of the long, wide hall went out.

Across from her, the buttery glow from the brass lamp on the credenza provided the hall's only light. From below came the muffled sound of footsteps on marble and the click of the butler's door as it closed.

Tess didn't move. She just stood there, clutching what he'd given her and listening to the silence.

The enormous house suddenly felt as empty and lifeless as Tut's tomb. Yet it wasn't just the house that felt that way. Something about glimpsing a bit of warmth from a man who was a virtual stranger had somehow magnified what she'd felt for a long time now. Empty. Drained. And more lost than she would ever have thought possible.

She pulled a deep breath, pushed back her hair and turned to the room and the little boy now helping her by unpacking his suitcase himself.

She was just tired, she told herself, setting the pager on her nightstand before picking up the T-shirts that had fallen to the carpet. That was the only possible explanation for why she'd felt abandoned all over again when Parker had turned his back on her. He was her bodyguard. His job was to keep her from being harassed. It made no difference that he disturbed her in ways she couldn't explain. It didn't even matter that she'd sensed the disapproval he was so careful to mask. All that mattered was that with him around she felt…safe.

Mikey had no problem falling asleep. He awoke, however, at four o'clock the next morning. Since Tess was awake by then, too, she had him crawl into bed with her, where they cuddled and read their respective books until he complained of being hungry. By then it was five-fifteen and light outside, so she dressed herself, dressed him, and they both headed through the quiet house to the kitchen where she poured him a bowl of granola and a glass of milk and tried to figure out the coffeemaker.

At the palace, she could have rung for coffee and had it brought to her room or been served a cup from a silver pot on a terrace. Under normal circumstances at her parents' home, in another hour or so she would have found a carafe of it on the sideboard in the family breakfast room. When she'd been married, the live-in help had made it or she'd gotten it from the Starbucks on the first floor of the building she'd lived in.

Never again would she take her morning coffee for granted.

Since staring at the machine with its levers and buttons provided few clues to its use, she searched the drawers in the hope of finding some sort of manual.

That exercise proved just as futile.

She knew she needed water and coffee, so she filled the glass carafe, found a bag of beans in the refrigerator and decided that she'd have to wait until Parker woke and ask him how to get the thing to work. In the meantime, with Mikey occupied on the kitchen floor with his robot that transformed into a tank, she would use the kitchen computer to check out the local real-estate market.

By six-thirty she'd found three houses she wanted Parker to call about, but even if he'd been up, it was too early for him to make an appointment with the Realtor.

By six thirty-five she'd entered the back hall to listen for some sign of life from the room he was using.

Mikey scrambled past her on his hands and knees, making motor noises as he pushed his tank. Turning around a few feet past Parker's closed door, he stood up.

"What are you doing?" he wanted to know.

She dropped her voice to a whisper. "Listening to see if Mr. Parker is up yet."

"Why?"

"Because I need his help with something."

"Why?

"Because I can't do it myself."

At three, he had no trouble comprehending that rationale. "I'll look," he announced and reached for the door.

Tess's eyes widened, but she'd barely opened her mouth to tell him that checking wasn't necessary before he'd pulled down on the handle and pushed the door open.

Parker wasn't there.

She dropped to her knees in front of her too-helpful little boy. "Honey, we don't do that." Relief at not having found her bodyguard in bed collided with puzzlement over where he might be. She knew she hadn't heard him leave. She'd been listening for him. "This is Mr. Parker's private space. We don't open closed doors. Okay?"

"Then how do we get back in our bedroom?"

"That door is all right. We don't open doors to other people's rooms. Not without permission." Rising, she took his hand. "Let's see if we can find him."

If there was anything she knew about the guards she'd encountered, body or otherwise, it was that they were incredibly fit. They didn't get or stay that way without work. Considering the amount of muscle Parker needed to keep in condition, she figured he might be in one of three places: out jogging or running, in the pool doing laps or in the workout room her mom had had equipped for her dad and his trainer after his doctor told him to get more exercise or deal with rehab after he had a heart attack.

If Parker was running, she'd just have to wait until he returned. If he was swimming or working out, he could tell her how to make the coffee machine work and they could each get on with their morning.

He wasn't in the pool.

He was, however, in the mirrored exercise room off the sauna—wearing nothing but baggy athletic shorts and running shoes.

The counterpart to the pager he'd given her lay on the floor by the machine he was using. She noticed it only because it wasn't far from his feet, which was where her glance landed after moving the entire length of his hard, honed body.

The sculpted muscles of his shoulders and back gleamed with sweat as he slowly lowered the incredible amount of weight he'd loaded onto the machine.

With Mikey heading for a big blue exercise ball on a yoga mat, she watched Parker rise from the black bench seat. Concern slashed his features as he reached for the blue hand towel on the arm of the machine and wiped it over his face.

"Is there a problem?"

She was staring. She knew that as she ventured into the mirror-lined room that reflected him from every angle. Yet she couldn't seem to help it. She'd seen statues of magnificently sculpted warriors and gods in Rome and Florence. Perfect male bodies immortalized in marble and bronze. She just wasn't accustomed to such a blatantly masculine male in the flesh. At least not a nearly naked one.

From six feet away, she jerked her attention from his powerful thighs to his beautifully carved stomach and chest. Feeling strangely warm when she met his eyes, she swallowed and gave a small shake of her head.

"Just a minor one," she began, hugely relieved that she sounded quite normal. "I'm not sure how to use the coffeemaker. We've been up for a couple of hours and I could really use some caffeine."

"Jet lag?"

"Major," she murmured, remembering the elusive bit of warmth he'd allowed when they'd said good night. Or maybe what she'd glimpsed had been sympathy. "When you're finished, will you show me how to make the coffee?" she asked, torn between wishing she could again see whatever it had been and knowing she'd only feel worse when that warmth was gone. "Or just tell me now and you can get back to what you're doing. That way it'll be ready for you, too, when you're finished. If you drink it," she hurried on. "Maybe you don't put things like caffeine into your body. You obviously take good…care of it."

Seconds ago, her glance had moved from his stomach to his pecs. It now faltered and hit the floor.

"I don't abuse it," he allowed, a little surprised by how flustered she suddenly seemed. "But I do allow certain indulgences."

She cleared her throat. "Like coffee."

"Among other things."

He couldn't remember ever having seen a woman blush. But there was no mistaking the pink beneath the peach blusher on her cheeks. That provocative bit of innocence didn't fit at all with her sophistication. Or her reputation. It seemed to him that a woman who claimed she could never be happy with just one man would be accustomed to variety at most or, at least, the sight of a bare chest.

He wasn't an immodest man. Or a particularly modest one, for that matter. But he was now conscious himself of his state of undress. Especially with her looking every inch the lady of the manor in a cocoa-colored sleeveless turtleneck, matching capri pants and touches of gold on her ears, neck and low-riding chain belt. There was a certain decorum to maintain between them. There were boundaries. Less than twelve hours ago he'd made a point of drawing them himself.

Sweat trickled down his chest. Taking an absent swipe at it, he was about to tell her he'd be upstairs in a few minutes when he tossed the rectangle of terry cloth over the machine. It promptly slid to the floor.

Swearing to himself, he bent to snatch it up. So did she. Her fingers had barely skimmed the terry cloth when his shoulder hit hers, she flew back and his hands shot out to catch her.

With his fingers curled around her bare upper arms, he jerked her upright.

He'd hauled her to within inches of his chest when he thought he heard her breath hitch. He knew for certain that his own stalled somewhere behind his breastbone. The breath he'd drawn had brought her scent, that combination of innocence and seduction that moved from his lungs to his blood at the speed of light, taunting nerves every centimeter of the way.

Beneath his palms, her skin felt like velvet. Her slender muscles were as taut as bowstrings. But it was the confusion he sensed in her when his glance moved from the temptation of her lush mouth and his eyes met hers that told him she wasn't immune to him, either.

That was dangerous knowledge to possess.

No longer fearing she'd wind up on her appealing little backside, he reminded himself of all the reasons he needed to keep his thoughts off her body and his hands to himself and slowly released his grip.

The pink blushing her cheeks seemed even deeper as she crossed her arms and stepped back.

"Are you okay?"

"I'm… Yes, of course," she assured him. "I'm…fine."

Seeing how her hands covered where his had been, his brow pinched. "Did I hurt you?"

"No. No," Tess insisted, suddenly conscious of what had his attention.

Apparently aware that she was holding in his heat, she dropped her hands and picked up what neither of them had managed to get. As if utterly determined to appear composed, she rose with the rectangle of blue terry cloth. "You dropped this."

Impressed by her aplomb but not at all fooled by it, he lifted the towel from her hand and hung it around his neck. She'd already put another arm's length between them.

"Give me twenty minutes and we'll deal with the coffee." The job, he reminded himself. Just focus on the job. "What's the agenda today? You said you want to look at houses. Do you prefer me in a suit or more casual?"

"Casual. Thank you," she murmured, then turned to collect her son from where the boy had draped his little body over the ball and coaxed him out the door.

Tess honestly didn't care how Parker dressed as long as he showed up wearing something less distracting than those gym shorts. She couldn't believe how he'd rattled her. She'd admit to having been more sheltered growing up than most women her age, but she'd hardly been raised in a convent. She'd been married. Heaven knew she'd seen male bodies on beaches and in magazines. He'd just caught her off guard was all.

Or so she was telling herself when he emerged from his room exactly twenty minutes later with a shaving knick on his chin, one above his right ear where he'd apparently continued with the razor right on over his head and wearing khakis and a cream-colored polo shirt that made him look only slightly less formidable than he did in a suit.

He barely made eye contact with her as he walked past the kitchen table, where she was flipping through a cookbook and Mikey was coloring and watching cartoons on the small television mounted beneath one of the cabinets. A strange sort of restlessness seemed to follow in his wake.

"Let's see what we have," he announced, heading for the far counter and the coffeemaker, "and we'll get this going."

He barely glanced at the appliance and what she'd left in front of it. Within seconds, jaw working, he'd assessed the situation, told her the reason it looked complicated was because it was also a cappuccino machine and moved into action, opening one cabinet after another much as she had yesterday.

He told her the beans needed to be ground when she walked up behind him, so they'd need to find a grinder. They needed a filter, too, so he explained what a paper coffee filter looked like.

There was no hiding the fact that she was domestically challenged, but he did nothing to indicate what he thought of her limitations. The man was all business, which suited her fine just then. Within minutes they'd found what they needed, he'd figured out how to get the machine going and the heavenly scent of brewing Arabica filled the kitchen.

She would have felt infinitely more grateful at the prospect of finally getting a cup of coffee had it not been for the faint tension that radiated like sound waves from his big body. Even with the island now separating them, it snaked toward her, surrounding her, tightening her nerves and making movement essential.

With him waiting by the coffee machine while it dripped, she headed for the cookbook she'd left on the table.

"Mind if I get something to eat?" he asked.

"Of course not. Please. Help yourself." She started to tell him he was welcome to join Mikey, who'd decided he was hungry again. Remembering how adversely he had responded to her offer for him to eat with them last night, she offered only the food instead. "If you can wait until I figure out how to make scrambled eggs, you're welcome to have them and toast."

Mikey looked up from his coloring. "I want some," he announced. "They're my favorite."

Parker's brow furrowed. "I thought pasta was."

"It is."

Not quite sure what to make of that dubious logic, he looked back to the boy's mom.

Her attention was on the cookbook.

Restless, hungry, he took her up on her offer to help himself and moved past the spotless sink and counters to the built-in refrigerator. When he'd done a final check of the house before he'd gone to bed last night, the sink had been full of pots, pans and plates. He'd put his own dishes away, partly because he expected no one to clean up after him, mostly because the neatness and order drilled into him in the military suited him, but he had left everything else where it was. Just as he had no intention of babysitting, he'd told himself he wasn't playing maid to her and her son.

From the way she'd cleaned the kitchen first thing that morning it was clear she'd expected nothing of the sort from him.

Wondering if that morning had been her first experience with dirty dishes—suspecting it had been—he opened the fridge. "I'll make his eggs."

"Thanks," she replied, "but I need to learn how."

As last night, her tone held insistence. Or maybe what he heard was simply determination.

Reluctantly drawn by her efforts to learn to do for herself, he pulled out a carton of eggs, grabbed butter and milk. "Then you can make them for both of us. Come on. I'll walk you through it."

"What about a recipe?"

"We don't need one."

As with the coffee and the marinara sauce last night, he explained what she needed to do. Then, with the coffee ready, he poured them each a cup and stood back to coach her through the preparation. With her at the stove, he leaned against the counter behind her, mug in hand, long legs crossed at the ankles.

Tess could practically feel his eyes on her back as she focused on her task. Tried to focus, anyway. As she glanced around from the pan she'd poured the eggs into, she found that he was, indeed, watching her. Only now, instead of reserve, what she saw in the carved lines of his face looked very much like curiosity.

She was curious, too. About him. She had been ever since she'd noticed the kindness in him when he'd first smiled at her son. She'd become even more so since he'd mentioned that his mother was a concert violinist.

After being put in her place so soundly last night, the last thing she wanted was for him to think she was getting personal. But she desperately needed to think about something other than how she'd felt branded when he'd caught her and the odd quickening in the pit of her stomach when his glance had landed on her mouth. The disconcerting sensation of feeling his heat seep into her wouldn't leave. Even now, she could practically feel the strength of his hands on her arms.

"Is your father a musician, too?"

Parker watched her turn with the empty mixing bowl in her hand. The white apron she'd tied loosely over her top and capris did a fair job of camouflaging her slender shape. That he had no trouble imagining her shape anyway was something he tried to ignore as he focused on her logic. It was as mystifying as her son's. He had no idea what route her thoughts had taken to get from pouring the eggs she'd beaten into the pan to his father's occupation.

"As far as I know, my father has no musical talent at all. That's Mom's thing."

"So you grew up with the arts? Symphonies? The theater?"

"And football," he expanded, as if to balance things out.

"Is your father a coach?"

"He's a Marine."

Parker caught the rise of her eyebrows as she set the empty bowl in the sink beside him. "Is he in Special Forces like you were?"

"How did you know I was?"

"From the information Bennington's e-mailed me. It indicated that you'd been a lieutenant-colonel."

He'd forgotten about the background sheet.

"Special Ops was my thing. He's a general. Three-star. Or maybe," he amended, lifting his mug to his lips, "by now, it's four."

Tess blinked up at him. She didn't know which fascinated her more at the moment—his parents' diverse backgrounds or his unexpected lineage. She couldn't imagine what a concert violinist and a military general would have in common. Except, perhaps, for the enormous discipline necessary for each to succeed.

She had the feeling that their son had inherited that trait in spades.

He'd lowered his mug. Realizing that her glance had fallen to his mouth, she hurriedly turned to the eggs shimmering in the pan and asked what she should do with them now.

He told her to let them set for minute, then give them a slow stir.

"You said your mom plays with the Philadelphia Symphony," she continued, fishing the spoon she apparently still needed out of the sink. "Did she join symphonies wherever your dad was stationed?"

"She's been where she is for twenty years. They were divorced when I was sixteen."

She hadn't anticipated that. "Then you lived with your dad," she concluded.

Two parallel lines formed between his eyebrows. "Why do you say that?"

"It just sounds as if you'd have wanted to." She gave a small shrug. "You followed in his footsteps. That says a lot about the respect you have for him."

The drip of the faucet into the bowl coincided with the clang of his mug on white tile as Parker slowly lowered it to the counter. He had little respect for his father at all. Never had. Never would. The man had refused to be there for his family. He'd chosen to marry and have children, yet he had never been a husband or a father in any way that had counted.

"My sister and I lived with Mom. And respect had nothing to do with my decision to join the military." He'd long ago reconciled himself to the bitterness he'd felt over his father's failure to be part of his family's life. None of it mattered to him anymore. That part of his life was over, never to be recaptured and certainly never to hold any influence over him again. "I joined to get his attention. The only reason I stayed in for so long was because I liked doing what I was trained to do and I was good at what I did."

"Then why did you leave?"

"Because when it was time to re-up, a headhunter for Bennington's made me an offer I couldn't refuse."

His apparent fondness for covert operations was something Tess knew she would never understand. What he might have had to do in those operations and where he'd had to do them wasn't something she cared to think about, either. Considering what he'd just so unexpectedly shared, she found herself far more interested in the desire he'd had for a relationship with what sounded like a rather difficult father.

"Did you get your dad's attention?" she asked quietly.

For a moment he said nothing.

"You'd better stir those," he finally said.

Parker wasn't closed about his personal life. With his head in his projects, he simply didn't think about it much—until someone reminded him he had one. He just had no idea what was prompting her interest. Or why it seemed so important to her that he answer when she did what he'd instructed and she turned back to him.

"Did you?"

"To a point." He wasn't closed about his past, but he rarely ventured into this particular territory, either. "He seemed interested enough while I was moving up the ranks. He acted as if I'd betrayed him when I didn't stay in."

He spoke easily, his deep voice utterly dispassionate as he revealed far more than Tess had expected to hear. Or maybe, she thought, more than he even realized he'd admitted. He had wanted his father's approval, but the only time he'd had it was when he'd been marching to his father's drummer.

She knew exactly how it felt to have a father who totally disregarded how his actions could affect those he should care about. She just wished she could be as unaffected by paternal betrayal as he appeared to be. She truly envied him that seeming indifference.

Her voice dropped. "He has it backward," she said, speaking of his father. "He's the one who betrayed you.

"Tell me," she murmured, the conviction in her tone turning to something less definable, "do you think it's possible to ever regain respect for a parent who turns out to be a hypocrite?"

Parker had no more anticipated her conclusion about who had betrayed whom than he had the genuine sympathy in her eyes. But it was the hint of hurt behind her question that jerked at his niggling suspicion that all wasn't quite as it seemed to be with her.

She'd made her query sound theoretical. Yet it was as clear to him as the agitated way she stirred breakfast that she had lost respect for one of her parents. Given that she wanted to be in her own home before her parents returned and how difficult she'd implied it would be to live there with her father, he would bet his next assignment that parent was her dad.

Once more he reminded himself that certain aspects of her personal life were none of his business.

"Sometimes acceptance is easier." It was the best advice he could give her, no matter who she was talking about. "People are what they are, whether we like it or not."

His glance skimmed the tense line of her back. When she said nothing, he reached in front of her and took the spoon from her hand. "Easy on those. You'll make them tough. I'll dish these up. You get the toast."

Accepting that her father was a hypocrite wasn't something Tess was prepared to do. She didn't know what else to do, though. Given how William Kendrick had always preached duty to family, then snuck around on her mother and had an affair, she wasn't sure she could see him any other way.

She wasn't sure, either, if the man now telling her son that breakfast was on its way was a cynic or if he just tended to be coolly objective about his relationships. All she knew for certain was that she wasn't accustomed to talking about a problem with a member of her family with anyone outside it.

Thinking it best to let the matter go before she gave away something she shouldn't, she buttered the toast when it popped up and poured two glasses of milk. One tall. One short. Thinking of her father reminded her that she had no time to lose finding a house of her own. The sooner Parker ate, the sooner she could show him the Realtor listings she'd pulled off the Internet so he could call and make an appointment.

## Chapter Four

"These are the properties I'd like to see."

With Mikey sprawled on the floor with his tank, Tess turned from the computer in the kitchen alcove and held out a notepad. Behind her, the computer's monitor displayed the home page of Vandree & Associates Realty, a company promising "exclusive homes to discerning buyers. 1M and over."

Towering over her, Parker took the pale green notepad, glanced at what she'd written. "These are just street names."

"That and a short description of the property is all the information they give. Peter Vandree is the name of the contact for each one." She pointed to where she'd neatly written the realty's phone number right below the man's name. As she did, her arm brushed his. The impression of bumping into steel coincided with the sensation of warmth. Conscious of the scents of soap and his citrusy aftershave, she took a step back. "I'd like to see them as soon as possible."

Parker said nothing else. He simply tossed the pad back onto the desk, picked up the phone and punched out the number, only to punch the end button and cancel the call.

"Is this number blocked? I don't want 'Kendrick' showing up on their caller ID."

Pulling her glance from where his biceps strained against the short sleeve of his shirt, she told him it was.

He hit redial.

She took another step back. Busily wishing she wasn't so conscious of him, she listened to him ask for Peter Vandree and give whoever had answered the names of the properties she wanted to see.

Nerves made her want to pace. The need to not miss a word he said kept her rooted right where she was.

"Ridgeline Road," he said after a moment, "Fox Hollow Lane and Kirkland Road. Parker," he continued, because whoever had answered apparently asked for his name. "No problem. I'll hold."

"Is he in?" Tess whispered.

"She's checking."

"She doesn't know?"

"I'm sure she does," he assured her, then hit the button for the speaker phone so he wouldn't have to repeat his entire conversation.

In the time it took the receptionist to relay what he wanted, the sound of elevator music gave way to a courteous male voice. "Mr. Parker. Peter Vandree here. You're interested in estate property."

"Are those three still on the market?"

"They are. If you'll come by and answer a few questions for us, I'll be happy to show them to you."

Parker's voice remained completely unconcerned as he echoed the man's phrasing. "I'll be happy to answer them now."

"Actually, what I need is for you to fill out a couple of forms. I'm sure you understand that homes of this caliber require a little more information about a prospective buyer than the usual photocopy of a driver's license and a license plate number." The man spoke easily, making it sound as if anyone asking to see such expensive homes would necessarily be aware of formalities. "The owners trust us to limit traffic only to those seriously in the market. You can provide us with either the name of your banker and an account showing availability of funds or a letter of credit. Either is perfectly acceptable."

Tess felt her heart sink. Parker barely hesitated. "And how do I protect my privacy?" he asked, absently flipping the edges of the pad with his thumb. "I understand your clients trust you with their property, but I don't want anyone to know I'm looking in this area. Maintaining privacy is of utmost importance to me."

"I see," came the thoughtful reply. "I certainly understand your concern, Mr....Parker," he said, now clearly questioning that to be his real name. "We still need a bank's letter of credit and positive identification to show the homes, but rest assured that confidentially is the cornerstone of my business. Our listings are exclusive. Their nature alone indicates that we deal with a clientele that expects discretion about their private surroundings. I've owned this realty for twenty years. Without my reputation, I have no business."

"What about your staff?"

The disembodied voice coming through the speaker bore no offense at the blunt question. "They also pride themselves on discretion at both ends of a transaction. Without it, they have no job."

Parker nodded to himself. To the man on the other end of the phone he said, "Thanks for your time. I'll get back to you."

He set the receiver back on its base. From the even way he looked at her, Tess thought he might remind her that he'd tried to tell her yesterday that there was more to looking at homes than making a phone call. As his glance moved from her to the little boy now flying his tank through the air like a plane, he apparently decided she'd figured that out for herself.

"I assume a letter of credit is not a problem for you."

Like her siblings, Tess had a trust fund that had become fully her own when she'd turned twenty-five. She had income from various Kendrick Corporation investments. A prenuptial agreement had, fortunately, protected it all. Money, she had. Confidence in a stranger's word, she did not.

"I can provide whatever they need, but then they'd have my name."

They'd both heard what the man had said about maintaining clients' confidentiality. Parker didn't remind her of that, either, though. He just picked up the phone, punched in another number and nonchalantly checked out the view of Jackson riding by on the lawnmower while he waited for his call to be answered.

"Yeah, Emily," he said after a moment. "It's Parker. Do me a favor and check out a Vandree & Associates Realty in Camelot, Virginia, will you? Owner's name is Peter Vandree. Says he's been in business for twenty years. Call me back on my cell." He chuckled, the sound rich, deep and surprisingly easy. "Of course I'm behaving myself. You be good, too. Thanks."

He was still smiling when he hung up. His expression was back to business when he said, "She'll call back."

"A friend of yours?"

"She and her husband both are. Emily's the background specialist at Bennington's. She looks into ownership and incident records of places our clients want to go if there's any question of their safety. She also runs checks on new clients.

When we get a request for protection from someone no one has ever heard of, we check them out."

"Why would you check out someone coming to you for protection?"

"We don't send our people into situations where there might be illegal activity. So what do you want me to do?" he asked, moving from his end of the business back to hers. "If this Peter Vandree is as reliable as he claims to be, do I make the appointment?"

Tess drew a deep breath, slowly released it. She'd told him last night that she no longer knew who she could trust. He also knew that she either had to trust him to protect her and her privacy as she was paying him to do or she would have to stay where she was and live with her parents.

"Emily's fast, but she's also thorough."

It seemed he sensed her struggle.

"If you're comfortable with what your colleague finds, then please," she murmured, "make the call. Just let me know what I need to do."

He gave her a nod. "It should only be an hour or so before the search comes back," he assured.

As he spoke, Mikey flew his tank into the space directly in front of him. "I can make this into a robot," he said, holding his toy up to him. "Do you want to see how?"

Tess, ever conscious of her son's manners and mindful of how often he'd been dismissed by such men, immediately reached to move him away. "Honey, we don't interrupt…"

"He's fine." Parker caught her shoulder to stop her. Conscious of how she went still, more conscious of how he hadn't thought to not touch her, he let his hand slip from where it cupped the top of her arm.

"Sure, sport," he replied, deliberately keeping his focus on the boy. "You can show it to me while we wait for a phone call."

\* \* \*

The room Parker temporarily called home had a double bed and a dresser on one end, a love seat and a television at the other and a bathroom with what he swore was the world's smallest shower. Pink cabbage-rose fabric and wallpaper covered nearly everything. A man's room, it was not. It did, however, provide a private space for him to work and a phone line for him to connect to the Internet. That was all he really cared about.

The writing desk by the Priscilla-draped window had his focus as he closed the door behind him.

Tess was on the phone to her banker. The information Bennington's had provided about Peter Vandree showed the man to be an upstanding, churchgoing, Little League-supporting member of everything from community organizations to the Virginia Realtors Association, where he'd been salesperson of the year five years running.

After trading phone calls with the man who probably suspected he'd been pretty thoroughly checked out, arrangements had been made to meet at his realty office at nine o'clock tomorrow morning. Tess had clearly wanted to look at the properties that day, but the need to make arrangements for the letter of credit to be delivered and with the owners of the homes for showings had pretty much thwarted that part of her plan.

To her credit, she hadn't acted upset, petulant, irritated or otherwise put out by that circumstance. She had simply looked a little disappointed and accepted with an admirable sort of grace that she needed to readjust whatever schedule she'd set for herself, thanked him for his help and, since she had no need for a driver that day, given him the rest of the day off.

Grateful for the extra time and relieved to be on his own,

his plan as he reached the desk was to get his last case behind him before moving on to the one coming up. That meant going online to review the reports the individual team members should have filed by now on the job they'd completed last week. The secret wedding of two movie stars on a private beach in Cancun had required ten Bennington's security personnel and the cooperation of the local police. Except for a few paparazzi who wound up being arrested for trespassing and a drunk guest who'd tripped over a tent cable and required stitches, the event had gone as planned. But until he read the reports, noted what could have been done better and assessed each guard's performance, he couldn't close the file.

If there was anything he hated it was paperwork. If there was anything he hated more than paperwork it was having it hanging over his head. The case he was on or the one coming next always held more interest. Except for lessons learned from errors, looking ahead held far more appeal than looking back. He applied that same philosophy to what little there was of his personal life.

He pulled his laptop from his leather briefcase and set it on the mauve blotter. With a frown for the dainty chair in front of it, he moved the chair aside, retrieved a sturdier one from the kitchen table while Tess, on the phone, made notes at the desk in the alcove and returned to seat himself in front of his computer.

He'd booted up and waded through the first five reports when he noticed movement outside the window beside him.

Tess had apparently done all she could on the phone for now. Between the edges of the open lace curtains he could see Mikey on the freshly mowed lawn, chasing something. A butterfly, Parker realized when he tipped back to get a better look and caught a flash of orange.

Tess, calling something inaudible, moved right behind him.

She still wore the cocoa knit top that hugged her throat and bared her arms and the matching capris that matched her flats. The tail of the gold belt she wore low on her hips swayed as she ran. She was hardly dressed for a romp in the parklike setting, but she didn't seem to pay any attention at all to the possibility of grass stains when Mikey turned and tackled her.

She landed on her bottom with Mikey sprawled across her legs. Lifting him, she turned him around and tucked him to her chest, laughing as she cuddled the giggling child.

She didn't seem to care if her little boy wrinkled or stained her clothes or smudged her makeup. At least that was the impression Parker had when she kissed the top of his head and Mikey turned around to hold her face between his little hands and give her a big kiss back.

Parker started to smile at the engaging child's wholehearted affection, only to feel that smile die as something uncomfortable settled in his chest.

He felt like a voyeur watching something he wasn't supposed to see. Tess's smile lit her pretty face, radiating a kind of warmth that touched him in a place he hadn't even realized existed.

Puzzled by her, not wanting to be, he looked away—only to find himself compelled to look back again.

At first glance, she appeared carefree, relaxed, untroubled. There was an exuberance about her that hadn't been at all apparent before, a natural sort of joy that existed simply being with her son. Yet the more he watched, the more he had the feeling that what he was seeing wasn't at all what it seemed to be.

Mikey pushed himself upright, using her shoulders to balance himself before he spun away to run off all that little-boy energy. As he did, Parker watched Tess's smile fade, her expression grow pensive, then troubled.

It was then that he realized it wasn't lightheartedness he'd sensed about her. Or anything so free as joy. What he'd seen had been more like her natural spirit struggling through, fighting not to be suppressed. Or maybe it had simply been a show for her son so he couldn't see how dispirited she truly was.

The disquieting thoughts had barely registered before the quality of her consternation changed and she looked toward the house. Specifically toward the window through which he watched her.

Preferring that she didn't catch him so brazenly analyzing her, he let the front chair legs hit the carpet and faced his computer.

He wanted to think that Tess Kendrick had created her own problems and that whatever she had to struggle with or overcome had been her own doing. That conclusion didn't feel anywhere as certain as it had less than twenty-four hours ago, but he wasn't going to question it. In two weeks, this assignment would be behind him and he'd be in Minnesota making sure no one nefarious got anywhere near the hotel he and his team were in the process of securing. Tess and her little boy would then just be another assignment summary in a file.

By one o'clock he'd closed the Cancun file and received the call he'd been waiting for from FedEx in Camelot. Tess and Mikey hadn't yet come back to the house, so he left a note on the island in the kitchen telling her he'd gone into Camelot to pick up a delivery from Bennington's and to call him on his cell phone if she needed him.

Tess found the note when she came in to change her and Mikey's clothes for a horseback ride around the lake. When they returned a few hours later, she found another note from

Parker indicating that he'd gone back to the FedEx office to send off something on another project he was working on and that he'd be back by seven or so. She was to call if she needed him before that.

She was in her bedroom undressing Mikey for his bath when he called at six forty-five to ask if she wanted him to bring back a pizza for Mikey's supper. He was at a sports bar where he'd stopped for dinner himself.

"We made peanut-butter-and-jelly sandwiches," she told him, cradling the receiver with her shoulder while she tugged her little boy's grass-stained shirt over his head. "But I appreciate you asking." She thought his offer terribly nice, too, considering he was on his own time. "You know, Parker," she said, wanting to reciprocate somehow, "you don't have to drive into Camelot for your deliveries. You could have them addressed to Ina or Eddy and the truck can come here."

"It's not worth the risk. The driver might catch sight of you or Mikey. This works fine for me. If everything is okay there, I'm going stay and finish watching the game."

She was tempted to ask about the other project he was working on. She wondered what game it was that held his interest. Not wanting to consider why she didn't want him to hang up just yet, she did neither. She'd given him the day off. He was free to do as he liked.

"We'll be upstairs when you return. Mikey's had a long day."

"I'll see you in the morning then. What time do you want to leave?"

"Eight forty-five."

"I'll have the car ready. And Miss Kendrick..."

"It's Tess."

He hesitated. "Tess," he finally said, his tone business-as-usual. "I suggest you dress in something inconspicuous.

I really don't think you need to worry about Vandree, but we have no way of knowing who might be in or around any of those houses."

Her smile for his concession to informality died.

*The owners' staffs,* she thought.

"I thought he said he'd make sure we were the only ones there."

"I imagine he'll do what he can," he assured her. Then, apparently not wanting to deal with her any more on his own time, he said, "I'll see you in the morning."

Apprehension and anticipation kept Tess totally preoccupied as she'd bathed her little boy, bathed herself and laid out their clothes so everything would be ready in the morning. She'd always prided herself on being punctual, partly because her mother had driven it home early on that everyone's time was equally valuable, no matter who they were. But mostly because Tess didn't ever want to be perceived as thinking herself more important than someone else by making anyone wait on her account.

Her son, however, had not yet developed an understanding of staying on schedule.

The digital clock on her nightstand read eight twenty-two when she picked Mikey up outside their bedroom door the next morning and, in the interest of time, carried him and the stuffed dinosaur he'd chosen as his companion for the day down the long curving staircase, through the dining and breakfast rooms and into the kitchen.

Parker had already been there. The welcome aroma of coffee greeted her as she hurried through the doorway.

"Bless you, Parker," she murmured. "Go sit at the table," she said to Mikey, standing him on the floor. "I'll get you some cereal."

"And milk."

"And milk," she repeated over the sound of footsteps behind her.

Glancing over her shoulder, she saw Parker emerge from the hall, frowning at his watch. "I thought you wanted to leave at a quarter till."

"I did. Do," she corrected, taking granola from the pantry. "We would have been down sooner, but Mikey got into my lipstick while I was dressing and I had to clean him up and change him."

"It was pink," said the little boy.

It sure was, Parker thought, taking a closer look at the child holding his dinosaur by its tail. Tess had dressed him in a navy T-shirt and little khaki pants much like those Parker wore with a white polo shirt himself. Just the miniature version. There was no mistaking the faint rosy stains on the boy's cheeks and forearms. He'd missed his lips, if he'd even been aiming for them, but from the stains it seemed he'd managed to draw slashes that might have made him look like a little warrior had the color not been so...pink.

"He had it all over his arms and legs," Tess explained, grabbing milk from the fridge and a bowl from the cabinet. "It took a while to scrub it off." Shifting what she held so she wouldn't drop anything, she took a spoon from the drawer in the island. "His legs were the worst. That's why he's wearing long pants."

"I drew a boat."

"And it was a lovely boat. But we don't draw on our skin."

"Not with anything," came the sober conclusion.

"Not with anything," she repeated, carrying his breakfast to where he'd climbed into a chair.

She poured milk and cereal into the bowl but kept the spoon as she returned to snatch a hand towel from a drawer.

Having nothing to secure it with, she tucked the ends into the back of his collar. "I don't have time to change you again," she explained, handing him the spoon. "Be careful, all right?"

Receiving her son's nod, she dropped a kiss to the top of his head and made a beeline for the coffee. "We'll make it on time," she said, assuring herself as much as the man checking her over from head to heels as she passed him once more.

Parker's glance made another journey over her lithe, leggy shape as she filled a cup, inhaling the rich brew as if it contained the essence of life itself. The woman looked incredible. Her makeup perfect, her hair freshly washed and smoothed back to fall unrestrained below her shoulders. There was no mistaking her polish or the delicacy of her elegant features. Anyone who saw her would notice them.

"Only if it doesn't take you long to get ready."

"I am ready. We just need to wait for Mikey."

"I thought you were going for low-key," he said, wondering if she understood what *inconspicuous* meant. "If you don't want to be recognized, you need to rethink a few things."

"What things?"

His glance went straight to her mouth. "Start with the lipstick."

Looking confused, she shook her head. "I'm not wearing any. It's just gloss."

"Whatever it is, it attracts attention to your mouth. And your hair," Parker continued, thinking like a professional, afraid he was reacting like a man. "You need to cover it." He hadn't seen it down before. But he didn't want to think too much about how soft it looked or how incredible it would feel in his hands. There were other distractions she needed to work on.

"You should dress down, too."

Tess glanced at what she wore. "I *am* dressed down."

She had chosen the most basic and nondescript clothing she owned—a white wrap blouse tucked into slim-legged jeans. A simple silver necklace and earrings. She didn't know how much more dressed down she could get, but she would do whatever he suggested. Being recognized was the last thing she wanted.

"I'll put on sunglasses," she told him, because she'd intended to do that anyway. "And a ball cap. I don't know how to cover up any more unless I wear a trench coat. It's going to be eighty out there today, but I'll do it if you think it will help."

He took a second look at her attire, tried to ignore the shape underneath. "Definitely on the sunglasses and the cap. Make it tan or beige if you have one. And tuck your hair up under it, too. Don't pull it through the back or leave it down."

"Anything else?"

A coat was out of the question. It would attract attention itself simply because it would be so inappropriate this time of year. Not that it would have done much good anyway, he thought.

"That should do it," he muttered, thinking she'd have to be covered from head to toe in a tarp for a man not to be aware of her, and headed out to bring around the SUV.

Tess had always loved the little town of Camelot. Colorful pots of flowers hung from the lampposts that lined Main Street and surrounded the town square. Art galleries, boutiques and wonderful restaurants shared block after block with specialty bakeries and markets. There had been a time when Tess had taken for granted an afternoon at the day spa or meeting friends for lunch at the charming bistro across from the huge forested park.

As Parker pulled the SUV up to the Realtor's office two blocks off Main and she glanced out the tinted windows that concealed her from view, her only thought was that she wanted to get out of there before someone saw her.

"I'll only be inside for a minute, " Parker told her. What he really wanted to say was, *Relax.* "Stay put and I'll be right back."

Relaxing didn't seem to be something she looked capable of doing just then, he thought. Had she not been confined in the car, the fine tension he sensed in her told him she would have been pacing. He just wasn't sure if she was nervous about being in public or anxious about the houses.

Figuring it was some combination of both, he left her and her son in the SUV and walked through the bronzed glass door, where he was promptly greeted by a neatly bearded and mustached fifty-something gentleman of average build in a navy sport coat and tie. Parker identified himself as exactly who he was—his new client's bodyguard. From the way the man had checked out his shaved head before his glance settled in the middle of his chest, Parker figured he probably knew that even before he explained that she wasn't going anywhere without him.

The man he dwarfed didn't appear to have any sort of problem with that at all. He hesitated, however, when he asked if he could drive them to the homes in his car and learned that they had a child with them.

"Our clients don't normally bring small children into our homes."

For fear they'll destroy something, no doubt, Parker thought.

"He's a good kid," he assured the fastidious-looking man and informed him that they would follow him to the first house in their own car—which was where Tess, seeming hesitant but trying not to look it, met him herself.

The Realtor held out his hand within seconds of emerging from the silver Lexus sedan he'd parked in front of the SUV.

"Peter Vandree," he said, trying not to be obvious as he looked over the beige Ralph Lauren cap that covered her hair and smoky sunglasses hiding her eyes. "It's a pleasure to be of service to you, Miss Kendrick. And I suppose I should say welcome home. You've been away for, what, a year now?"

Tess felt her stomach tighten as manners made her remove the sunglasses to make eye contact and return his handshake. The man seemed to mean well and he looked far more curious than disapproving, but it felt decidedly awkward to meet one of the undoubtedly well-informed locals who thought he knew all about her past, sordid and sensational as the media had made it seem.

"Thank you, Mr. Vandree." Retrieving her hand, she slid her sunglasses back into place.

"And this is your son?"

Her hand tightened on Mikey's even as she felt Parker move behind her. "So how many bedrooms does this one have?" she asked.

Either the man who'd somewhat skeptically eyed her child was the epitome of tact or he was too interested in a potential sale to press for polite conversation. With a speculative glance toward her and a more guarded one for the blond, literally pink-cheeked little boy smashed against her leg, he pulled a wad of keys from his pocket and headed for the lockbox by the stately Colonial's front door.

"This home has five bedrooms and five and a half baths. The garage is five-car with guest quarters above."

He opened the front door, entering first so he could see his infamous client's reaction to the spacious entry.

"You have antique wood floors throughout," he said when she walked in. "As you can see through the front salon over here and the living room in that direction, the house has been situated to take full advantage of the views."

The views were stunning. Drawn by the expansive views of gardens visible through the distant rooms, Tess glanced into the salon next to her, then cautiously looked down the hallway of the beautifully furnished home for any signs of life. Seeing none, she moved farther into the entry.

"How many acres are there?"

She watched Mr. Vandree check the clipboard in his hand. "Twenty-two. They include orchards and woods and an in-ground pool." He lowered his notes. "What is it you're looking for in a home, Miss Kendrick? The three you've chosen are all quite different."

From behind her, Parker watched Tess glance into the living room as she held her little boy's hand. He had no idea himself what she was looking for. He wasn't even sure what might appeal to her. It seemed she didn't either.

"You'll have to forgive me," she asked. "This is the first house I've seen. I'd just like to see what my options are."

"Of course," the man said as if he understood completely. "Perhaps if you'll tell me what your requirements are in a home, I can be of more help. How large a staff will you bring with you? Do you plan to entertain in small groups or large? Will you need space for overnight guests?" He looked to Parker. "And their assistants?"

Tess did little more than draw a breath, but Parker swore he could see the tension in her slender shoulders as they rose.

"Perhaps you could just show me the house?" she asked.

Vandree dutifully took a step away, only to turn back to look at the wide-eyed child behaving himself so beautifully. "Perhaps you'd like to start upstairs. There is a room that can easily be converted to a nursery. It has an adjoining room for

a nanny or au pair. Did his nanny come with you from Luzandria or will you be looking to hire here?"

Parker saw her stiffen.

The man was clearly making assumptions based on what
he could see and on what he knew—or thought he knew—
of her and her lifestyle. Parker couldn't blame him. He'd
made assumptions himself. Broad, condemning ones. He
would also concede that the man needed to know a client's
interests and needs to steer her toward the right property. Yet
the questions he asked made Tess uneasy enough that her disquiet seemed almost palpable.

To him, anyway.

"Why don't you show her the kitchen?" he suggested, just
to get things moving.

Tess's glance darted to him. He gave her a shrug, which
earned him a slight but grateful smile.

Peter Vandree was nothing if not quick. It took only a few
more conversational-sounding questions and a few more
nonanswers for him to realize that his client wasn't interested
in talking about anything but the house, and he turned his attention to expounding its merits.

Though Tess said little herself, it seemed to Parker that all
she really liked about the large, rambling residence was the
view. After a quick tour of the main level, she said she'd seen
enough. Since she didn't bother to have him show her the upstairs or any of the outbuildings, they were in and out in minutes.

"It's nice," she said to Peter on their way out the door. "But
I'm afraid it's too big. I don't need anything with rooms for
a housekeeper or a nanny."

The man's eyebrows shot up. He'd been given precious
little from her personally to go on, but he'd clearly thought
he had nailed her need for quarters for staff. The man recovered quickly enough, however, to keep any question he had

about his discovery to himself. "So you're looking for something without servants' quarters."

"Exactly."

"Then the next one might be more to your liking. There is a maid's room off the kitchen, but it could be used for storage. I believe it also has slightly less square footage." He flipped through his notes, lifted his neatly bearded chin. "Yes," he murmured to himself, having filed away what precious little she'd given him. "It is smaller."

It was. By two rooms. It was also the architectural opposite of the home they'd just seen. The only thing the angular, modern structure had in common with the Colonial they'd just left was the size of the acreage it sat on.

"Still too big," she concluded, so they headed for the third home on her list.

A beautiful reproduction of a Virginia farmhouse shared the same size problem with the first two. Perplexed but undaunted, Mr. Vandree mentioned another property a few miles away that she might want to see.

Within minutes they were back in the SUV, following the silver sedan, her and Mikey in the backseat, Parker chauffeuring.

"Do you mind if I ask you something?" he asked, glancing at her in the rearview mirror. "You had to know these houses were big from their descriptions. Why did you choose them?"

"They were the only ones with land. But I want that land outside," she informed him, apparently thinking of the house they'd just left. "I have no idea what I'd do with a twenty-by-twenty plant atrium. I'd just kill anything green and growing."

"Have your gardener take care of it."

"I'm not going to have one."

His attention darted once more from the tree-lined country

road to her image in the mirror. "How will you take care of a lawn and the grounds?"

Her brow furrowed as she considered the practicality of her decision. "A gardener, then," she agreed, sounding as if she were negotiating with herself. "But only someone who comes in once a week."

He didn't get it. He didn't get her. But he kept his thoughts to himself as Mikey claimed her attention by pointing to the horses grazing in a field and she entered into a conversation with him about the ride they'd taken on one of her father's horses yesterday.

With Mikey talking about how his teeth had hit together when the horse had started to trot, Parker considered the remoteness of the properties she had selected and her lack of desire for the staff that could be a deterrent to trespassers who might breach her security.

He was wondering if she'd considered just how vulnerable she'd be living alone and isolated when the Realtor's car turned and he followed it down a long drive that led to a neat little Williamsburg Colonial. White columns graced the porch. Charcoal-gray shutters flanked the windows and echoed the color of the front door.

There was no mistaking the interest in Tess's face when he opened her door and released Mikey from his seat.

"This one needs a little work," Mr. Vandree said the moment he walked over from his car, "but it has only four bedrooms and three baths. It also has a duck pond out back and its own orchards."

With Mikey at her side, she took his hand to follow the man who'd turned toward the house.

Mikey, who had already been led through three houses and missed his nap, immediately pulled away and held both hands in the air.

"I want up."

"Oh, sweetie, you're too heavy to carry. Just hold my hand, okay?"

"Nuh-uh," he insisted, coming as close to a whine as Parker had ever heard from him. "Carry me."

"Hey, sport." Tugging at the knees of his khakis, Parker crouched in front of the child. Until now the boy had been golden. "How about a piggyback ride?" He glanced to his mom. "Is that all right with you?"

Between her sunglasses and the brim of the cap shadowing her face, he couldn't see much of her expression. He could, however, hear the uncertainty that entered her voice.

"I don't know. He's never had one."

"You're kidding."

Parker figured every kid got piggyback rides. Certainly his dad would have given him one, he thought, only to cancel the assumption when he thought of how the child's father had been deprived of that pleasure. His own father had played the little game. He'd been younger than Mikey at the time, but his mom had a picture of him on his dad's shoulders to prove it.

"He wasn't around his grandfather and his uncles that much before we left for my grandmother's," she explained, seeming to overlook the child's father completely. "But if you're careful…"

The footsteps behind them stopped. Seeing that his client was occupied, the real-estate agent hitched his thumb toward the door. "I'll wait at the door," he told her.

Tess assured him that they'd be right there.

Parker never took his eyes off the little boy staring solemnly at him.

"You don't want to walk, huh?"

Mikey shook his head.

"Why not?"

"'Cause."

"Because you're getting tired?"

He gave a small nod.

"Then tell you what—you don't have to walk. If you'll climb up on my back and put your arms around my neck, I'll give you a ride."

For a moment Mikey didn't seem to know what to think of the offer. He clearly understood what it was to ride on the back of a horse. A ride on the back of human with only two legs required a little more reasoning. After a few seconds of consideration, he apparently decided that a ride beat walking no matter how it was accomplished and let Parker help him into position.

The moment her son's sneakers left the ground, Tess grabbed his shoulder to steady him, then watched, anxious, as his big brown eyes grew wide when Parker rose to tower above her. For a moment it seemed Mikey didn't know what to think about being up so high. A second later he giggled.

"Breathe, Mom," Parker murmured. "I'm not going to drop him."

Apparently aware of how uneasy she'd looked, she blanked her expression, tipped up her chin. "I didn't think you would."

*Liar,* he thought but let that bit of maternal protectiveness go in favor of getting the tour over with.

He fully expected another rejection on this house. Within five minutes he was sincerely hoping for one.

The moment they'd pulled into the drive he'd noted the lack of a privacy wall. But when he noticed the security pad for the alarm system inside the front door—specifically the make and model which had been discontinued some twenty years ago— his own alarm system had gone from standby mode to alert.

No rejection on her part was forthcoming, though. Within

five minutes it became evident that she was actually interested in the house with the spacious family room that looked
out on the Virginia hillside. Within fifteen, having discovered
a doggy door off the newly remodeled kitchen and learning
that the pond was actually large enough to float a small boat,
she was ready to take it.

"How much is this?" she asked Vandree.

From the Realtor's smile, it was clear he'd caught her interest, too. "A million five, but they're motivated sellers. I
think they'll negotiate."

"If I buy it, how long will it be before I can move in?"

"The present owners will be moving in two weeks," came
the quick reply. "They want to be settled in their new home
before school starts."

"So I can get a decorator in here to paint and hang new
drapes by the end of the month?"

Parker didn't quite hear all Vandree was saying about es-
crow and closing. He was too busy lowering Mikey to the
floor. Catching Tess's eye, he shook his head and motioned
to the doorway beside her.

Her response was a frown of incomprehension before she
looked back to the neatly bearded man standing next to her
in the family room.

"So you wish to make an offer?"

"Actually, I'll have someone contact you, but—"

"Not just yet," Parker concluded for her.

He'd come up beside her, with Mikey holding his finger
because he couldn't reach to hold his hand. Since she'd
missed his more subtle hint for a moment alone with her, he'd
have to go for something more overt.

"Will you excuse us?" he asked the man who now looked
puzzled, too.

Taking Tess by the elbow, he steered her through the doorway into the living room. He knew she was anxious to get into a house. He just hadn't realized she was so anxious that she'd buy the first thing she didn't hate.

Her voice dropped to an incredulous whisper. "What are you doing? I want this house."

"No, you don't."

Her eyebrows shot up even as her voice dropped another notch. "Excuse me?"

"It's not what you want," he insisted, his voice lowering to match hers. "You need to keep looking."

"What's wrong with this one?"

"Just trust me on this." A faint shuffling sound had him looking up. Vandree had moved into the hall, supposedly to collect the briefcase he'd left on the entry table, more than likely to catch what he could of their conversation. "This isn't the place to talk."

Tess opened her mouth, only to let out a breath of pure disbelief before she closed it in the interest of not creating a scene. Since she wouldn't be handing her Realtor a check that moment anyway, she glanced to where the heat of Parker's big hand permeated her blouse, took Mikey's hand when he pointedly released his grip on her and headed into the hall herself.

From beyond her, Parker watched the Realtor study him as if he was no longer sure of the scope of his duties or of his interest in the displeased young woman slipping her sunglasses into place. Bodyguards didn't tend to get involved in their clients' business or personal decisions. He certainly hadn't before. But then, most of the clients he had worked with hadn't been floundering around in the deep end of the real-world pool on their own, either.

"Are there any questions I can answer for you?" the Realtor asked, cautiously looking to each of them now.

"Not at the moment," Tess replied. "But thank you."

"We'll get back to you," Parker said from behind her and followed her and Mikey out the door.

## Chapter Five

Tess fully expected to ride in the back of the SUV with her son. Parker had other plans. No sooner had he strapped Mikey into his seat than he opened the front passenger door for her.

"It'll be easier to talk if you sit up here."

Since talking—or at least hearing his explanation for what he'd done—was exactly what she wanted, she got in, tried to ignore how small the spacious area seemed when Parker climbed behind the wheel and waited to see what he had to say.

He'd just started the vehicle and glanced around to back away from the Realtor's car when she decided that the ten seconds she'd just given him was ten seconds longer than she was willing to wait.

*Trust me* wasn't good enough.

"Would you please tell me what you were doing back there?"

Moving his arm from the back of her seat, he cranked the wheel around and focused on the driveway ahead. His arresting features remained frustratingly inscrutable.

"My job," came his succinct reply. "There's no way you and your son would be secure in that house. The alarm system belongs in the Smithsonian, the monitoring system only had two cameras and there was no peripheral system at all. Even if you replace what's there, have a wall built around all twenty acres and buy yourself a couple of guard dogs, the whole place is too exposed."

Her annoyance with his interference evaporated like steam. While she'd been looking at room layouts and thinking in terms of what she could manage by herself, he'd been checking for monitors and access and doing a little weighing of his own.

"Will you answer something for me? You don't seem to want any staff," he continued, clearly more interested in getting a response than permission as he turned onto the road. "You said you don't want a housekeeper or a nanny. And no gardener unless he lives off the property. Forget for a moment that there's safety in numbers. Why do you want to do everything on your own when you can afford to hire help?"

"Because I don't want a home run by staff." It had only been a couple of evenings ago that she'd become aware of how empty a house could feel with only her and her son in it. She'd become accustomed to feeling alone. What she hadn't considered in her fledgling attempt to fly on her own was the difference between feeling isolated and actually being that way. "I don't want to have to guard every conversation I have or have to worry about someone being upset with me if I have to let them go and selling whatever they've heard in my home to the tabloids. As for a nanny, that's the last person I want around."

She glanced between the seats. Mikey's head rested against the side of the car seat. He clutched his dinosaur in one hand, his eyes closing more slowly with each blink.

She turned back, lowering her voice as much to protect her little trouper from her realities as to keep from disturbing him.

"Aside from the fact that my ex-husband paid the one we'd had to report my every move to him, I don't want my son raised by anyone who doesn't love him. He deserves better than what he had," she quietly insisted. "That's why I want him to live as private and normal a life as every other little boy. I want him to be able to get dirty or make noise without someone telling him he's bad or getting after me to make him behave." The calm in her tone held a hint of steel. "I want him to know he's totally accepted. I want him to…have a puppy."

For a moment Parker said nothing. He simply considered the lovely, exasperated and utterly determined young woman silently daring him to tell her she couldn't do exactly as she planned.

The feeling that things might not be as they seemed with her had just compounded itself. In the space of seconds she'd raised questions from everything to why her ex had needed— or wanted—an informer on staff to who would have cared so little for her son. Her comments about giving Mikey more than he'd had and her desire to protect him from authoritarian or repressive behavior also made him wonder why Mikey's father hadn't stepped in—until he considered that Bradley Ashworth could be who she'd wanted to protect Mikey from.

The possibility stopped him cold.

"I don't think I'm being unreasonable," she defended. "It shouldn't take half a dozen people to take care of two. Plenty of people live on their own."

He had questions that demanded answers. But he was there to do a job and that job came first.

He hated to burst her tenacious little bubble.

"I appreciate what you want for Mikey. And I don't think you're being unreasonable," he conceded, because all she wanted was pretty much what every child should have. "But you are being unrealistic. Alone, you're vulnerable. So is your son. It's obvious you want a big yard for him to play in, but if you're going to live alone, your best bet for safety is in a high-rise condo or an apartment with a key to your floor and a guard in the lobby."

She seemed completely undeterred. "Camelot and the countryside around it don't have high-rises. And I'm not going to live in the city," she informed him, removing that possibility before he could even suggest it. Stubbornness suddenly sounded more like self-preservation. "That's where I lived when I was married, and I've never been so miserable.

"I know I can't get my old life back," she admitted, moving quickly past that admission, "but I can at least give him the freedom of the outdoors that I knew as a child."

She wanted to give her son the childhood she'd known growing up on the estate. The freedom to run on vast lawns, roam woods, paddle in a boat. To simply be a little boy. That was now as clear to Parker as the anxiety she busily suppressed as she looked out the window beside her.

What wasn't so clear was which part of her old life she was referring to—or why he ignored his own sense of self-preservation when it told him to leave her personal life alone.

"Which life are you talking about? Your own childhood...or the life you had before you left the country."

Her glance darted to his, moved self-consciously back to the road.

"The life I had before I married," she finally, quietly, said. "You said you know what's been written about me, so you know what's happened to my reputation." She absently rubbed one perfectly manicured nail. "I'm not that person."

He already rather strongly suspected that. "From what I understand, you've never said anything to make anyone think otherwise."

"I know," she murmured, still rubbing, and changed the subject before he could ask why that was.

"I want a place with land," she reminded him. "And water. A small lake or a pond. And trees."

She clearly wanted him to let her lack of self-defense go. Considering how long she'd gone without defending herself—to anyone, it seemed—he had no reason to think he'd get anywhere if he pushed for a reason. He would do as she wished. For now.

"An isolated place inside the goldfish bowl?"

"Exactly."

She wanted a place where she could protect herself and her child from the intrusions of the curious, the malicious and those interested in making a living off her misery. A place where she could raise her son simply and in peace.

The fact that her child seemed to be the focus of her life had touched him before. It touched him again now—and tugged at a sort of protectiveness that didn't feel familiar at all.

"You also said you want 'normal,'" he reminded her, thinking how incredibly difficult it would be for her to survive on her own. "But normal people don't have to think about buying a place that can be fitted with security cameras and fencing to keep the weird and the curious from walking right up to their front door. Or about someone snatching their son while he's chasing butterflies because they have millions to spare to get him back. Or about having paparazzi stake out their windows or stalking them when they go out for a walk. You hired me, remember? You know all this."

Tess sat silent. She did know all that. She'd grown up knowing it. She'd just totally forgotten to consider such things as she'd moved through the rooms of the charming old Colonial with its manageable size and wonderful views from every room. The house had simply felt safe.

Or maybe, she thought, remembering feeling that same way as Parker had walked away from her bedroom the other night, it had simply been his solid presence that made it seem that way.

"Other than a high-rise," she asked, not about to offer how he made her feel as defense for her oversight, "what sort of place should I look for?"

The quiet, no-nonsense tone of her voice drew his glance. She looked at him much as she had when she'd waited for him to proceed with her first cooking lesson. She knew what she had to do. She just didn't quite know how to go about accomplishing it.

She needed help. His help. Knowing she had no one else she felt she could turn to should have made him feel uneasy. Instead all he felt was the odd protectiveness that didn't want to let go.

"Let me see what I can find. Now that I know what you need, I can go through the listings with Vandree and check out some properties myself. If I find something suitable, I'll take you to look at it."

"You'd do that?"

He lifted his shoulders in a dismissing shrug, nodded his head toward the child now asleep in the back seat. "It'll be easier on him," he said, as if he was only thinking of her son.

Then, to keep from thinking about what her smile and her scent did to the fit of his pants, he headed for Camelot, grilling her about her preferences for architecture and how much work she was willing to have done on a place.

\* \* \*

Lunch was fast food from a drive-through, a first for Mikey, who treated a burger in a box with a toy as if it were the world's best treat. Dinner consisted of the pork loin Ina had bought for their dinner the night they'd first arrived. It took a preoccupied Parker all of two minutes to tell Tess how to roast it with the fresh vegetables he'd picked up from a roadside stand she'd spotted, but as before, he took his into his room to eat while he watched a baseball game on television and she and Mikey again ate outside on the veranda. In between, she'd made her bed, stripped Mikey's and put on fresh sheets, since that was where he'd gotten creative with her lipstick, and gathered the laundry that had accumulated at an alarming rate. She'd never realized before how many clothes her son went through in the course of a day.

Since she'd run out of time before dinner, it wasn't until after she'd cleaned up the kitchen that she found herself in the laundry room trying to figure out the machinery.

She was having no luck at all when she felt a warm tingling at the back of her neck and looked around to see Parker leaning against the door frame of the cabinet-and-counter-lined room. Mikey stood at the dryer beside her in his blue dinosaur-print pajamas, his hands behind his back to keep himself from opening the door she'd told him to leave closed.

She saw Parker smile at the child, that easy smile that was always gone by the time he looked to her.

"You look confused." He nodded to the lipstick-and-grass-stained pile of miniature clothes piled atop the front-loading washer. "Need help?"

Tess looked from the directions on the box of soap she'd found in the cabinet above her to the keypads on the computerized machine. "Thanks, but you've already gone above and beyond today. If this is anything like the dishwasher, I'll figure it out." Eventually.

"I don't doubt that you will." With that totally unexpected vote of confidence, he unfolded his arms from across his chest, straightened his big frame and came up beside her. "But I can probably save you some time."

She clearly had to learn all the basics from scratch. Yet, rather than remind himself of how spoiled he'd thought her to be, he now considered only that she was operating from a distinctly disadvantaged position.

Checking over the keypads himself, he asked her what she wanted to wash first, then had her punch in the water temperature and fabric type before telling her she'd need to spray stain remover for the grass and lipstick.

"You might want to wash that red shirt by itself or with a load of darks," he suggested while she treated the lipstick streaks on a set of sheets and a little white T-shirt and tossed them into the washer. "Otherwise the whole load will be pink."

Curiosity danced in her delicate features as she looked up at him. "That sounds like the voice of experience."

The chips of gold in her deep brown eyes almost seemed to glow when she smiled. But it was the curve of her mouth that put the warmth low in his gut. "Yeah, well," he muttered, not wanting to notice things like that about her. He'd come only to see if he could help her out. That was all. That's what he wanted to believe, anyway. "Years of trial and error teach you a lot. I think you've got a handle on this," he continued, reluctant to move, doing it anyway. "So I'll let you get to it."

He turned to her son.

"See you in the morning, sport," he said, giving the kid a smile.

He looked back to her, that same smile still in place.

"Let me know when you're ready to move on to the vacuum cleaner," he told her and saw her hand settle over her heart as he walked out the door.

Twenty hours later, Tess still wondered at the way her heart had squeezed when he'd smiled at her and at his casual, almost teasing offer to instruct her on other household machinery. She had no idea what to make of the man who managed to ease her with his presence and scramble her nerves at the same time, but she wasn't going to worry about the phenomenon. Electrical appliances weren't all she needed help with. As she moved and lifted the boxes she'd had stacked among old storage chests and furniture in the crowded attic the next morning, what she needed was some muscle. Unfortunately that muscle was with her Realtor.

She eventually found what she was looking for among the things she'd left in her parents' safekeeping after she'd escaped Brad. With nothing else to do until Parker found a house for her to look at and needing to stay occupied so she wouldn't start second-guessing her decision to come back, she'd decided to see how much work was left on her proposal for the Kendrick Foundation's women's scholarship program.

In the past few years her life had narrowed to escaping a miserable marriage and the legacy of its aftermath. The two things that had saved her sanity during much of that time had been her son and work she'd done for the foundation. A lot of that work had been fund-raising with her mom, sister and a small committee of like-minded women. But her heart had been in her desire to help the children of the underprivileged moms who won the scholarships the fund-raisers provided.

She'd always loved children, had always wanted to work with or for them. That was why she'd earned her degree in child development when her friends had been majoring in art history and business. Her sister had taken over the scholarship screening after their mom relinquished some of her duties to focus on other charities, and Tess had focused on the day-care center the foundation provided. As the foundation had grown, it had became apparent one center wouldn't be enough. It had been Tess's hope to add two more centers where their scholarship mom's children would be safe, educated and entertained while their mothers attended school.

All that had gone on hold when she'd left for her grandmother's. By then, it had been decided by the foundation's board—which consisted not only of family members but prominent members of the financial and business community—that her visibility on any project would be considered a drawback, and her regular work had been taken over by others. Since it had sounded as if any proposal she made wouldn't be acted on anyway, she'd left the project behind along with nearly everything else that had been important in her life.

She didn't care if she got credit for the idea or not. Given the low profile she wanted to keep, she'd rather come in under the radar, anyway. She would complete her proposal, then perhaps give it to her sister to present.

It was with that thought that she lugged the boxes into the comfortable family breakfast room and she and Mikey unpacked the boxes of blueprints used for the existing center, her rough sketches for the new ones and the now-outdated lists of potential sites and budgets.

She had spread everything over the long mahogany table and gone through about half of what was there when Parker returned late that afternoon carrying two sacks of groceries.

He wore faded jeans that hugged his powerful thighs and

a white dress shirt with its collar open and its sleeves rolled to expose his hard, sinewy forearms. The muscles in his broad shoulders shifted against that crisp cotton as he set the sacks on the island.

"What blew up?" he asked when he saw the paper-strewn table through the kitchen doorway.

She was already through the doorway herself, eager for his news. "That's just a project I'm working on. Did you find any houses?"

"Are those house plans?" His glance swept the hint of hope in her face as he pulled milk from a sack, then nodded toward the blueprints.

"They're plans for a day-care center. I was working on it before I left." She reached into a bag, pulled out bananas. "So did you?"

"Only one. It's about five miles away, on the other side of Camelot." Seeming to set his curiosity aside to satisfy hers, he spoke while he shoved two gallons of milk into the refrigerator. He did the same with the orange juice she handed him. "It doesn't have a lot of land, but it doesn't have servants' quarters, salons, guesthouses or atriums either."

So much for what it didn't have. "No land?"

"Not as much as you've asked for," he conceded.

"Is it even close?"

"The place has a lot going for it."

He reached back into the bag. Stepping closer, she ducked to catch his eye. She took his response to mean something like *Not even.*

"Is this one of those 'trust me' things?"

She wasn't sure what she saw enter his eyes. She wasn't even sure if whatever it was was there because of what she'd asked or because she'd suddenly gotten so close. She was within inches of him, close enough that his heat radiated toward her, close enough to see the way his eyes seemed to darken when his glance fell to her mouth.

"Just take a look at it. Okay?" Deliberately pulling his glance to his task, he took a step back. "Vandree will meet us there at ten o'clock tomorrow, if that time is all right with you. If you don't like it, we'll move on to something else."

Paper rustled as he offered the assurance and reached into another bag. "You have the makings for fajita salad or tortellini." He held two butcher-paper-wrapped packages in one hand—one large, one small—and three packages of fresh pasta in the other. "Which do you want to practice tonight?"

He seemed to take it for granted that he would be her tutor again. It also seemed he suspected she wouldn't want to see what he'd found if he had to answer too many questions about it.

"Ten o'clock is fine," she replied, wondering what was wrong with the place. She wondered, too, if he had any idea how much he could rattle her with little more than a look or how very much she appreciated what he was doing for her. "And, Parker," she began, needing him to know the latter, "thank you…."

"Not a problem." He clearly wasn't interested in her gratitude. "So which is it?"

It struck her then, as he stood with his eyes on hers waiting for her to make a decision, that he wouldn't be comfortable hearing how much she appreciated his help. Though it was hard to imagine him feeling awkward with much of anything, she wasn't about to press. "Which is more complicated?"

He told her they were about the same. He'd bought her seasoning packets for the meat and the guacamole, so the fajita salad was mostly a matter of slicing meat and veggies. The pasta was as easy as the kind she'd made the other night.

In the interest of expanding her minuscule repertoire, she told him she'd go for the salad and started reading the seasoning packet he handed her. She was thinking how cooking might not be all that difficult if everything came with Parker and little packages when she heard him talking to her son.

"Put this in the pantry, okay? Bottom shelf."

Standing even with Parker's knees, Mikey reached up to take the box of cereal the big man handed him, then walked over to where he knew the food was kept. He did the same with a box of granola bars and the other items he was handed, looking very pleased with himself each time he returned from the pantry for another assignment.

"And this is for you."

Tess looked up to see Parker holding out a small football.

Mikey took it with both hands.

"Lookit, Mommy!" He held up his prize. "Mr. Parker gave it to me!"

The pure excitement in the child's eyes was unmistakable. So was his uncertainty when, still holding it up, he turned to the man who'd given it to him. "What is it?"

Tess told him.

"I think the shape has him puzzled," Tess explained when Parker looked just as confused. "He probably doesn't remember the football his uncle Gabe gave him." She had packed it away before they'd left and stored it upstairs with everything else she hadn't considered essential to take. "All he knows are round balls. They don't play football in Europe. Not the kind we do here."

He immediately understood. "What they call football, we call soccer."

"I have a soccer ball," came the little voice from between them.

"And I still need to unpack it," she reminded herself.

Parker handed her an empty bag to fold. "They had those at the checkout. You like to be outside with him, so I thought you two could toss it around."

Mikey held the ball higher. "You do it, please."

Tess's first reaction was to distract Mikey by saying that the two of them could play catch on their own. Even though she was paying Parker handsomely to work for her and even though he'd somehow become willing to help her with her housing and domestic challenges, she didn't want to impose on him any more than she already had. She especially didn't want to impose her child on him—even if he did seem awfully good with Mikey.

It seemed Parker hadn't expected the request either. He also looked very much as if he hadn't actually intended to play with the child himself, until the plea in brown eyes so like her own had him caving in to the request.

"If it's all right with your mom," he finally said.

"It's okay," Mikey assured him, then sat on the floor with the ball between his legs to wait. The moment his bottom hit the floor, he looked to her. "Can my friend eat dinner with us, too?"

His friend.

Mikey was clearly oblivious to the lines drawn between her and the man whose glance jerked to hers. Yet it wasn't maintaining her and her bodyguard's respective roles that concerned her. It was the fine tension that tended to surface every time Parker's glance would drift to her mouth as she spoke or he would touch her or she would find herself next to his big body. She could ignore that tension until it seemed he could sense it in her himself and would move away as if he really didn't want to be so close. Then she simply did her best to pretend that the awareness wasn't there.

She did her level best to pretend it wasn't there now.

"Mr. Parker is welcome to join us whenever he wishes," she said, offering the invitation her sense of self-protection would have prevented her from offering again on her own.

The knowledge that the child regarded him as a friend apparently made it difficult for him to decline the request. Either that or he was getting tired of eating alone.

"Then, thanks," he said, looking at her, speaking to Mikey. "I think I will."

The round wrought-iron-and-glass table on the spacious veranda overlooked the back lawn and formal gardens. Yet the pleasant view, the lovely early-evening air and the peaceful sound of birds calling to each other from the sweet gum trees were lost on Tess.

In the ten minutes since they'd brought their dinner to the table, Mikey had barely stopped talking. Not to her. To Parker. The man comfortably seated across from her while he ate didn't seem to mind the litany of esoteric questions the inquisitive child usually hit her with during their meals. *Can I feed the ants? What do bugs eat?* If anything, he seemed equally amused and impressed by the workings of a three-year-old's mind. What had her attention, though, was the way Mikey kept glancing at Parker's shaved head.

She'd noticed him staring at Parker on occasion over the past few days. But always before, he would be distracted by something else and forget his curiosity. Since Parker had given him the piggyback ride yesterday and Mikey had found himself so much closer to all that skin, that curiosity had apparently gone into overdrive.

He now sat gazing intently at the man to his right, fork in his fist, completely ignoring what was left of his meal. Having never seen him quite that focused on Parker before, she was thinking she should whisper that it wasn't polite to stare when Mikey's little brow furrowed.

"Where's your hair?"

Tess nearly choked on her sip of iced tea. Hurriedly setting down her glass, she leaned toward him and lowered her voice.

"Mikey, honey, we don't ask such personal questions."

"Why?"

"Because it's not polite."

"Why?"

"I don't mind."

Parker sounded totally unoffended. Glancing up, she saw that he didn't look at all surprised, uncomfortable or otherwise embarrassed either. If anything, he appeared to be stifling a smile as his glance shifted between Mikey's innocent brown eyes and her faintly discomfited expression.

His attention settled back on Mikey. "I shave it off."

"Why?" came the question Tess could have warned him was coming next.

"Because my sister got sick a few years ago and was going to lose her hair. As much as it bothered her, I thought it would be easier if she wasn't bald alone." With a shrug, he forked up a bite of his salad. "I've just kept it shaved since."

Mimicking him, Mikey stabbed his fork at his lettuce, too. "When I got sick, I didn't lose my hair."

"You were sick?"

His face screwed up. "I couldn't breathe through my nose."

Every bit as serious as the child, Parker lifted his chin, gave a thoughtful nod. "You had a cold, huh?"

Curiosity suddenly became more important than his malady or mimicking the man he had clearly taken to. The fork landed on his plate with a clatter. "Can I feel your head?"

Tess didn't know why she felt as if she was holding her

breath. But Parker didn't seem to mind her son's curiosity at all as he pushed back his chair. As easily as if he'd been dealing with children all his life, he reached over and hoisted Mikey into his lap.

Mikey knelt on his thighs. Without a moment's hesitation, he gripped the white shirt covering one muscular shoulder to balance himself and flattened the other on the crown of Parker's bare head. As he rubbed, he giggled.

Parker grinned. "What's so funny?"

"It feels soft."

"What did you think it would feel like?"

Mikey's shoulders nearly reached his ears with his shrug.

Parker's response was to tousle her son's hair, which made Mikey giggle again. Mikey then wanted a high-five, something his newly discovered friend had apparently taught him to do while they'd tossed the football and she'd finished making dinner.

It was becoming more apparent by the minute to Tess that the big man with the impossibly sexy smile had a huge heart. He'd shaved his head to make chemotherapy easier for his sister.

She had already considered that he might have become accustomed to the look in the military and had simply kept it up after he'd left. Or that it suited the work he did now. Or because it was trendy or that he'd already lost a little hair and had decided to beat Mother Nature at her own game. Yet, of all the possible reasons he could have had, she had honestly never expected the one he'd offered.

"How is your sister doing now?" she asked, thinking how special his relationship with his sibling must be.

With Mikey demanding his attention, she almost missed Parker's brief hesitation.

"She died last year."

Blissfully unaware of the nature of the conversation, Mikey held up his hand again. "Another one," he insisted.

"I'm sorry," she murmured. That left him with only his mother. "Very sorry."

His charming grin was gone. What replaced it was merely a quirk of a smile.

"Me, too."

The admission came as easily as her child's giggle when their palms once more slapped midair.

"You were close."

She spoke the conclusion quietly, wanting to acknowledge how much he'd lost. What she'd lost with her siblings seemed almost insignificant by comparison. She felt bad enough that she no longer had their respect or the ability to feel comfortable with them. She could only imagine how awful it would be to never be able to see any one of them again.

"We were," he admitted frankly. "Jan never let me forget I was part of a family. She always called to check on me. And when we'd get together for holidays, she was the one who made them special."

"What about your mom?"

"She misses her, too."

"I'm sure she does," she murmured, watching him turn her totally captivated son around in his lap, "but doesn't she check up on you, too?"

"Mom and I both tend to get caught up in what we're doing and forget to pick up the phone. But, yeah," he told her, the admission seeming to remind him that it had been a while, "she does. And I call her. We just don't do it as much without Jan nagging us."

Beneath his formidable facade, the former-Marine-turned-bodyguard continually proved to be more intriguing and far kinder than she would have ever suspected. Her son obviously responded to that kindness. Family, no matter how small, seemed important to him, too. And that made her respond to him in ways that touched the very core of who she was.

Family was all that had ever truly mattered to her.

"Did she have children?"

"She never got around to it," he replied in that straightforward way he had of answering what was asked.

"Do you have a child of your own, then? I just wondered," she explained, in case she'd stepped on sensitive ground. She could easily see him as a father. She could easily see him missing a son or daughter, too. "You seem to have spent time around a little one."

"The only kids in my family belong to cousins. But it's been a while since I've seen any of them."

Since his sister died, she guessed.

"I probably should see them before they get much bigger," he muttered as if making a mental note to himself. "But for me, I can't ever imagine having one. I travel too much, and a kid needs his dad around."

The dismissal in his tone had been matched only by his conviction. Thinking how terribly final his decision sounded, Tess considered the little boy now nestled so comfortably in his strong arms.

Mikey clearly craved male companionship and a role model. Parker sat leaning back in his chair, one ankle crossed on the opposite knee. Leaning back against his solid chest, Mikey crossed his ankle over his other knee, too.

She couldn't help the defensiveness that tested her smile. It came unbidden and too suddenly to stop.

"Being there is only part of it. A child needs his father around only if his father loves him." He knew that, she thought. He had missed a lot as a child himself. Whether he wanted to admit it or not, he was probably paying for that lack right now. "A man can do too much damage otherwise."

There was another way a man could hurt a child: he could allow that child to care about him, then disappear.

The thought of how attached Mikey could get had her ignoring the sudden interest in Parker's expression as his glance narrowed on her face.

She'd never met anyone who seemed as comfortable with himself and who he was as Parker did. He seemed to be a man who held no secrets, a man who wouldn't be proud of his faults or his failures but who would admit them, learn from them and move on. What you saw with him was what you got. And what she saw held far more appeal for both her and her son than she was comfortable with.

The lights that illuminated the formal garden clicked on. An instant later, the lights surrounding the veranda followed suit.

The Fates—or the automatic timer, at least—had just provided the perfect excuse for her to put a little distance between Mikey and the man to whom they could both too easily become attached. If she were inclined to ever get involved with a man again, which she was certain she was not, and if Jeffrey Parker were the sort of man who wanted a home and family, which she now knew *he* was not, she could find herself being even more attracted to him than she already was.

"I should get him washed up."

With the scrape of iron chair legs on wood decking, she rose to lift Mikey from his lap. His little sneakers had barely hit the deck when she reached toward Parker's plate. She was about to ask if he was finished eating when his hand stalled her motion and bumped her heart against her ribs.

With his fingers curled above her wrist, her glance darted to his.

"Are you always so protective of him?"

She hadn't intended to be so obvious. Or so discourteous. Half of his dinner remained untouched.

"I'm sorry." The apology was quiet, sincere. "I didn't mean to be rude. You've been so good with him."

"You didn't answer my question."

She was aware of that. She was also hoping he'd overlook it when she realized that he wasn't so much looking *at* her as he was *into* her. His intense blue eyes searched hers as if he honestly wanted to understand whatever was responsible for her actions and reactions with her son. And maybe, just maybe, as if he simply wanted to understand...her.

The need for him to possess that understanding caught her as unprepared as the empty sensation opening in her chest. Something that felt as if it were dying inside her responded profoundly to his silent invitation to talk to him. There was just so much she couldn't say. She wanted so badly to unburden herself of the lies, deceit and deception. But the part that needed to protect the people she loved kept it all locked up right where it was.

"I've had to be protective," she admitted anyway and eased from his touch because something inside her responded profoundly to that, too.

The rattle of silverware hitting the table told her Mikey had decided he was finished even if no one else was. He'd picked up his plate and started for the back door.

"Excuse me," she murmured and, looking as disturbed as she felt, headed after him.

Parker watched her go, his glance fixed on her slender back. He'd noticed her protective instincts with Mikey almost from the moment he'd met her. Yet what had his interest now wasn't her unmasked concern that he might get too close to the child himself. It wasn't even his growing certainty that

she'd had to protect him from his own father. It was the be-
traying unease he felt wondering if she'd had to protect herself, too.

## Chapter Six

Tess had already suspected that the house Parker had found wasn't something she would ever have considered on her own. She knew that for certain the moment they drove through the gates of an exclusive walled and gated community built above a small private lake.

Land was at a definite premium. Every one of the twenty-one newly built homes sat on little more than an acre, and every acre was surrounded by eight-foot-high stone walls that reminded her of villas in Europe.

She knew the moment she saw the guard at the main gate and the small security camera at the double arched gate leading into the villa Parker wanted her to see that the security aspects of the newly constructed property met or exceeded his requirements.

Within a minute of pulling in behind Mr. Vandree's car and walking through the cobblestone courtyard with its tiered and peacefully cascading fountain, she began to suspect it might meet or exceed her revamped requirements, too.

She'd no sooner stepped inside the large, light-filled entry than suspicion turned to anticipation. She faced another court-yard and another fountain, only this fountain was surrounded by newly laid grass and a travertine patio.

The house inside was unpainted, uncarpeted, unfurnished. Everywhere she looked she saw nothing but high ceilings, windows and light. With the majority of the house situated around the center courtyard, every room she walked through made her feel as if the outdoors had come inside. Yet, for all the space and airiness, she had the feeling of utter privacy and seclusion.

She hadn't hesitated to trust Parker's professional insights where her and her son's privacy and safety were concerned. It hadn't occurred to her that his insights had extended to knowing how much she craved space and openness, too.

Or at least the illusion of it.

"This is wonderful."

She barely whispered the words. With Parker behind her as she held Mikey's hand, she moved from the spacious mas-ter bedroom and bath around to the room that would be Mikey's, past one she had no idea what she'd do with, past a sizable office and on around to a living and dining room that led to a kitchen with a long granite island. That island faced an open family room with a huge stone fireplace.

She could easily envision working in the kitchen with Mikey, making the cookies she'd promised herself she would learn how to bake, watching television with him in front of a cozy fire.

"Parker, I love this." It had been so long since she'd felt anything resembling true excitement that she almost hadn't recognized the first unfamiliar hints of it. She couldn't dismiss the feeling now. She *was* excited—and getting more so by the minute as she grabbed his arm.

"It's perfect," she insisted, too caught up in the potential around her to consider how easily she'd reached for him. "Especially the courtyard. Mikey can play out there and I'll be able to see him from just about anywhere."

She would be able to see him from the kitchen, from the office. The office was perfect, too. It would be the ideal place to do her work for the foundation. But it wasn't the room itself or any room in particular that made her feel just a little lighter than she had when they'd arrived. It was the new beginning the house represented.

She might have mentioned that had she not suddenly become conscious of how hard Parker's flesh felt beneath her hand and the smile in his too-blue eyes as his glance drifted over her face. With her heart doing a funny little flutter against her ribs, she fell silent instead and simply smiled back.

That smile caught Parker square in the chest. The more he discovered about the woman looking up at him, the more he realized that she'd been living in shadows for longer than he cared to consider. Yet, for that moment, the shadows had parted enough for him to feel the warmth she radiated like sunshine.

He couldn't believe how good it felt to absorb that warmth or to know he had helped put that light in her eyes.

His awareness of her grew by the hour. Or maybe it was the minute. With the feel of her small, soft hand on his arm, he decided it had actually narrowed to seconds.

His glance fell to her mouth. Had the Realtor not been in the next room, he would have been tempted to forget who she was and see for himself if her lips were as soft as he'd imagined them to be. With her looking at him as if she'd make no effort at all to stop him, he was almost tempted anyway—if for no reason other than to get the idea out of his head.

"I thought you might like it," he finally said. He wanted to think of her as just a problem waiting to be resolved. But no problem he'd encountered had ever left him feeling as edgy and restless as she did whenever he got a little too close. Or when she got too close to him. "We should find Vandree so you can tell him."

"Tell me what?" the Realtor asked, walking in with his clipboard.

He saw disquiet enter Tess's eyes as her hand quickly slipped from his forearm. He didn't doubt for a moment that that unease was there because she'd so completely dropped her guard with him. He just wasn't sure if she was more concerned about him having realized that or the possibility that her Realtor had when she stepped back to meet the curiosity in Peter Vandree's neatly bearded features.

"That I want this," she said, clearly hoping to deflect any interest he might have had in their close proximity. "What do I have to sign?"

"That's our house?"

"It will be. The man we just left has to present our offer to the builder, then our family attorneys will take care of everything from there."

"Oh." Mikey's nose wrinkled as his little mind raced. "And I have a bedroom and you have a bedroom?"

"You'll have the one right next to mine."

"And Mr. Parker has a bedroom?"

With his hands on the steering wheel, Parker's preoccupied focus remained firmly on the road.

"Mr. Parker will only be with us for another week or so,"

Tess replied to her son. "He'll be gone before we move into our new house."

"Oh," Mikey said again, then went silent.

That silence sounded dishearteningly like disappointment to Tess. But concern about her child's growing attachment to the man driving them back to the estate lasted only seconds before Mikey's endless curiosity took over and he asked if they would have a television.

Tess encouraged the questions. Without the distraction, she was too aware of the man beside her and of the subtle edge about him that made her feel strangely restive herself. That restiveness had been there pretty much since the moment she'd realized she wanted him to kiss her.

It had been a mistake to drop her guard with him. It wasn't as if she'd planned to do it. It wasn't as if she'd even been conscious of what she was doing at the time. She'd reached for him simply because she'd felt so excited, and it honestly hadn't occurred to her to exercise restraint. Reaching for him had just seemed like the natural thing to do. Or maybe, she thought, it had simply seemed necessary to the part of her that craved a connection with another human over the age of three.

Ever since those moments on the veranda with him last night, those moments when it had seemed he wanted to understand, she'd found herself even more resentful of her inability to talk about the anger and awful powerlessness eating at her over her ex-husband's duplicity, the hurt she felt for her mom over her father's betrayal and how adrift she felt no longer fitting in where she had once belonged. Yet, as hard as it was to have no one to confide in, it had felt just as hard to rein in the anticipation that had caused her to reach for him to begin with.

She was so tired of having to keep so much of what she

felt in check, but she needed to remember that her protector wasn't there to share her evolving life with her. He wasn't there to share anything at all. It didn't matter how grateful she felt to him for how kindly he treated her son or how he'd allied himself in her quest to prepare for her future on her own or even that he made her feel so safe. She needed to remember that he was with her only because she had hired him to be.

The thought did nothing but add an entirely different edge to her restiveness. Needing to do something with that odd energy, she headed for the phone as soon as they arrived at the estate to call the head of the law firm her family had used for years and find out what she needed to do to purchase a home with funds from her trust.

Five minutes later she told Parker there was nothing for her to do until she learned whether or not her offer had been accepted and that she was going to walk Mikey to the lake to feed the ducks. The afternoon was his to do as he chose.

As far as Parker was concerned, that was the best news he'd had all day. With nothing required of him just then on his other project either, feeling edgy himself, he changed his clothes and headed out for a ten-mile run.

The exertion relieved the worst of the restlessness he'd felt confined with Tess inside the SUV. He wasn't some teenager whose hormones jerked into overdrive at the mere sight of a desirable woman. But he was hardly a monk, either. He was a physical man. He knew his body, its needs, its demands. If he took care of it, it would take care of him—and anyone relying on his abilities. He prided himself on physical and emotional control in every aspect of his life. Yet, the more he was around Tess Kendrick, the harder it became to block his mind to the slow-burning heat her scent put low in his gut or ignore thoughts of how the soft curves of her body would feel beneath his hands.

He managed to pound the latter images from his head along about the fifth mile, which took him through the park in Camelot, where he bought a bottle of water and a newspaper from a vendor, downed the water and headed back along the two-lane country road he'd taken in. Getting her out of his head completely wasn't going to happen, though. Not until he'd turned her over to the bodyguard he was filling in for.

Reminding himself that he could put up with anything for another week, he turned his focus to the pounding of his heart as he ran, the burning in his muscles, the scream of his lungs for air—until five miles later when he was reminded that Tess didn't have the luxury of moving on as easily as he did.

He was breathing hard as he let himself through the main gate and walked up the drive to the mansion's servants' entrance. Sweat made his tank top cling to his back and chest, and most of his thoughts were on getting a shower when he absently opened the thin newspaper to kill the last minute of his cooldown. He would admit to a certain curiosity about the area that had drawn Tess back from halfway around the world, but it wasn't the paper's focus on the quiet community that caught his attention. It was Tess's name in bold print in the People section in the *Camelot Crier.*

Either her Realtor had a leak in his office or someone had watched them on a security monitor in one of the homes they'd toured.

Considering what he read, his money was on the latter, especially since a specific home was identified. It was the one she'd first wanted to buy. Even as antiquated as its security system had been, its cameras had worked well enough to ruin her attempt to remain anonymous.

The short paragraph stated, "Tess Kendrick, youngest daughter of William and Katherine Kendrick, whose scandalous divorce from Bradley Michael Ashworth III last year rocked the Virginia social scene, has reappeared after a year-long absence. It is widely believed she spent at least part of that time living with her maternal grandmother, the queen of Luzandria, either at the royal palace or at the queen's summer residence in the Alps. Tess is apparently looking to buy in the area and recently toured the 1.5-million-dollar residence of Simon and Shelley Weiss with a small child believed to be Bradley Michael Ashworth IV and an unidentified male companion who seemed quite close to little Bradley and to Tess herself."

According to the columnist, she and her "male companion" had been seen having "a disagreement" while at the property but had otherwise seemed quite "in tune" with each other.

The bit of wholly unashamed hearsay ended with speculation about whether or not they were looking to buy property together.

Parker folded the paper in disgust and let himself in the back door. It never ceased to amaze him how the press could take something insignificant, take it out of context, put their own spin on it and make it sound so totally like something it was not. The gossip columnist hadn't even gotten Mikey's name right. Tess never called him Bradley.

He was thinking the misinformation wasn't necessarily a bad thing from a security standpoint when he tossed the newspaper onto the island in the dim and empty kitchen. He would shower the sweat off, then track Tess down and show her the article. Or so he was thinking when a piece of paper fluttered to the floor. The newspaper had knocked it off on its short slide across the island's slick surface.

He recognized Tess's neat script even as he snatched up the piece of pale sage notepaper.

*Parker—I found a recipe for pasta that called for the pancetta you bought the other day. Yours is in the refrigerator if you didn't get dinner out. It's actually edible. Just reheat it. Mikey and I are going to our room. See you in the morning. Tess*

He felt his mouth curve even as he tossed the note back onto the counter. He wasn't going to worry about how touched he was by her efforts or how thoughtful it had been for her to think of his care and feeding. He wouldn't give another thought, either, to why he actually felt relieved to spare her the article until morning. There was no need. He'd be gone soon.

"How come Mr. Parker can't live in our new house with us?"

Tess was normally a morning-shower person. Without anyone to watch Mikey for her, however, she'd found it necessary to bathe in the evening while he wound down with his books and cars on her bed. That was why they always retired to her room so soon after supper.

He was playing on her bed now, freshly bathed himself, while she watched him from her bathtub.

"Because he's only working for us for a little while." Reclining in the blissfully warm, verbena-oil-scented water, she dangled a thick white washcloth from one big toe and waited for the question to come.

"Why?"

"Because," she explained, smiling at his predictability, "that's when the lady bodyguard we wanted will come to work for us."

"Why?"

"Because," she concluded and left it at that because she

didn't want to think about Parker no longer being with them. She narrowed her glance through the bathroom's open door-way. "What are you playing with?"

"A thing."

From where she lay soaking, the "thing" looked like the remote control for the television. If he punched the wrong buttons, he'd mess up the cable reception again. "Put that down. Okay?"

She barely heard his quiet "'Kay," before the click of a latch joined the slam of her bedroom door against the wall. In the space of a heartbeat, Mikey's glance jerked up. Her own eyes widened on the mountain of muscle in a U.S. Marines T-shirt and sweatpants suddenly filling the space at the foot of her bed.

Every ounce of Parker's body was tensed to move as his glance jerked from Mikey smiling up at him from the piles of cream and blue pillows and swept around to freeze on her in her bath.

She'd already bolted upright, steamy water sluicing from her arms and bare breasts. Grabbing for the washcloth floating at the end of the tub, she covered herself as best she could.

Mikey held up a book.

"Will you read to me, Mr. Parker?"

Tension radiated from him in waves. "Not now."

That same tension drew his features taut, honed his voice with an edge of razor-fine steel. "My pager went off," he said to her.

Her only response was the uncomprehending shake of her head.

Parker's mind worked in overdrive. Even as he took in the layout of the room, he drew instantaneous conclusions for himself. The high cream brocade curtains were drawn and still. No feet were visible beneath them. A quick whip upward of the ruffled bed skirt revealed the box spring too low to the carpet for anyone to be under it. The upholstered wingback chair angled from the corner sat too low for anyone to hide beneath and was too short for anyone other than a child to hide behind. Likewise the daybed visible in the sitting area.

His body primed with adrenaline, he swept his glance back to the bed. The pager he'd given Tess lay among an assortment of pillows, blocks and books.

Snatching up the small device, he looked to the child so innocently watching him.

"Did you push any buttons on this?"

Mikey's fine blond hair brushed his eyebrows with his slow, suddenly uneasy nod.

Adrenaline competed with the image burned into his brain of Tess's wet body. "Never," he said, "ever," he emphasized, "touch this unless you or your mom are in danger. Do you know what danger is?"

Eyes wide, Mikey barely shook his head.

"Danger is when someone comes through the window while you're sleeping. Or when a stranger grabs your mom and tells you to be quiet or he'll hurt her. It's a fire that's blocking your way out…."

"Parker!" Water splashed wildly against the sides of the tub. "That's enough!"

Tess grabbed the bath towel from the wide marble ledge. As she did, she bumped into bottles of bath oil, conditioner, shampoo. Something landed in the tub, the rest on the floor. She had no idea which had gone where. Her little boy's eyes had grown wider by the second. Mikey didn't know what danger was. Not in the context Parker so bluntly described. As protected as he had been, the child could be frightened simply by the explanation.

"I'll take care of this," she insisted, sloshing water every-where as she stepped onto the bath mat. "Please."

Parker went silent.

Tess stood dripping onto the rug. She had a large bath towel gripped in front of her. With her free hand, she shoved back strands of damp hair that had escaped the knot wound atop her head.

· As her hand fell past her bare shoulders, his glance fell with it. The towel angled to one side, exposing the water droplets on her slender thigh, the shapely calf of her leg.

His jaw locked as he tossed the pager back onto the bed. Without another word, he strode from the room.

Tess couldn't sleep.

Mikey, however, was dead to the world.

If he had been traumatized by his introduction to the dan-gers that could threaten their lives, he hadn't acted it. She'd explained what she felt her three-year-old might compre-hend without giving him nightmares of bogeymen and as-sured him that she would always do everything possible to make sure he was safe, but when she'd asked if he had any questions, he'd wanted only to know if Mr. Parker was mad at him.

She had no idea how Parker felt about anything at the mo-ment. She did not, however, want her son worrying, so she'd told him she was sure everything would be fine, and he'd turned his attention to picking out the story he wanted her to read.

He'd fallen asleep shortly after that.

That had been well over an hour ago, but she had yet to find anything to calm her own restless mind. Reading proved impossible: she couldn't seem to concentrate. Watching tele-vision with earphones proved futile; not a single program caught her interest. An attempt at yoga occupied a few minutes, but she totally lacked the mental discipline that evening to achieve anything remotely resembling inner peace, much less balance or harmony. She would barely start to focus on her breathing before her mind would wander to what she'd seen in Parker's expression as his glance moved over her body—and to what she'd felt when his eyes had met hers.

No man had ever made her feel such heat with just a look. What had left her so shaken, though, was how she'd been drawn by the hunger she'd seen in him.

That undeniable circumstance had her questioning her judgment on a number of levels in the moments before she unfolded herself from her position on the floor, checked her soundly sleeping son and, pulling on her short pink robe, headed down the stairs in search of anything chocolate. Chocolate ice cream had been on the grocery list Parker had filled in Camelot the other day. She would start with that.

Or so she was thinking as she stuck a spoon into a pint of Häagen-Dazs and turned from the freezer to face the man who'd driven her to eating straight from the carton.

Parker stood at the far end of the kitchen. He still wore the faded blue U.S. Marines T-shirt and light gray sweatpants he'd changed into after his run. The tense set to his jaw hadn't changed since she'd last seen him, either.

"I heard noise," he said, his eyes steady on hers. "I just wanted to check it out."

Now that he knew who was there, Parker turned to go back to staring at the talking head on CNN.

His conscience allowed him only one step before he took a deep breath and turned right back.

He owed her an apology. Not for bursting into her room; he would react exactly the same way were the situation to present itself again. When a client's night pager went off, he always assumed the worst until he knew otherwise.

"I shouldn't have been so short with Mikey."

His impatience had actually had far more to do with himself than with what the child had so unwittingly done. For a few precious seconds, the sight of her in her bath had totally sidetracked him from his purpose and robbed him of an instant that could have made the difference between harm and safety had the circumstances not been so innocent. He'd been trained to expect the unexpected. He knew that distractions were dangerous. Yet it wasn't only his momentary professional lapse that had seemed so dangerous to him. It was the unwanted and relentless pull he'd been fighting toward her pretty much since the moment they'd met.

"I hope I didn't frighten him." Even as he offered the admission, he tried to get the image of her barely covered body out of his head. She stood there barefoot, in a pink silk robe that hit her midthigh. By lingerie standards, the thing was almost virginal. But he knew how tempting she looked under it. "I'll talk to him if you want me to. Now. Or in the morning. You name it."

Tess moved to the counter, set down the ice cream chilling her hands. His concern seemed as palpable to her as the tension that radiated toward her, surrounding her, making it a little hard to breathe.

"You don't need to do that. He's…fine," she concluded. "I should have kept the pager with me."

She didn't move. Except for the jerk of a muscle in his jaw as he considered her, neither did Parker.

"I should apologize for embarrassing you, too," he finally said.

Tess opened her mouth to tell him she hadn't been embarrassed at all, only to promptly close it when she realized what she'd be admitting. Of all the things she'd felt when his eyes had locked on hers, embarrassment truly hadn't been among them. As surprised as she was bewildered by that, she was about to remind him that he'd just been doing his job when he drew a deep breath and cupped his hand at the back of his neck.

Her hesitation had him glancing away.

"It might be best if I call someone else to take over until your first request arrives. I think you wanted Stephanie Wyckowski." Hard muscles shifted as his hand fell. "If you agree, I'll call Bennington's in the morning to see if another female can take over until she's available."

"No! No," Tess repeated, forcing the insistence from her tone. "There's no need for that." She didn't understand the quick panic that shot through her. She knew only that she didn't want him to go. "Please. Stay," she requested, more calmly. "You only have to put up with us for another week."

Putting up with her wasn't the problem. The problem was the unexpected plea in her lovely eyes and the unguarded urgency he'd heard in her voice. He'd had no idea how she would react to any part of the unforeseen incident upstairs. He just knew he hadn't anticipated what he heard and saw in her now.

He had the feeling that if he closed the distance between them, she would do nothing to discourage his touch. It was that kind of purely feminine vulnerability softening her features.

The suspicion did nothing to alleviate the tension coursing through his body. The woman was the most impossible combination of innocence and seduction he had ever met. She was also the only woman to tear a chunk out of his prided ability to stay totally focused or who had ever made him seriously consider leaving a job.

He had been spared compromising that record. He wouldn't back out on this assignment. What he would do, however, was keep his distance.

"If you're sure you're comfortable with that."

She did no better masking her relief than she had her panic. "I'm sure. Really," she added so he wouldn't change his mind. "Let's just forget all this. Okay?"

Like that was going to happen, he thought. "Okay," he agreed, willing to give it a shot, anyway. "Consider it forgotten."

"Thank you."

His mouth formed a hard line as he lifted his chin, gave her a nod. "Good night, then."

"Good night," she echoed and watched him walk away for the second time that evening.

Parker made it halfway down the hall before he remembered the newspaper. It still lay on the island, open to the column he'd intended to show her in the morning.

The desire to protect her a while longer from the knowledge that she'd been discovered immediately went to battle with his need for distance.

The mental skirmish lasted mere seconds.

The woman was seriously messing with his head. His job was to protect her privacy and her safety and deal with whatever repercussions arose from her having been identified. It was not his job to protect her from being distressed by what was put into print about her.

He entered his room and closed the door behind him with a decisive click. Yet even as he deliberately blocked the sounds of her moving about the kitchen, his logic did nothing to alleviate the twinge of guilt he felt leaving her to discover the news on her own.

Parker swore.

Swearing again, he jerked the door back open and headed for the kitchen.

He was too late. Tess stood at the island, her ice cream forgotten as she looked up from the newspaper.

"They're not going to let it die." Sounding far more unaffected than she looked, she shook her head in defeat. "They couldn't just identify me as William and Katherine Kendrick's daughter. They had to remind everyone about Brad and the mess of my divorce."

Parker thought for certain that her first concern would be paparazzi. The national syndicates would pick up the local article in no time.

"Are you okay?" he asked.

She gave him a brave little nod. "I'm fine," she replied, picking up the carton of ice cream, leaving the paper. "This was bound to happen sooner or later. I'd just hoped for a little more time."

From the small smile she gave him, it almost appeared as if she was taking the matter in stride. Anyone else watching her would have thought just that. Yet he couldn't dismiss the concern he'd felt as unwarranted. From the way she took the entire pint of ice cream with her as she said goodnight, he had the strong and certain feeling that she was doing what she did with all the other things she wouldn't talk to him about—shoving down what troubled her to deal with on her own.

They wouldn't let it go away.

It had been over a year, yet the first thing she'd seen printed about her had brought up what she'd desperately hoped everyone would let her move beyond. The rest of it, the conjecturing about Parker and what role he might play in her life, was easier to dismiss. That speculation would go nowhere because he would soon be gone. The scandal that had ruined her reputation would apparently haunt her forever.

That distressing thought remained stuck like lint to black wool in the back of her mind as she spent the next morning on the phone with Martha Talbot, the no-nonsense real-estate attorney assigned by the head of the law firm to handle the purchase of the villa. Her offer had been accepted. Between the calls to and from the lawyer, Mikey's need to run off a little energy outside and her dismay over the story in the paper that would eventually alert the paparazzi to her presence, she had little time to worry about why she felt so relieved that Parker had stayed. She just accepted that she was so very thankful he was there…somewhere. The last she'd seen him, he'd been outside on the lawn, pacing a trench in it while he talked on his cell phone.

She had more calls of her own to make.

With Mikey now down for a much-needed nap, she left her bedroom door open so she could listen for him, descended the stairs and headed back through the formal dining room to the space that had become her office of sorts. The other rooms she might have used—the den or the library— had dustcovers over most the furniture.

That had left the light and airy breakfast room, with its row of tall, multipaned windows, large mirror above the sideboard, family pictures on the walls and plenty of space to spread out. One end of the long mahogany table remained overtaken by her foundation project. The other end was now covered with the papers she'd been faxed and her notes on the sale of the house.

The house would be hers in a matter of days. Her parents would return in a matter of weeks. That meant she had no time to waste arranging for paint, carpeting, window coverings and furniture. At least in that territory she knew what she was doing. She had a good eye for color and texture. She knew what she liked and what she didn't. She knew she wanted kid-friendly fabrics and none of the stark, hard edges and smudgable surfaces Brad had favored. She also knew the best way to expedite the process would be to hire an interior designer with major connections, which was why she had looked up Virginia Hellerman-Mays's phone number in the Rolodex in her mother's office at the other end of the house. Her mom had raved about the work Ginny had done for her on the remodel of the Hamptons house and mentioned more than once how dependable and conscientious the woman was.

Tess sat down in a chair near the head of the table. Picking up the portable phone she'd brought in from the kitchen, she punched in Ginny's number. The woman's answering machine picked up on the third ring. Her message indicated that she was either out or on another line. Hoping it wouldn't take Ginny long to get back to her and hoping, too, that she'd be available—and willing—to take the job, Tess left a message asking her to call at her earliest convenience. She'd barely hung up and started looking through the Yellow Pages for car dealers so she could check that item off her list when the phone rang.

Thinking the designer might have been screening her calls and was calling her back or, possibly, that it was her lawyer again, Tess didn't bother to glance at the caller ID before she snatched up the phone with a quick "Hello?"

Seconds later, she felt her heart sink at the sound of her ex-husband's voice.

## Chapter Seven

"I'm surprised you came back, Tess."

Hearing Brad on the other end of the line, Tess slowly rose from the chair at the end of the cluttered table. With one hand over the sickening thud of her heart, her other gripping the phone, she quelled a definite and totally pointless urge to run.

"This is my home," she quietly reminded him.

"Ah, yes," came his murmured reply. "The rolling hills of Virginia. Have I ever told you how much that place bores me?"

"Several times."

"At least in Palm Beach there's a little excitement," he continued, the well-modulated tones of his voice utterly conversational. "The weather's gorgeous here. How about there?"

Knowing he was four states away somehow made it easier to breathe.

"Typical for late July." She drew a calming breath, hoping she sounded conversational, too. "Why are you calling?"

She thought she heard him sigh. Or maybe he'd just blown smoke from one of the expensive cigars he favored. "Can't I just call to welcome you back to the States?"

He could, but she sincerely doubted it. Brad didn't do anything without a motive. "Is that why you're calling?"

"Actually, no." The admission came with a hint of what sounded suspiciously like displeasure. "Mom heard about some article in the *Crier* that said you were in Camelot with your boyfriend."

"He's not my boyfriend," she cut in, wanting to head that impression off from the start. The last thing she wanted for Parker was the hassle of being hounded by paparazzi himself. Not that he couldn't handle them. "He's my bodyguard."

"Muscle. That's okay, then," Brad muttered, as if she needed his permission for a personal life. "Listen," he continued before she could even react to the thought, "Mom wants to see the boy when they get back in a weeks."

*The boy.* He couldn't even call his son by name.

Calm slipped as her unease increased. "Your parents are welcome to see Mikey. He's their grandson."

"Yeah, well, they're on me to see him, too. They finally quit nagging me about it after I told them you wouldn't let me see him at your grandmother's, but now that you're back, I suppose I should."

She could practically see Brad's patrician features pinch at the thought. She knew he couldn't care less about being with Mikey. He did, however, care very much about what his parents thought of him.

"You could have seen him anytime you wanted." The hand over her heart drew into a fist. "But you never asked," she reminded him. "You know the judge didn't place any restrictions on visitation."

Only the knowledge that Brad would never use the privilege had kept her from panic when he had been granted full visitation rights. Her attorney had given his attorney the number to call to make arrangements. Yet not *once* had he so much as pretended he wanted to see his son.

"You can see him with your parents." And with her. As hard as it would be to bear the senior Ashworths' censure, she wasn't about to turn her son over to people who to Mikey would be virtual strangers. At least Brad's parents were good people. When she'd seen them with him before, she'd never doubted that they cared about their grandchild.

This time he sighed for certain. "This isn't about the legalities, Tess. I told my parents that every time I called to make arrangements, you said you'd tell the palace guard not to let me in. I told them that if they called to see him, you'd do the same thing. I know they'll bring it up when you get together. I want you to confirm that story."

Anger slammed into disbelief. "I am not lying to your parents. You know I never…"

"You'll say what I tell you to say," he countered easily. "We have an agreement, remember? You either go along with me or I release the photos I have of your father. The ones you didn't see. And by the way," he continued, his voice chillingly calm with the power he held, "if you feel like disappearing again, that's fine with me. It would just back up my story about how you're keeping me from my son."

The desire to tell him to go to hell was the strongest urge Tess had felt in months. With every fiber of her being she craved the freedom to tell him she wasn't going anywhere, that she and Mikey were staying right where they were because she'd just started reconstructing the life he'd taken away from them. Yet she could vent none of that. She didn't doubt for an instant that if she defied him in any way, he would use the threat he held over her or somehow make her situation even more untenable than it was. The man she had married cared about nothing other than protecting the golden-boy image his parents and everyone else seemed to have of him. The man could exude charisma, excitement, charm. He drew people to him with enviable ease. She just wished she'd realized how totally self-centered and self-serving he was when he'd first turned that charm on her.

Hating how powerless she felt, the fight drained from her voice. "Have your mother call me," was all she could say.

Brad wasn't the type to gloat when he knew he'd won. His manner was more insidious. He simply took victory as his due and somehow made it sound as if she'd been silly to think the conversation would end any other way. "I knew you'd see it my way, Tess. Take care of yourself," he had the nerve to add and left her listening to the dial tone.

From behind her came the thud of a closing door.

Hearing heavy footfalls in the kitchen, she hurriedly punched End Call on the phone. Only then did she realize she was shaking.

She'd just set down the phone and jerked back her hand when she looked up to see Parker in the doorway. Looking like a man on a mission, his glance swept from the toys on the Persian rug beneath the table to the papers on top of it as she crossed her arms over the knot in her stomach. He said nothing, though, in the moments before his brow slowly furrowed.

Parker knew Tess had been consumed with the purchase of her house. Every time he'd seen her that day she'd been on a call, just making one or just hanging up. Because she hadn't needed him to take her anywhere, he'd spent that time with calls of his own and was about to make sure she still planned to stay put so he could go for his daily run.

That plan went on hold as he took in the rigid way she stood with her arms wrapped around the coral shell tucked into her white capris.

Something wasn't right.

"What's going on?" he asked.

Wondering if the house deal had fallen through, he watched her hug herself a little tighter.

"He never even asked if his son was okay."

Parker went as still as the massive oaks beyond the windows. "That was your ex?"

She drew a deep breath, gave him a tight nod.

"What did he want?"

What the man had wanted was none of his business. At that moment Parker didn't particularly care. Tess looked as pale as milk. From the way she held herself and the anxiety that robbed the light from her eyes, she also was either angry or frightened or both.

Anger at an ex-spouse seemed typical. Fear did not.

He already suspected that she had somehow protected her child from Bradley Ashworth. Seeing her now, the suspicion that she'd had to protect herself from him, too, became concrete.

"You're afraid of him."

At the flat conviction in his deep voice, Tess's glance flew to his. An instant later it fell to the floor. She couldn't deny his insight. Yet she wasn't in a position to admit it either.

It seemed her silence spoke for her.

"Did he ever hit you?"

The blunt question caught her as unprepared as his conclusion.

"Parker, please."

"Please what? You need to talk to me, Tess. If there's any

chance he might harm you or Mikey, I need to know about it." Her history could no longer remain off-limits. If the possibility existed that she or her son were in any sort of jeopardy, her personal business had to become his. "Is he here? In Camelot?"

"He's in Florida. He won't come here." He hated the country. "He really doesn't want to have anything to do with me. I'm just…insurance."

"Insurance? For what?"

That his image stays intact, she thought.

"Parker, I can't go into this." Her voice begged for understanding even as she ached to dump it all at his feet. "If anything I say gets out…"

Realizing what she was saying, she cut herself off. Even explaining what could happen would give away too much. But trying to stop the man assessing her every word was like trying to stop a tank.

He took a step forward, his bulk blocking her view of everything but the pale yellow cotton covering the wall of his chest. His voice dropped like a rock in a well. "What happens if you tell me what's going on?"

The knot in her stomach seemed to clone itself.

"Tess, come on. I'm not saying anything to anybody." His blue eyes lasered into hers. "Did he hit Mikey, too?"

"No! No," she repeated more quietly. Brad's transgressions were great enough without embellishing them. "I just couldn't risk that he might."

"Is that why you left?" Concern slashed his features. For her son. For her. "To protect Mikey?"

Tess had already confirmed far more than she had intended. Yet, seeing what she did in his expression, the fierceness of it, she realized she didn't feel at all anxious that he now knew what she'd kept hidden from everyone else.

She had no idea how he had figured out how ugly her marriage had become. She just knew there was something terribly freeing about the fact that he had.

"I left for both of us," she finally, quietly admitted. "His impatience and criticism had become bad enough…."

"But then his abuse turned physical," Parker concluded. A muscle in his jaw jerked. "How long did it go on?"

"Longer than I'd been willing to admit to myself. The verbal part, anyway. It only took once with the other for me to leave."

She had made herself overlook the early changes in her marriage because, as Brad had begun to point out, she wasn't as adept as her mom and her sister at balancing work at the foundation, running a new household and managing their social lives. He'd wanted her available to him for his business trips and dinners. He'd wanted her to entertain his business associates. She'd wanted to do all that, too.

She told Parker that, quietly adding that because her experience had been limited in those arenas, she'd honestly thought the fault was hers when she hadn't been able to do it all as perfectly as her husband had expected. When she would put on a dinner she was proud of or manage a weekend of his houseguests, he would complain of her looking tired or not being totally up around the people he wanted to impress. He'd liked having her on his arm, been proud of having her for his wife. She just hadn't realized until he'd eventually thrown it in her face that that was the only reason he'd married her—for the prestige her name would bring him and his family.

"Then I ruined the image he wanted of me when I became pregnant," she continued in that same quiet voice. "I'd had a rough pregnancy and wasn't as available to him as I was apparently supposed to be. After Mikey was born…"

She shook her head, shaking off the confusion and hurt she'd felt when he'd made it clear that she could be a mother if that was what she wanted but that she was still to attend all her social and business obligations as his wife. She wasn't to expect his life to change in any way.

"We never argued where we could be overheard because of the nanny and the housekeeper, but we spent a lot of time 'discussing' Mikey's demands on my time," she told him, moving on to all that mattered now. "That's what we were arguing about when he shoved me across the bedroom." And yanked her back up so hard to slap her that she'd had to wear long sleeves for weeks.

Her stomach clenched at the memory.

"That was when I left," she confided, blocking the worst of the memory. She still wondered if Brad would have lost his temper had any staff been there. Both women had been off that night, so there'd been no witness to what he'd done. "I wasn't going to stick around for him to turn on the son he'd never wanted. He'd just never said he didn't want children until after Mikey was born."

For a moment Parker said nothing. He simply stared at the woman holding herself tightly enough to crack a rib. He had already found her to be the antithesis of the person portrayed by the press, and it sickened and relieved him in ways he didn't care to consider that there had been far more to her divorce than anyone realized. He just didn't understand why she'd allowed herself to be sacrificed as she had.

That lack of comprehension narrowed his eyes, drew in the dark slashes of his eyebrows. The desire to reach for her was as strong as the desire to do serious bodily harm to her miserable ex. "Why didn't you say anything? Why did you let everyone think you left because you got bored with the marriage?"

"Because I *couldn't* say anything." The insistence in her

voice faded as she turned away to pace. "I still can't," she explained, turning back when she reached the mahogany sideboard. "I hadn't said anything before I left him because I'd thought it was my duty to make the marriage work. In this family you don't complain about something you regard as duty. You just do it. Then when things started getting worse, my pride wouldn't let me admit I'd made a hideous mistake marrying a man who was just using me to begin with. Mom and Dad both thought things happened awfully fast between us, but I was head over heels and didn't want to wait."

Neither had Brad, she admitted, pacing back. But Brad hadn't been crazy in love with her. He just hadn't wanted to give her a chance to change her mind.

"What about Mikey? Why didn't you confide in someone about his attitude toward him?"

"Because no one would have believed it. Brad was a model of fatherhood when others were around, but the minute there was no one to witness his performance, he either ignored Mikey or told me to take him to the nursery so he didn't have to listen to him fuss. If I didn't get him out of the room fast enough, he'd storm out of the room himself."

A small plastic soldier lay on the wood flooring beneath a window. Parker watched her pace off the rug and pick it up. For as much as she'd revealed, she'd yet to say a thing that would have prevented her from defending herself against Ashworth's claims. Or so he was thinking when she paced back and came to a stop a few feet away.

"Remember I told you that the nanny was being paid to do more than help with Mikey?"

"You said Ashworth paid her to report your activities to him."

"I found out about his arrangement with her when I went back to our penthouse the next day to get my things. Mom and Dad were both traveling, so I'd left Mikey with Olivia and

Rose," she explained, speaking of her parents' cook and head housekeeper. "I was in the bedroom when Brad came home from work. The nanny had returned that morning and called him to let him know I was taking my things.

"I told him I was going to file for divorce," she continued, sparing them both the details of the encounter that had been horribly, chillingly civil. "He said that if there was a divorce, he would be the one to file for it. I told him I was the one with grounds. That's when he took an envelope out of his safe and showed me pictures he had of my dad with another woman. He said he had some that were even more explicit and that if I accused him of anything, he would release the photos to the press."

Parker felt something dangerous knot his gut. "Do you know who this woman is?"

Tess couldn't seem to meet his eyes as she shook her head.

"How did Ashworth get them?"

"He said he took them with his cell phone. He'd been at a meeting at a hotel a couple of months before and seen them together." Her fist went white around the little soldier. "He said he'd had the feeling they'd come in handy and that the only way he wouldn't turn them over to the press and tell them all that he saw was if I took full blame for the divorce."

"He blackmailed you into silence about his abuse?"

The incredulity in his tone made her wince.

"I'd thought that would be the end of it," she defended, her voice precariously close to cracking. "But now he's piling on more lies. He told his parents that I was the reason he didn't see Mikey this past year. He told them I'd kept Mikey from him and that I would have done the same to them had they called. I never would have done that, Parker, but he's threatening to release the pictures if I don't go along with that, too."

He had seen her agitated before. He had seen her uncertain, uneasy, protective and maybe even a little brave. He'd sensed loneliness in her. But he'd never seen her the way he did now. She looked utterly lost and far more alone than he could stand.

"Is there anything else he's demanding of you? Money?" he asked as he walked over to unfold her hand from around the toy biting into her tender flesh. "Access to bank accounts or corporate information?" The Kendrick conglomerate was huge. Insider information on any of its businesses could be worth a fortune.

With her head bent, she slowly rubbed the red marks on her palm.

"Making himself look blameless seems to be all he wants."

"While he totally destroys your reputation."

Looking down as she was, he couldn't see her face. He didn't need to know that this latest assault on her reputation hurt her as much as knowing her father had cheated on her mom.

The protectiveness he felt had nothing at all to do with his job.

He settled his hand on her shoulder, felt the tension in the taut muscles there. Heaven knew he'd rather take on a deranged stalker than deal with a woman's tears, but he wasn't going to question what he was doing. There was no one else to offer her reassurance. No one else to take away the lonely, fearful look he'd seen in her eyes.

"I wish you'd told me all this before."

Tess would have asked him why, but the comforting feel of his hand increased the pressure in her chest, made it hard to speak. That reassuring touch did the same to the sting of tears she desperately fought. She didn't want him taunting her precious control. Or so she thought before he coaxed her forward and gathered her against the solid wall of his chest.

Her breath leaked out. Along with it went anything re-motely resembling resistance. Leaning into his strength, sur-rounded by it, she shamelessly burrowed her face into his shirt. She hated how needy she felt, how defeated. All she'd wanted was to come back home, to blend in, to move beyond the lies. Only the lies were being compounded and she had no idea how to silence their source.

As if he sensed how helpless she felt, Parker's arms tight-ened around her. It had been so long since she'd been held. Longer still since she'd felt anything resembling comfort or consolation in a man's arms. Yet that was what she felt now. Comforted. Protected.

She felt his hand smooth her hair, felt his breath against her temple.

"Are you okay down there?"

With her forehead pressed to his chest, she gave her head a negative shake.

The weight of his arm shifted as he settled his hand on the back of her head. "I was afraid of that," he murmured, stroking her hair.

He let himself stroke the length of that warm silk again. And again, slowly, calming her the only way he could. He didn't know what else to do. Or what he could say that would take away the distress tightening every muscle in her slender body. With her burrowed into him like a kitten seeking warmth from the cold, it seemed all he could do was hold her and be grateful that she hadn't caved in to the tears he'd heard threatening in her voice.

Nothing about her breathing or the rise and fall of her shoulders told him the tears had won. But just to be sure, he hooked one finger beneath her chin and tipped it so he could see her face.

He should have left well enough alone. Her dark eyes glistened as her breath shuddered in. Tears he could have handled. Watching her struggle to keep them from falling was far tougher to take.

He lifted his hand, cupped her face. With the pad of his thumb, he traced the fragile line of her jaw, carried that touch to the corner of her mouth. Her soft, subtle scent filled his lungs. The feel of her body quietly taunted his. But it was the need to let her know she didn't have to struggle alone right now that drew his head toward hers.

Tess felt his mouth brush her lips. Her breath caught at that contact. His mouth had looked too grim to feel so gentle, too hard to feel so soft. She moved closer as his mouth settled over hers, her heart beating a little rapidly as she gripped his shirt in her fists.

He was letting her know she could cave, let go and, maybe, lean on him for a little while. She so desperately wanted to do all that. But she couldn't. If she caved in, if she admitted defeat, Brad would have taken her spirit, too.

A small sob escaped at the thought. Parker drank in the tiny sound. Easing his hand the length of her back, he drew her closer. It was almost as if he knew what she battled and, for now, that he would be her shield between her and all the anger and hopelessness she fought. She felt safe in his arms and, at that moment, as far from harm's way as she'd felt in longer than she cared to remember.

She kissed him back for that. Kissed him hard, clung tighter. She desperately needed the sense of safety he made her feel. But it was what she felt when his tongue touched hers and a delicious heat spread through her body that made her aware of other needs that felt almost as essential.

Just kissing her, he pulled sensations from her that she hadn't known existed—and made her want in ways that would have frightened her to death had she not been so desperate to escape the fear that she might never be allowed to regain control over her life.

With her hands gripping his shirt, her body and mouth urgently seeking his, it was all Parker could do to remember he shouldn't be doing this at all.

He had honestly never intended to act on the pull he'd felt toward the woman playing utter havoc with his nervous system. When he'd reached for her, he honestly hadn't been thinking of how badly he'd wanted to do exactly what he was doing now. Yet one touch of her lips to his, one taste of her on his tongue, and his thoughts had moved straight from offering comfort to how incredible she felt beneath his hands.

She would feel even more amazing in his bed.

The thought made him groan. Or maybe it was the feel of her molded to the length of him that pulled the guttural sound from his chest. All he knew for certain was that wanting her threatened to overtake his common sense. His job was to protect her. From himself if necessary.

Ruthlessly ignoring the demands clawing at his body, he eased her arms from around his neck and pressed her head to his chest. Wondering if he'd just qualified for sainthood, he slowly ran his hands over her back, calming himself, soothing her.

It occurred to him vaguely that Mikey could have walked in and he never would have heard a sound.

That thought did an even better job of pulling his thoughts back on track. Still rubbing her back, he lifted his head, glanced around to see that they were still alone.

Relieved by that, and needing to kill the awkwardness that threatened, he asked, "What do you want to do about your ex?"

At the quiet question, the calm Tess had started to feel being soothed by his big hands disappeared like smoke in a stiff wind.

Feeling thoroughly unsettled by what he must think of her for practically crawling inside his shirt, she eased away and glanced toward the empty doorway herself.

"I don't know what to do," she admitted, worried all over again. Wanting badly to move straight back to him, she started to pace. In the protection of his arms, everything had seemed so much easier to handle. "The only real choice I have is to go along with him."

The thought of her having anything at all to do with the man responsible for her agitation did dangerous things to Parker's blood pressure. But he was a practical man, a methodical one, and he knew a cooler head had distinct advantages over emotion. He needed to focus only on what would accomplish the mission.

"There's another choice," he countered. "You can put an end to this."

Hope clashed with doubt. "How?"

"Get him on the phone again and I'll tape your conversation. Or wait until you have to see him," he suggested, even though he hated that particular idea. "You can usually get more out of someone in person. It's too easy to hang up a phone. I'll wire you so we can record what both of you say. Once he's incriminated himself on tape, you can have him prosecuted for blackmail."

Tess honestly hadn't thought her life could get any more bizarre than it already was. She was now, however, convinced that it had officially turned surreal.

The man who'd just sensitized every nerve in her body was actually explaining that he could have equipment sent to him so he could hook her up. A courier service could have it there by tomorrow.

"Microphones are really tiny these days. We can clip it inside your shirt or to the underside of a jacket collar. If you go for the personal approach, I'll make sure I'm close enough to get to you if he decides to get physical. If you think you can get what you need on the phone without tipping him off, I'd really rather go that route."

"How do you know so much about wiring people? I thought you were a bodyguard, not a spy."

"I keep up with military intelligence techniques." His massive shoulders lifted in a shrug. "I have to," he explained. "I still teach them."

"You teach them?"

"I do a couple of sessions a year. To Special Ops trainees."

"I thought you weren't in the Marines anymore."

"I'm not. I work as a civilian contractor."

Her voice went as flat as the bug Mikey had squashed yesterday. "You're kidding."

"I like the challenge," he defended. A hint of animation had returned to her eyes. He hated to kill it. "So what do you want do?"

What Tess wanted to do was to stop talking about something that would never happen. Sending Brad to prison or, better yet, having him rot in the dank and abandoned dungeon of her royal grandmother's castle, held a certain visceral appeal. Unfortunately that bit of payback would help only her.

Her internal agitation demanded movement. Methodically she began to gather the notes she'd made and slip them into their respective folders. One for the house. One for the decorator. One for the bank.

"Having a father in prison isn't a stigma I want for my son. And bringing charges against Brad won't protect my family from the damage prosecuting him would cause. To bring charges, I'd have to explain about the pictures he has of my father."

Her motions restive, she picked up Mikey's drawings and

put them in a folder, too. "That means his affair would become public knowledge and the worst of the pictures would find their way straight to the nearest tabloid." Those were the pictures she hadn't seen—and those she had had been incriminating enough. "I don't want my mother embarrassed and hurt like that. So I'm not going to call him," she concluded, thinking that the other thing she wanted was to turn around and bury herself against the rock-solid chest a few feet away. "Or meet him. Or tape any conversations."

She made herself look from where she wanted to be to the frustration in Parker's expression. "I appreciate your offer. I really, truly do. But I'm not going to do anything but go downstairs and run a couple of miles on the treadmill and think about my new house." Running outside would put her too far away from her son. Escaping with yoga was out of the question. She had too much energy to work off to even think about seeking serenity. "Would you please listen for Mikey for me and come get me when he wakes up?" She glanced at her watch. "He's been asleep for almost an hour. He might even wake up when I go get my running shoes, so I'll just take him with me. But if he doesn't, I don't imagine he'll sleep more than another fifteen minutes or so."

The telltale muscle in his jaw jerked at the quiet plea in her eyes. She wanted space.

"Sure," he muttered, intimately familiar with the need. "Go on."

Her smile said thank you even before she murmured the words and hurried through the formal dining room and on to the foyer.

Jamming his hands into his pockets, Parker watched her go. It was his nature to take over, to take charge, and nothing frustrated him more than running into a roadblock. At the moment, that roadblock was Tess herself.

There had to be a way to get her jerk of an ex off her back, but she was so intent on protecting her family that the obvious solution clearly wasn't the best.

He finally understood the reason she'd allowed the press to do a slash-and-burn on her character. He understood the reasons for her silence with her family and her friends. But all that understanding did was make him want to find some other way for her to get out of the mess she was in. There was only one problem with that. She had willingly accepted his help on a number of levels, but she hadn't asked for his help with this. She had, in fact, quite pointedly turned it down.

He had also just overstepped his bounds big-time with her.

The good news was that she hadn't seemed to mind. That was the bad news, too. The thought that she might come to him willingly did nothing to make him want to keep his hands to himself. Her life, however, was complicated enough without him adding to the mess. Having no desire to complicate his own, he decided the best course of action would be to forget those moments of spontaneous combustion, think in terms of cold showers and, once Mikey woke up, make himself scarce unless she needed him to drive her somewhere. As far as he knew, she wasn't going anywhere until tomorrow.

Tess's plans remained unchanged. With the house already scheduled to close tomorrow she moved on to the rest of the to-do list that kept her from worrying too much about the strength of the attraction she felt toward the man helping her with all she had to accomplish. She had an appointment with the decorator at the house that afternoon. But before that, she wanted to enroll Mikey in preschool. He needed to be around children. Without siblings, he had no way to learn to share with his peers.

She'd known from the time he was born that he would attend La Petite Academie. Not only was it *the* place for any child who hoped to get into one of the exclusive private primary schools in the area, but she was personally familiar with it because of her charity work with its owner/director a couple of years ago.

She'd dismissed the idea of making an appointment, though. Her experience with various facilities when she'd researched them for her foundation preschool project had taught her that she was more apt to see what typically went on if the staff didn't have time for advance preparation.

She just wanted to pick up an application, anyway, which was why she told Parker it wasn't necessary for him to accompany them inside. As small as the school was, she didn't doubt that she'd have to wait for an opening. But the earlier she got Mikey's name on the list, the sooner he could be with children his own age a couple of days a week.

The vestibule of the Colonial-style building with its bell tower on top held two bright red sofas and a coffee table lacquered primary yellow. A closed door marked *No Admittance Without Authorization* occupied the end wall. To her right, a glass window slid open a moment after a faint buzz announced her and Mikey's entry.

A college-age woman with braided auburn hair flashed a dimpled smile. "May I help you?" The smile faltered with recognition. "Oh. My. It's you. Miss Kendrick." Color flooded her cheeks as she gave her head an embarrassed shake. "I'm sorry. I mean Mrs. Ashworth. I'm…"

"It's Kendrick," Tess offered politely. "And no apology necessary. I'd just like to fill out an application and perhaps let my son look around, if it's not too much trouble?"

"Oh. Sure." Looking flustered in the face of someone so famous or, possibly, Tess feared, someone so infamous, she held up her hand. "Wait just a minute."

A minute turned into two. Two into four.

Tess was about to tap on the glass to ask if she could just fill out the application and leave it when the No Admittance door opened.

A stylish, late-thirty-something blonde in a childproof T-shirt and denim skirt looked from her to the little boy holding her hand. Behind her, children and their voices filled a large space alive with primary colors and activity.

"Miss Kendrick."

Tess smiled. "Pamela," she said, extending her hand. "It's good to see you again. It's been, what, two years since we worked on the children's literacy campaign?"

She had met Pamela Whiting at a fund-raiser for the event that had led Tess to touring this very facility. The woman she remembered as being so welcoming didn't seem interested in recalling their shared interest, however, as she withdrew her hand.

"About that, I believe," she replied but said nothing about it being good to see Tess, too.

"I'd like to fill out an application for my son. I'm sure your waiting list is forever long," Tess hurried on, "so I don't expect he'll be able to start this term. I'd wanted him to see the school, but if now isn't a good time…"

Since Pamela's smile looked more cautious than welcoming, Tess thought for certain she was about to be told that the timing really wasn't good. Instead Pamela stepped back and motioned her and Mikey inside.

The security door closed with a solid click.

"Why don't we have him join the children while we talk?" The woman's smile turned softer as she placed her hands on her thighs and bent to her son. "Your name is Bradley, isn't it?"

Tess mentally winced. The woman had obviously read

the piece in the *Crier,* the one that had identified him by
his first name—and reminded everyone of why she'd left.
"We use his middle name," she quietly advised. "He's used
to Michael or Mikey."

"Then hello, Mikey," the woman said kindly and motioned
to one of the teachers trying not to be obvious about staring
at Tess. The two dozen children at various play and work sta-
tions around the open room paid her no attention at all. "Miss
Linda will introduce you to some of the other children. You'll
be able to see your mom right through here," she told him,
motioning to an office with floor-to-ceiling glass walls.

Tess had to convince her son that it was okay to go play
with the other kids, but it wasn't long before another little
boy was showing him a computer and Tess was led into an
office of bright colors and books. It also held some of the
only adult furniture in the place. Everything on the other side
of the wall was child-size. Yet what Tess noticed most was
the awkwardness filling the room as the preschool's owner
motioned her to a green barrel chair and settled herself behind her large blue desk.

"Miss Kendrick…"

"Please, it's Tess."

Pamela acknowledged her with a nod. She did not, however, indulge in the informality.

"I'm flattered that you want to enroll your son in our
school. Someone such as yourself needs to be very particular about who she entrusts her child to. We're concerned as
much about maintaining a safe environment at all levels for
our students as we are with the content of our curriculum."

"That's why I want him here."

"Of course." A pen lay next to her telephone. She picked
it up, absently toyed with its clip. "It's why the majority of
our parents want their children here. It's because of that that

I can't accept your son's application. There's too much potential for disruption when parents are having custody disputes. I won't put myself or my staff in the position of letting a child go to the wrong parent, no matter who we feel the child should be with."

The woman's disapproval was as obvious as the way she avoided Tess's eyes. That disapproval stung. All the more because Tess hadn't been prepared for it. At worst, she'd thought that the woman might have been reminded of the old scandal because the newspaper had reminded everyone who'd read it. She hadn't anticipated that what Brad had told his parents about her keeping Mikey from him had become public knowledge.

She needed to be careful how she defended herself.

"I'm not sure what you've heard," she began, though she had a fair idea, "but there is no custody dispute." She spoke with calm assurance as her fingers knotted more tightly in her lap. With Brad, even that simple statement could come back to haunt her. "I assure you there will be no problems with Mikey's father. I'd already planned to volunteer my time here on the days Mikey attends," she hurried on, thinking her presence might further ease the woman's mind. "I can read to the children. Or prepare snacks. It's really important that he be around others his age."

Pamela had the grace to look uncomfortable. "I appreciate that. And I'm sorry we can't provide him that opportunity. As for you volunteering here, that would present an entirely different obstacle. I'm afraid your presence would cause problems with our other parents.

"I'm sorry," she repeated, rising. "But there's really nothing else I can do. I'm sure you understand."

## Chapter Eight

Tess practically vibrated with fury. She managed to keep that anger in check as she thanked Pamela Whiting for her time and escaped the preschool with a quiet dignity that would have made her mother proud. But that sense of offense lay a scant centimeter below the lightness of her voice when she explained to Mikey that they couldn't stay because she had another appointment and hurried him into his seat in the SUV.

She knew Parker could see how mad she was the moment he saw her face. Her anger reverberated in her tight "Not now," when he asked what was wrong and in her lock-jawed silence when, a mile down the road, he glanced to the white-knuckle clasp of her hands in her lap and detoured to a deserted parking lot at the far end of Camelot's half-mile-long park.

In one swift movement, he cut the engine and pulled out the keys. "Come on."

"What are you doing?" she asked, but he was already out of the vehicle and opening the back door to say something to her son.

Since movement seemed like a truly fine idea, she got out, gave the short jacket of her black capri pantsuit a yank and watched him walk around the front of the bull-nosed vehicle. It had come as a huge relief that he seemed as intent as she did on ignoring how desperately she'd clung to him after Brad's phone call. What relieved her far more at the moment was not having to guard what she said to him.

The breeze rustled the leaves of the lush oak and magnolia trees protecting the park's play areas, sitting gardens and jogging trails. The laughter of kids practicing baseball drifted from the field just beyond them.

With a glance to where he'd left Mikey in his car-seat with his book and snack pack of fish-shaped crackers, Parker motioned her beneath the branches of a sweeping oak. With no one else about, the SUV in plain sight less than ten yards away and her in shadows, he simply said, "Talk to me."

She hadn't trusted herself to say anything within earshot of her son. It was as clear as the concern carved in his face that he knew that.

"She won't accept Mikey's application." She hadn't said that before because she wasn't sure she could say the words without adding everything else jammed up behind them. Speaking the words now brought her fury front and center. "She's denying an innocent three-year-old a little bit of normalcy because she thinks his father and I are involved in a custody dispute. Apparently everyone thinks that," she ranted, turning away to pace, turning right back around again. "The only way that could have happened is for Brad or his mother to have told someone else I was keeping Mikey from him. Which Brad knows I'm not. But his mother doesn't, so whoever she told clearly sympathizes with her and with him, and the worst part," she continued without a breath, "is that Pamela acted as if Brad might be the better parent!"

She wasn't yelling. Only her eyes were. The flecks of gold in those dark depths looked like pure flame.

"Who's Pamela?"

"The owner of the preschool."

"Is there anyplace else you can enroll him?"

He was being reasonable. But just then, reasonable wasn't something she wanted to be.

"That's not the point," she insisted, though it was certainly part of it. "The point is that what people think of me isn't getting better, it's getting worse. I'll never be accepted here if he keeps making up lies about me. She didn't even want me as a volunteer because my presence would apparently be a problem for the other parents." That hurt. "It's as if what I'd done...or what they think I did," she corrected, because she hadn't done a thing any one of them wouldn't have had they been in the same situation, "would somehow influence their offspring.

"And now it's starting to affect Mikey," she hurried on, because that was the worst. "Even if I do find another preschool, I can't control the other kids. Children repeat what they hear, and if they hear their parents saying bad things about me, that's going to get back to him."

"He's only three, Tess."

"And then he's four and seven and ten and getting into fights because kids are calling me names."

"You don't know that will happen."

"You doubt it? He's either going to beat up someone defending me or get beaten up because he'll know he's not supposed to fight. If he's anything like his uncle Cord, he will fight back, then he'll get a reputation like Cord had and it won't be his fault."

She was projecting big-time. But Parker couldn't blame her. He couldn't even find much fault with her worst-case scenario.

"I just have no idea how to shut Brad up."

Her frustration with that obstacle threatened to turn what Parker saw as healthy resentment into something infinitely less positive.

There was no doubt that Ashworth held the upper hand with her and that the man could jerk her around at will. What wasn't so clear to Parker just then was why he was rapidly discarding his own plan to disregard the fact that she didn't want his help on this particular score.

Not wanting fear to take hold of her again, he glanced at his watch.

"Do you want to reschedule your next appointment?"

Tess checked her watch, too. She had an hour until she was to meet the designer. The house wasn't hers yet, but the real-estate agent had agreed to let them in so the woman could measure for paint and carpeting.

She had no intention of allowing that plan to be derailed, too. "We have time to get there."

"I was thinking more of you taking some time to get yourself together. If you want to keep the appointment, then why don't you take a few minutes and go for a walk or take Mikey to the swings?"

He nodded beyond her. A few children played on the little merry-go-round. Two women in shorts and tank tops— apparently their moms—visited with each other at a nearby picnic table. A couple of bigger kids were knocking a tetherball around its pole. The swings were deserted.

"The swings," she finally said. "And thank you."

"I didn't do anything."

"You let me unload." It had been surprisingly easy to do, too. It had also felt better than anything had in a long time. Except for when he'd held her. Then there'd been that kiss....

"Yeah, well, you've probably needed to do that for a while now."

She jerked her thoughts from being in his arms to simply being grateful he was there as he turned away to get Mikey from the SUV.

Parker stayed back while she pushed her son on the swings, close enough so it was clear to the other women that he was with the pretty brunette and not some pervert out stalking kids but far enough away that he wasn't part of their activity. Far enough to have a decent view of who and what was around her. Far enough to not be distracted by her himself.

The kids ignored her, except for one little girl who wandered over from the merry-go-round and asked Tess if she'd push her on the swings, too. As engrossed as they'd been in their conversation, the young moms probably wouldn't have paid her any attention at all, except for how stylishly she was dressed for a playground. And for him. It was pretty hard to ignore a six-foot-three-inch, two-hundred-and-ten-pound bald guy wearing dark glasses, a dark polo shirt and dark jeans. But if they figured out who she was, they did nothing to bother or embarrass her, and that was all he cared about. Or so he told himself.

Tess tiptoed from her sleeping son. Leaving the door of her bedroom ajar, she hurried down the wide hall to the staircase and began to descend.

Now that Mikey was fed, bathed and asleep, she wanted to look again at the carpet and fabric samples Ginny Hellerman-Mays had left with her and that Parker had helped her carry into the breakfast room. During her first consultation on the phone, she had mentioned to Ginny that she preferred natural colors—russets, browns and creams. Sage-greens and shades of autumn gold. The stylish brunette in the rhine-stone-trimmed glasses and trim black suit had shown up with her tape measure and a contract and the assurance that if Tess couldn't find what she wanted among the stacks of samples she'd brought, she would bring her more.

Tess was thinking of the paint chips still in her purse when her pace began to slow. She wanted to be excited. She wanted to let her mind play over possibilities. Yet each step became slower than the last, and by the time she reached the bottom, she had to admit that she simply couldn't find the enthusiasm she was looking for.

Standing on the last of the stairs, she looked around the shadowed and empty foyer with its empty urn on the center table and sat down in the middle of the stair runner.

She'd walked into her meeting with Ginny trying desper-ately to put her encounter with Pamela Whiting out of her mind. She'd wanted to focus only on how their meeting would bring her closer to moving into her new home. Within a minute, however, it had become clear that the woman who had seemed friendly enough on the phone was more reserved in person. And while she'd seemed eager enough to work on the new home and she'd immediately understood Tess's vision for it, by the time Tess had signed the contract and set their next appointment—with the understanding that Tess was free to call Ginny at any time, of course—Tess had had the uneasy feeling that it was only the promise of a sizable commission and the woman's relationship with her mother that had kept the well-connected designer from showing the disapproval she had encountered at La Petite Academie.

The foyer was lit only by the light spilling faintly from the hallway lights she'd left on in the wing above her. She hadn't bothered to turn on the main chandelier when she'd taken Mikey up for his bath because the twilight coming through the windows had made it light enough to see. Now, with only the deep blue of evening beyond the leaded glass, the space was pretty much shadows—until the butler's door beneath the stairs opened and a slash of light cut across the marble floor.

The sound of familiar footsteps had reached the middle of the foyer when she saw Parker glance toward her. He'd changed into a polo and khakis after his run.

Parker had sensed her before he'd seen her. Wondering how long she had been there, he checked the lock on the front door as he did every night and walked over to where Tess sat between the curves of the carved railings

She had said nothing else to him about what had happened at the preschool and very little about her meeting with the designer. While the women had talked and done whatever it was women do when surrounded by squares of carpet and fabric, he'd taken Mikey and poked around in the various corners of the house. It would have been too hard on the kid to sit still that long, and even though he knew she worried about her son getting attached to a guy who wouldn't be there much longer, she knew Mikey was safe with him.

She'd seemed subdued when the meeting was over, though. Because Mikey had been right there, as he had been the rest of the evening, there had been no opportunity for her to say if something disturbing had happened. But Mikey wasn't there now.

"What are you doing down here in the dark?" He'd told himself he'd keep his distance. That meant he would keep his hands to himself. It didn't necessarily mean he couldn't listen if she needed to talk.

"I was going to look at the samples the decorator gave me."

"And got stuck here?"

The way she lifted one shoulder seemed oddly disheartened. Even in the pale light, he could see uncertainty in the delicate lines of her face.

"This was as far as I got before I decided I'd made a huge mistake coming back."

"To the estate?"

"To Camelot," she murmured, then looked from the eyes that had seen far more at times than she'd realized.

Pamela's response to her presence had given her a taste of what she could expect from the women whose children she and Mikey would encounter at swimming lessons, art classes, playgroup. Provided they were allowed to participate in any of those activities to begin with. Ginny's attitude had been more veiled at first, but it had been clear from some of her guarded comments that the gossip about Tess keeping Mikey from his dad had been around for months.

"I knew it wouldn't be easy to start over," she confided, now knowing for certain that she wouldn't be allowed to quietly slip into the fringes of her old circle. "But I hadn't considered the impact on Mikey."

"You're thinking about the owner of the preschool."

"And Ginny," she murmured. "I got more of the same from her."

Parker motioned to the step, arched one eyebrow.

At the silent request to join her, Tess moved over to make room for him on the stair and leaned forward again, her elbows on her knees, her chin in one palm.

Lowering himself beside her, he planted his size-elevens a yard apart and rested his forearms on his thighs.

He said nothing. He just sat there, lending her the support of his powerful presence and letting her decide when she was ready to tell him what was on her mind.

"She'd done a wonderful job of grasping what I wanted," she finally said. "So I mentioned how impressed I was with her understanding of my needs and told her that alone would make me recommend her." Her voice dropped, along with her glance. "She made it pretty apparent that a recommendation from me wasn't something she wanted."

Ginny had looked appropriately uncomfortable when that had become evident. She'd also attempted to soften the slight by telling Tess she had her mother's same exquisite taste in fabrics, but it had been utterly clear that Ginny would rather people didn't even know she was working with Tess.

"I think she's only doing this for me as a favor to my mom."

"If you're not comfortable with her, get someone else."

"I don't need her approval," she murmured, trying to toughen herself so she wouldn't be blindsided by the insults to come. "I just need her to do a job. Right now, I'm just wondering if I should even go through with the purchase of the house."

Parker's glance slowly skimmed the fall of hair hiding most of her profile. He hated to hear her say that. She'd been so excited when she'd seen what he'd found for her.

"Where would you go if you didn't live around here?"

"Back to my grandmother's."

It shouldn't have mattered to him, but he didn't like that idea either.

"Do you really want to let Ashworth do that to you?"

"Do what?"

"Make you live your life in exile."

Banishing her to live in exile is exactly what her ex would have accomplished if she went back. She knew that, too. Parker could practically feel her disquiet compound itself at the thought. Her response, though, was nothing but discouraged silence.

His first less-than-sensitive instinct was to point out the obvious. But as deeply distressed as she was by the events of the day, even he knew that now wasn't the time to tell her that the only mistake she was making was letting her ex-husband get away with character assassination. He'd liked it better this afternoon when she'd been angry and pacing. From the fire in her eyes and the starch in her spine, he'd had the feeling that her spirit could be bent but not broken.

What he sensed in her as she turned her head toward him now was that she'd been bent about as far as she could go.

"It's not what I want. But I have no idea how to stop him." The desolation in her eyes entered her voice. She was at the mercy of a man who had no conscience, no principles. "I don't even know what he might do next. When he called, I got the feeling he might even go after anyone he thinks I'm involved with."

The powerlessness she felt hit Parker like a fist. She clearly couldn't handle Ashworth alone. Yet he knew she didn't feel she could ask for help without compromising her family. Her own principles demanded that she protect those she loved. That need was exactly what Ashworth counted on.

Undeniably drawn by her loyalty, hating how it was being abused, his brow pinched. "You're not concerned about the thing in the paper, are you? About us touring that house?"

"I don't know," she murmured. "I didn't think I was." She shook her head, shoved her fingers through her hair. "Maybe I am."

It was all he could do not to sigh. "Don't be. You're giving him more power than he actually has," he insisted, clasping his hands to keep from reaching for her. "He's controlling you simply by making you worry about what he might do. Are you going to let fear dictate your actions?"

"Maybe it's not fear. Maybe it's practicality."

"Now there's a reach."

She shot him a sideways glance. Unfortunately that was the only bit of spirit she seemed to have left.

For a moment she remained silent. Then, considering, she looked back to him.

"I can't imagine you in my position," she qualified, "but if you were me, what would you do about the house?"

He didn't hesitate. "Buy it. You and Mikey need a home. As for what people are saying about you keeping him from his father, that's going to die when it becomes apparent to his parents that you're not doing any such thing. If for some reason things don't get better here," he added, covering all possibilities, "then sell it and move on. It's a good investment either way."

He made everything sound so simple. What he said also made sense. She and Mikey did need a home. And soon.

She really didn't want to live in exile.

Silence crept between them.

From the corner of her eye she saw Parker looking at his clasped hands, his focus on his thumbs as he rubbed one alongside the other. The movement struck her as thoughtful, contemplative. So did the expression in his profile.

"Parker?" Sitting beside him, feeling pensive herself, she mimicked his motions. "Have you ever wished you could go back to a particular point in your life and choose a different direction?"

He was quiet for a moment. "There are things I've regretted."

"Like what?"

She thought she saw a corner of his mouth quirk.

"Mostly a couple of relationships that I could have ended better. And not spending more time with my sister." Then there was the void he occasionally felt. The one that made him feel as if something was missing from his life. Growing up, he'd thought that absence was a relationship with his father, but as he'd grown older, the occasional hollowness simply felt like a need for a stronger connection with someone who cared about him. He regretted his emotional solitude at times, though he could think of no person or point in his life that would have helped him avoid it. "But it doesn't do any good to want the impossible." That void wasn't there now, though. That made it easy to dismiss. "I can't change what happened, so why waste energy wanting it."

"I envy you your acceptance. I'd give anything to go back and start from where I first met Brad."

The quiet tones of her voice held a hint of admiration and a lot of regret. The admiration he didn't deserve. He'd just had longer to come to grips with certain realities than she had. The regret bothered him.

"If that was possible," he asked, "what would you do then?"

That was easy. "Have nothing to do with him."

From somewhere beyond her came the creak of the house settling in for the night and the faint *bong* of the grandfather clock in the library.

"I think you'd want to reconsider that if you really thought about it. If you'd had nothing to do with him, you wouldn't have Mikey." Understanding in his voice, he lifted his hand, gently tucked a strand of hair behind her ear. "And if you didn't have him," he continued, letting his hand fall to clasp with his other again, "you wouldn't have discovered what a great mom you are. Or how much backbone you have. Or how strong you really are."

His quiet words soothed, empowered, strengthened. He had reminded her of the one thing to come of her marriage she could never regret. Beyond that, he made her sound far stronger than she felt, far stronger than she truly believed she could ever be. She could easily adore him just for that. Yet all that mattered to her just then was how badly she'd wanted the touch he had just withdrawn. It wasn't smart to want something that much. It wasn't practical or wise or any of the things she desperately wanted to be. It simply…was.

"You're right," she murmured, rising from the step. "I wouldn't have him." It was infinitely easier to not have Parker touch her at all than to be so close and be tormented by the possibility of being in his arms. "And you wouldn't be here having to listen to me go on about something I can do nothing about."

She tried to smile, to make light of having added "confidant" to his job description.

The attempt must not have worked very well. His shadow fell over her as he rose. With one step, he closed the protective bit of distance she'd gained.

"It's not that I have to listen," he clarified. "I want to. And just to keep the record straight, you can do something about Ashworth. We just need to figure out what it is."

*We.*

She didn't want the word to mean so much to her.

"Why would you want to get involved in this?"

"I don't know," he answered, being as honest as he could without telling her how bad he felt for her. "Haven't you ever just wanted something and not questioned it?"

In the pale light he saw her glance fall to his chest before she took another step away.

"Just because I want something doesn't mean it's going to happen. Or even that it's a good idea."

Her unease as she moved from him just then seemed almost palpable. That same disquiet had been evident when she'd moved moments after he'd pushed back her hair. He hadn't intended to touch her. He'd simply found himself reaching toward her before he'd had a chance to think about what he was doing—and pulled back the moment he'd realized how easy reaching for her had been.

It seemed that what had happened between them yesterday had its consequences after all.

"Would it help if I tell you it won't happen again?"

Confusion touched her features.

"I don't understand...."

"What happened yesterday. When I kissed you," he clarified, because he wanted no misunderstanding between them. "I was out of line. I'm not sorry you told me what was going on. But it's obvious that I've made you uncomfortable." A muscle in his jaw tensed. "That's the last thing I want you to be around me."

There was no discounting the man's sense of perception, Tess thought. He was the person she paid to maintain her peace of mind and he had definitely disturbed certain aspects of that peace where he was concerned.

He was also as dense as stone.

"Telling me it won't happen again doesn't help at all."

Talking to him was impossibly easy. Too easy, she realized, considering what she'd just admitted. He'd just gone as still as the marble columns in the formal gardens.

With his back to the light, his features were shadowed. Nothing in his expression betrayed what he thought of her admission as his eyes quietly searched her face.

"I need you to talk to me, Tess. I'll help you with Ashworth," he promised, when promises weren't something he ever made to a woman. "But right now—"

"There's nothing you can do."

"There has to be." There truly had to be some way around the catch-22 she'd found herself in. Short of arranging for

Ashworth to be airlifted off the planet, he just couldn't think of what that way might be. Not with what she'd just confessed drawing him closer. "But right now," he repeated, "I need to know what you want from me."

What she wanted was simple. She wanted to be in his arms again because she didn't want to feel as empty as she did standing there with him only an arm's length away. She didn't want to feel the sense of isolation that would accompany her up the stairs when he said good-night a minute from now and left her standing there alone. But she didn't know how to tell him that without baring so much of her soul.

Worse, she didn't know if what she needed would even matter. Her needs had mattered so seldom to anyone that she'd simply learned to suppress what wasn't convenient or acceptable or significant to anyone else.

As if he could sense her struggle, he slipped his hand over her shoulder. "If it's arms you need…"

Not just arms. *His.*

"Hey," he murmured and curved his fingers over her shoulders.

When her only response was to close her eyes in relief, he eased her toward him.

"Let it go, Tess. I know it's all weighing on you, but don't even think about any of it right now. Okay?"

*Don't think about it. Let it go.*

It made no difference just then that he really didn't know what had turned her so silent. His words seemed to drain the stiffness from her muscles. Or maybe it was the feel of finally being surrounded by his strength that dissolved some of the tension in her body as she rested her forehead against his chest.

As if he'd remembered the feel of her hair, he slowly sifted the length of it through his fingers, then curved his hand over the back of her neck. "Just let your mind go some-place where none of this exists."

In the space between them, she lifted her hand to toy with the front of his shirt. With her hair curtaining the sides of her face, she breathed in the musky male scent of him. The warmth of his embrace penetrated her skin, seeming to halt the chill that kept creeping deeper inside her. "I don't know where that would be."

"Invent a place. An imaginary island. A mountaintop."

She shook her head, felt the soft cotton of his shirt shift against her forehead. "I don't want to."

The tips of his fingers rubbed gentle circles along the side of her neck.

"Why not?"

Because with you I don't feel alone, she thought. Because you listen. Because I'm so tired of being scared, and when you hold me I'm not frightened.

"Because I'm standing exactly where I want to be."

The lulling motion of his fingers stopped a moment before she felt his fingers beneath her chin. He lifted her face. In the unreliable light, his eyes seemed to glitter on hers. But she had no idea what he saw in her expression. It might have been all the want she couldn't admit, for all she knew. She didn't care. All that mattered just then was the gentleness in his hands when he cupped her face and the feel of his thumb as he grazed the corner of her mouth.

Her vulnerability to him sat far too close to the surface. Parker had heard it in her guileless admission, could see it in her lovely eyes. He could feel it in her sigh when he tipped her head and covered her mouth with his.

She had no business being so susceptible to him. But then, he figured he had no business feeling such an over-whelming need to protect her—or indulging the sharp hunger that tore through him at the sweet taste of her lips. There was something insidiously dangerous about that combination. And later, a few seconds from now, maybe a minute, he would figure out what that danger was. He just couldn't do it with her opening to him, kissing him back as he coaxed her closer.

She didn't know how he'd done it. *Let it go. Don't think about any of it,* he'd said. She hadn't known how that would be possible. Yet all it had taken was the feel of him to banish thoughts of anything but the gentleness she once would have never suspected him to possess and the slow-burning heat he somehow created inside her. His breath moved into her lungs and became part of her very being. The feel of his tongue tangling with hers sent liquid warmth coursing through her body, weakening her limbs and making her aware of herself in ways she'd nearly forgotten.

That delicious, debilitating heat touched her breasts, moved lower.

She'd thought she had lost the ability to feel desire. She'd thought that what she'd known as desire was all that existed. She'd had no idea what it was to crave. Yet that was what he was teaching her. To crave. To yearn. To realize that there was more than she'd ever suspected. And all he was doing was kissing her.

It wasn't enough.

That yearning for more had her curving her arms around his neck. As tall as he was, her heels left the floor and she stretched herself against the hard wall of his chest.

The floor seemed to shift, causing her to sag against him when his hand splayed at the small of her back. Aligning her more intimately, his thighs brushed hers as he pressed her stomach to his zipper.

At the exquisite feel of her against his arousal, Parker

thought he heard her groan. Or maybe that small aching sound was his. All he knew for certain was that she had every muscle in his body feeling as taut as a tripwire and that if he didn't let her go now, he wouldn't.

Taking a ruthless grip on his control, he carried his kiss to her temple and eased her head to his chest. The woman in his arms had systematically destroyed his ability to stay detached. In another minute, she would destroy what little was left of his ability to think. She was like an illicit narcotic in his system. One taste of her had him craving more and feeling nearly desperate to get it.

"I'll hold you, Tess." There were times when she looked at him that he could feel her emptiness as if it were his own. If it would ease that awful sensation, he would hold her all night. He just couldn't torture himself with the feel of her body moving against his. He'd been too long without a woman to test himself that way. "But I can't do this."

Beneath his hands, the supple muscles in her back stiffened an instant before her arms slipped from around his neck.

Ducking her head, she tried to pull back. "I'm sorry. I didn't mean... I mean, I didn't..."

"Tess." He loosened his hold, but he wouldn't let her go. "Why are you apologizing?"

She shook her head, clearly not caring to answer.

"You didn't what?" he coaxed, wanting an answer anyway.

"I didn't expect... I mean, I never..." With her head bent, her trembling voice was barely audible. "I just didn't know it could feel like that," she finally admitted. "I don't want you to think..."

Her voice trailed off as she shook her head once more.

Even with desire clouding cognition, Parker realized she

thought he was rejecting her. Not about to let that idea linger, he caught her cheek with his palm and lifted her face to his.

The thought that she'd felt something with him that she hadn't with any other man all but wrecked his restraint.

"You don't want me to think you expect me to make love to you? Is that what you mean?"

She nodded. "Yes," she murmured. "No," she amended, making it sound as if she wasn't thinking too clearly herself.

He pulled her back to him, brushed his lips to her temple once more. "Just so we're clear, I never thought you expected that. But I want you, Tess. And I don't have a whole lot of willpower left." His voice was a little gruff as his lips grazed the incredible softness of her skin. The warm, satiny feel of it had him wondering how it would feel on her breasts, her belly, the insides of her thighs. It also had his voice turning to a rasp at the provocative images burning in his brain. "That's what I meant when I said I couldn't do this."

Her breath came out with a little, "Oh."

"Yeah," he murmured, lifting his head to smooth back her hair. "Oh."

She made no effort to move. She couldn't imagine him without his formidable control. Nor was it possible to imagine that he desired her anywhere near as much as she did him. But desire was what she felt in his body. It was what she'd heard in his dark, husky words.

With her palm on his chest, she could feel the heavy beat of his heart. It seemed to echo the erratic beat of her own. "What happens when your willpower is gone?"

Something feral slashed the shadows of his face.

"I take you to bed."

Swallowing hard, she touched the pulse beating at the base of his throat. "Promise?"

A dagger of heat shot through Parker at the plea in that

single quiet word. The rational part of his mind suspected that what she wanted had little to do with sex. What she wanted was comfort. Or maybe what she sought was escape from all the uncertainty and fear that had led her into his arms. With his body fully aroused and her naked need pulling him toward her, he was just having a hard time remembering why that fear was there.

That reason reared its ugly head a split second before his mouth touched hers. The moment it did, he deepened the kiss and eased her against him. He wasn't sure where the need came from, the almost primitive urge he felt to imprint his body on hers, but as he skimmed his hands over her back, there was no denying the distinct and compelling urge to drive every thought of her ex out of her mind.

Tess sagged against him. He kissed her slowly, thoroughly, weakening her knees along with any possible doubt about how much he desired her. Before, there had been no demand, no insistence. Just the slow, sweet seduction of her senses that had left her aching for more. Now what she felt in him was hunger, raw and restrained, as his tongue mated with hers and he shaped her body with his hands.

That hunger fed her own as he backed her across the dim foyer and into the shaft of light spilling through the butler's doorway. The light in the hall went out with the bump of his elbow to the switch. With his mouth on hers, his hands loosening the buttons of her blouse, memory and single-minded intent guided him to his room.

Moonlight spilled through the window, illuminating the outlines of the sofa, the desk, the bed. Then the moonlight was gone. Leaving her by the bed, he closed the drapes and flipped the nightstand lamp on low. In that soft light she watched him lift his hands to her face.

Something in the depths of his eyes had turned a little

fierce. But that thrilling intensity had no sooner registered than he was kissing her again, working at the clasp of her bra until it came free. He slipped her blouse from her shoulders. Her bra landed on top of it. A ragged heartbeat later, his hands moved up her sides, molding her waist, her ribs, her breasts.

"Your turn," he murmured and moved her hands to his shirt so she could tug it from his pants while he skimmed his lips down the side of her neck.

Tess had never felt bold before. She had never *been* bold. But then, she had never felt the kind of passion Parker unleashed as they fumbled with each other's clothing while their mouths clung and their hands caressed newly exposed skin. The hard muscles of his magnificent body felt like warm steel beneath her hands. He was all tension and heat, and the need to be in his arms became as essential to her as her next breath. But when the barriers were gone and he eased her back on the bed, he didn't pull her to him as she'd thought he would. His lips left hers to skim the length of her body, tasting every inch of it.

She couldn't tell if she was floating or falling. She hadn't realized that a man's touch could create such heat. She had known lovemaking as either pleasant or perfunctory and ultimately found little pleasure in the experience. But Parker had her aching.

She reached for him, needing to touch him as he touched her. He frustrated the attempt by murmuring that they had plenty of time, all night if she wanted. Then, taking up where he'd left off, he proceeded to erase everything she ever thought she knew about what went on between a man and a woman, along with all the inadequacies she'd been told she had and any doubt she'd ever felt about her ability to truly appeal to a man.

He told her she was beautiful, and made her believe it as he worshipped her body. He told her she was making him crazy and made her believe that, too, by the way he growled the words when he finally stretched out beside her and gathered her soft curves against the hard, honed length of his body. Tangling his fingers in her hair, his mouth devoured hers.

The hunger she'd felt in him suddenly seemed more like raw need. Or maybe it was her own need she felt as his arms tightened around her and their bodies strained toward each other. She felt sheltered there, safe in ways she'd never truly felt before. But mostly she felt desired, alive. And those were things she hadn't felt in longer than she could remember. This was what she wanted him to teach her. This mindless passion that sensitized every nerve, obliterated everything but the moment and made her think only of how he was melting her body along with her heart.

The thought drew a moan of pure yearning.

Parker drank in that small sound as he eased her to her back, rolled on the condom he'd pulled from his wallet and settled his weight over her. He'd told her they had plenty of time. He'd lied. The feel of her soft hands gripping his shoulders, the taste of her, the kittenish sounds she made, everything about her had his control hanging by a hair.

Poised about her, he whispered her name.

In the soft lamplight, he saw her open her eyes, lift them to his.

That was what he wanted. All of her. He'd never known the need to claim a woman before. But he couldn't deny that the wholly unfamiliar and primitive need was there as he slowly entered her heat.

He heard her breath catch, saw her eyes close. Then so did his in that split second before she arched to meet him and he caved in to the sensations that obliterated every other conscious thought.

Tess had no idea how long they lay in each other's arms before their breathing began to quiet and their pulses finally slowed. Parker had eased to his side, taking her with him, holding her with her legs still tangled with his and her head tucked beneath his chin. Listening to his strong heartbeat, she felt him smooth her hair from her cheek.

"Parker?" She murmured his name as she touched her fingers to the wall of his chest. "There's something I need you to know." The concern she'd felt earlier about him thinking she'd expected him to do what they'd done had been there because of her reputation. The anxiety she felt now existed for the same reason. She couldn't bear it if he believed even half of what he might have read about her supposed lovers. Considering what had just happened, how completely she'd abandoned anything even remotely resembling restraint or caution with him, he could easily believe every word to be true.

"I know I've asked you to believe it before," she murmured, "but I'm really not the woman people say I am."

Strands of her hair drifted against her shoulder as he sifted them through his fingers. "I already know that."

"I mean, I haven't had the relationships you might have read about. Any of them, for that matter. I've only been with one other man in my life," she admitted, feeling every bit as awkward as she sounded. "I just don't want you to think I'm…"

"Easy?" he cautiously suggested.

"That," she agreed. "I've always known that anything I did could wind up in print. Before I met Brad, I'd never met anyone worth risking a tell-all in some tabloid."

Parker had gone still. If he was hearing correctly, she had

just told him she'd found him worth that particular risk. She'd also just confided why it had never occurred to her that someone she had known all her life, someone she had once thought she could trust, could turn on her and tell lies that could be so damaging.

He didn't want to think about the man that had pretty much driven her into his arms. He didn't want her thinking about him, either. Rolling her onto her back, he lifted himself on one elbow. Her lips were swollen from his kisses, her face flushed from their lovemaking and, he would guess, a touch of discomfort at their topic. Having sex always seemed easier than talking about it.

Considering what all she had just confessed, he waited for the old and familiar need to escape to take hold. Tess wouldn't have slept with him unless her feelings had become involved, and once feelings were involved, expectations inevitably reared their ugly heads. Yet, as he brushed his lips over her forehead, he felt only a tiny twinge of that uneasiness. Mostly what he felt was guilt.

He knew her trust in him had to be total to have allowed what had just happened. He also knew that, despite the rather dangerous combination of protectiveness and pure male possessiveness he felt for her, he couldn't promise her any sort of future with him. The best he could do was be as honest with her as she'd just been with him.

"For what it's worth, I know the woman you are. And what happens between us stays between us."

Tess heard the promise in his voice. She saw it, too, in his eyes in the moments before his head descended and his hand moved up to cup her breast.

For her, for now, that promise was enough.

## Chapter Nine

The rain started around four in the morning, a soft drizzle that would turn the air sticky and humid with the heat of the day. Summer rains were simply part and parcel of August in Virginia. But had it not been for Mikey's inability to play outside that morning, Tess wouldn't have noticed the weather even had there been five feet of snow beyond the foyer's widows.

She stood near the right staircase, pretty much where she'd been when Parker had systematically stripped her of her senses, watching Mikey sock-skate across the shiny marble floor.

It totally defied the caution she had felt with every other man, but that natural guardedness had been missing pretty much from the beginning with Jeffrey Parker. She didn't know if that was because he had already proven himself by earning her brother's confidence or if she had somehow sensed his basic integrity and sense of honor. But as she had slipped from his bed when the rain woke her and climbed into her own, she'd realized that it had never occurred to her to not believe in everything about him.

The caution she hadn't felt before slipped belatedly to the surface when she heard him coming through the dining room.

She didn't have to turn around to know that he'd just showered. The clean scents of soap and his aftershave came with the breath that stalled in her lungs when he stopped behind her. He didn't touch her. Only his heat did when he bent his head to her ear.

"Are you all right?" he asked.

Her heart seemed to be beating a little too quickly as she turned to face the buttons on his white shirt. Lifting her glance past the strong line of his jaw, she offered a brave little smile

"Hi, Mr. Parker! I've been skating!"

"Hey, buddy," he replied, his glance never leaving Tess's face. "I don't know if I should apologize for what happened," he murmured, his voice low in deference to the child now sitting on the floor looking at the bottom of one sock. "Or take you back to bed."

Tess felt her pulse skip even as it occurred to her that she should be doing something to protect her heart. With her heart already involved, all she could say was, "Please don't apologize."

His eyes held hers. She thought she saw relief in their depths. She knew she saw heat.

"My sock's dirty."

She watched his glance fall to her mouth, then keep going and land on her son.

Conscious of Parker pushing his hands into his pockets, she took a step back herself.

"Then we'd better go find you clean ones," she said to the child frowning up at her. "We have to go buy our house."

"We'll be in commuter traffic," Parker reminded her, heading off to retrieve his suit jacket. "If you want to be in Richmond by ten, we'd better leave soon."

The doubts Tess had last night about going through with the purchase of the house had, thanks to Parker, given way to a cautious sort of excitement. That anticipation had grown as he'd escorted her and Mikey to the twentieth-floor offices of Liddy, Schwartz and Holloway. By the time he escorted them back with her hugging copies of her closing documents and with the keys to her new home secure in her purse, she might actually have been grinning—had it not been for Parker himself.

He knew she would rather not be noticed. That was why he stood in front of her in the crowded elevator, blocking her from the other passengers' view. It was why he discreetly slipped her into the SUV he'd parked by the basement elevator so she wouldn't attract attention going through the main lobby. He was doing his job, getting her in and out of where she needed to be with a minimum of fuss and totally focused on what surrounded them.

He remained in his detached, professional mode even after they'd pulled out of the parking garage and headed for the freeway. They had already planned to stop at a drive-through for lunch, since Mikey had been asking for a burger-in-a-box ever since his first one last week. She asked him now to drive her to her new home when they were finished, just so she could see it now that it was actually hers.

Though he said he'd be glad to, his disconnect from her seemed almost palpable. That detachment would have worried her, too, had it not been for the way he kept glancing in his side-view mirror.

"Is something wrong?" she asked, glancing over her shoulder herself.

"I don't know yet."

His tone was utterly devoid of emotion. So were his features when he changed lanes, then checked his mirror again.

"There's a car back there that came out of the garage right behind us."

Behind her she saw four lanes of traffic but nothing particularly unusual in the collection of cars, trucks and a couple of taxis.

"Which one?"

"The beige sedan. Four cars back. It's behind the red Mustang."

She barely glimpsed the car she wouldn't have noticed at all before Parker changed lanes again and checked his mirrors once more. The sedan was now blocked by a produce truck.

"I don't see it now," she murmured.

"It might be nothing," Parker replied, only to have his first suspicions confirmed when, nearing the freeway entrance, he pulled into a fast-food drive-through.

A minute later, the beige car with the dented left fender pulled in behind them.

Had Parker not called her attention to the car before, Tess would have thought nothing of it as the unassuming vehicle drove past them and headed for the back of the establishment's crowded parking lot. It parked, back end first, between two other cars before the driver's window lowered. A moment later, a large telephoto lens appeared.

Tess felt her heart sink even as she glanced over to see Parker quickly turn the wheel.

Concentration etched his profile. Since the idea was to keep distance between her and the paparazzi, she'd thought he would pull out and head for the road. Instead, looking utterly calm, he parked in the nearest space as if they'd changed their mind about the drive-through and were going inside.

"What are you doing?"

"Getting rid of him," he muttered, snapping off his seat belt. "It'll be easier than trying to lose him in this traffic. You don't want him following us to your house."

He moved from his seat and was out the door so quickly that Tess barely had time to unfasten her own seat belt before he'd slammed his door closed and was striding across the parking lot. Swinging around so she could wedge between the seats and see what was going on, she looked past Mikey and out the window beside him.

Pure purpose radiated from his big body as he headed straight for the small beige car. The large camera lens hastily disappeared. Seeing all that muscle bearing down on him, the driver of the vehicle apparently didn't want to wait to hear what he had to say. Rubber squealed on asphalt as he shot out of the lot, barely missing another car pulling in.

With her heart pounding from the near miss, she slid back into her seat and watched Parker climb back into his.

"Jerk," he muttered over the solid thud of his closing door. Sympathy crept beneath his annoyance. "I'm sorry, Tess."

He wasn't apologizing for going after the guy. His apology was for her loss of the low profile she'd wanted to keep. Where there was one parasite with a camera, there were more.

Her expression held a surprising degree of acceptance.

"I knew after the article in the *Crier* that it wouldn't be long before they showed up." With the arrival of the paparazzi, her relative freedom was now well and truly shot. "I guess now is where you really start to earn your keep."

From her faint smile, he knew she was trying to make light of something she found upsetting. Before she'd left, the press had been like flies on fresh meat with her. Considering the public's appetite for carrion and the gossip value of her return, they both knew she had every reason to expect the same treatment now.

"Then I'll do what you're paying me for and change your itinerary. We'll hit the drive-through and eat on the way back to Camelot. I think you should pass on going to the house for now. We don't know if he's working alone or if he has friends waiting for us to pull out. No sense leading them to your door."

Tess didn't argue with his conclusion. But then, Parker hadn't thought she would. She simply swallowed her disappointment at not being able to visit what she'd just bought and agreed that the last thing she wanted was for her new home to be discovered so soon. Like him, she wasn't concerned so much about paparazzi getting past the main gate of the exclusive development. A car couldn't get in without its own remote control unit to open the gate, a pass or clearance from the guard. But she needed time to make arrangements with the security company to pay for additional guards so her neighbors wouldn't be disturbed. She clearly didn't want to disrupt the lives of people who valued their personal privacy as much as she did her own.

It didn't occur to Parker to question his assumption that the man he'd been prepared to warn away from her had been a member of the tabloid press. At least it didn't until early that evening, while he was out for his daily run.

The rain that morning had left the hot air muggy. By that evening, the worst of the heat and dampness had started to dissipate, especially in the shade of the trees around the lake and along the footpaths at the back of the wooded estate's property. The damp earth was hard-packed, muffling the steady beat of Parker's feet. The faint breeze rustling the leaves cooled his sweat. He lapped the property twice. Once more and he'd have pounded out roughly three miles. That was two shy of what he considered his minimum, but he wanted to get back to the house. Tess was putting Mikey down for the night and would be downstairs after he fell asleep. She wanted Parker to look over the layout of her new home's security system. Now that the house was hers, she'd been given the wiring diagram.

Monitors and alarms were the last thing on his mind, however. He wasn't thinking about security at all. His mind was occupied with ways to help her escape the invisible prison she was in. Then there were the inescapable thoughts of how beautifully she'd responded in his arms last night—which nearly made him miss what he should have noticed long before he actually did.

He was twenty feet from the dented beige fender when he saw it protruding from the thick and tangled bushes along the rutted dirt lane. He was ten feet away when he'd slowed enough to come to a stop and note the D.C. license plate he'd already memorized.

The road was accessible from a lane nearly half a mile away. A chain and padlock secured a chain-link gate that allowed the gardener access to the back of the property that had been kept natural for the deer and the grounds' other wild inhabitants. Either the driver had cut the chain or the gardener had left the gate open. Either way, he had found the road and tucked his car where he'd thought it would be out of sight.

The windows of the car were down, undoubtedly to cut the chance of reflection. And detection. Parker had glimpsed the driver, a balding guy with a fringe of dark hair pulled into a ponytail, when he'd shot past him in the fast-food restaurant's parking lot. At the moment, the man was nowhere to be seen.

Having nothing else to do while he waited for him to show up, Parker decided to take a look through the papers scattered over the passenger seat. Ignoring the local map on the floorboard with the hamburger and candy bar wrappers, he reached through the open window and lifted out a hand-drawn map of the Kendricks' estate and the file beneath it.

It had barely occurred to him that someone personally familiar with the property must have drawn the meticulously detailed map when he started flipping through the correspondence in the messy file.

Within seconds, Parker felt his usual annoyance with those who invaded others' lives evolve to something bordering on pure, cold fury. The man wasn't at all who he'd assumed him to be. He wasn't a paparazzo. He was a private investigator.

The discovery that Parker would have assessed with cool detachment on any other job suddenly became very personal. And not just because the instructions in the letter to Ace Investigations from Bradley Ashworth included obtaining any information possible about the bodyguard employed by his ex-wife. Ashworth wanted any information possible about Tess's daily activities. He wanted photographs of her and any male she interacted with. He wanted the names of anyone she interviewed to hire.

Basically the man wanted anything he could possibly use to keep Tess from ever saying a word against him.

Leaves rustled near the back of the car, a branch breaking as someone worked his way through the foliage. Catching a glimpse of the same dark ponytail he'd seen before, Parker tossed the file back through the window and was around the back fender whipping the camera from around the neck of the balding PI before the man could do much more than swear and throw his hands up in front of his face.

"Take it easy," Parker muttered. It wasn't this guy's neck he wanted to snap. "I'm not going to risk an assault charge with you. I've got what I want."

"Hey, man." The guy lunged forward, snatching at the camera's dangling cord. Noting the size of Parker's sweaty muscles—or maybe just the deadly gleam in his eye—he jerked right back. "That thing's expensive!"

"So is bail." Flipping open the back of the camera, Parker popped out the film, exposing it in the process. Whatever images the guy had captured were now history.

Seeing his day's work destroyed, the guy with the paunch reddened. From the way his glance darted around him, he also appeared to be searching for the quickest possible escape.

"You're trespassing," Parker continued, shoving the roll of film into the pocket of his running shorts. He yanked down the hem of his tank, covering the cell phone and pager clipped to his waistband. "I figure you have about thirty seconds to get out of here before I call the police. In the meantime," he added, getting in the guy's face enough to let him think he might do him harm after all, "you might want to get on your cell phone and tell your client that Miss Kendrick's body-guard will gladly take care of you and anyone else he sends around disturbing her peace or invading her privacy." Arching one eyebrow, he shoved the empty camera at the stomach of the man backing away from him. "Are we clear?"

The man said nothing as he snatched his precious Pentax. Within seconds, the hapless private investigator had tossed his camera onto the papers on the passenger seat and was be-hind the wheel of his car. Seconds after that, he was bumping his way down the road for the back gate.

With his hands on his hips, his heart pounding from the run, anger and adrenaline, Parker started walking along the road behind him. He would check the gate to see how access was gained, then talk to both the gardener and the stable master so they'd know to be vigilant. He would also ask Tess if she wanted the PI picked up and charges pressed, but he already knew what her answer would be. Pressing charges against someone working for her ex would only result in publicity, and she would do whatever she had to do to avoid calling attention to herself or her situation in such a way.

His heart rate began to slow. His mind did not.

He very much doubted the PI would deliver his message to the man who'd hired him. More than likely the guy would quit the case cold or try to save face by telling his client he couldn't find anything and that he was wasting his money. Not that it would matter. There would be others like him.

Parker wasn't about to underestimate Bradley Ashworth. He also knew it was past time that something be done about him.

When he found Tess waiting for him with her diagrams an hour later, his first thought was to tell her just that. Seeing her uneasy smile, he decided to find out what was wrong first.

Tess glanced up the moment she heard Parker enter the comfortably cluttered breakfast room. He'd showered and changed into a crewneck shirt and khakis. It seemed he'd been in a hurry, too. He'd forgotten his watch. "I thought you were going for a short run," she said, wondering at everything she noticed about him. "You must have gone a full ten."

She couldn't believe how glad she was that he was back. Or how badly she wanted to slip into his arms now that there was no one else around. Having him hold her had been on her mind all day. Even more so since Ina had dropped off the envelope that had been delivered by courier that afternoon. The maid had answered the gate buzzer and signed for it herself.

She watched Parker's glance fall to her mouth. Memories seemed to darken his eyes before they moved back to the disquiet in hers. "I'd have been here sooner, but I stopped to talk to Jackson and Eddy." With the ease of a man who knows his touch will be welcome, he skimmed his knuckles down her cheek. "What's going on?"

She moved closer, so very grateful that with him she could share what she would have otherwise had to keep to herself.

"Brad sent me copies of the pictures he'd shown me before. They were delivered by courier while we were gone this afternoon."

Parker's hand stilled beneath her jaw, dropped to her shoulder. "Was there anything with them? A note? A letter?"

She shook her head. Brad wasn't stupid. He wouldn't write anything to her that could be used to prove blackmail. "Just the photos. I think he just wants to remind me of what he has."

"And yank your chain a little tighter now that you're back."

The venom in Parker's muttered words brought her head up.

"What did you do with them?" he asked.

"I haven't done anything with them yet. Ina just gave them to me a while ago. I'll find a shredder—"

"Don't do that."

"Don't destroy them?" Of course she would destroy them. It would be insane not to. "Why not? The last thing I want is for someone else to come across them." She stepped back, pulled the envelope from where she'd buried it beneath a stack of files. "The tabloids would pay a fortune for these. There's not a whole lot of doubt about what's going on in here."

To prove her point, she held the envelope out to him.

Clearly curious to see what it was she fought so diligently to keep from the rest of the world, he removed the half dozen prints. The stock was the sort used in home computers, the quality of the images quite superior.

Without a word, he began to shuffle from one to the next.

The woman with Tess's distinguished-looking silver-haired father appeared to be in her late twenties or early thirties. Definitely older than Tess but certainly younger than her mother. She was lovely, dark-haired, doe-eyed. In the first few photos, William Kendrick held her hands across a small cocktail table, their expressions intent on each other. There were two with his arm around her in a parking lot, another with her looking upset as he stood with his hands on her shoulders.

"These certainly raise questions," Parker conceded, "but they don't prove he's having an affair."

"Brad said he has others that do," she reminded him. "Besides, the press doesn't need proof. Those photos alone would do enough damage."

He seemed to agree. At least she assumed that was the reason for the solemn set of his features.

"I told you I talked to Jackson and Eddy." He slipped the photos back into the envelope. "I needed to put them on alert. We had an intruder on the property."

Totally puzzled by the change of subject, she took the envelope he handed her. "An intruder?"

"The guy who followed us when we were in Richmond. He wasn't who we thought he was. He's a private investigator. Your ex hired him."

The deep tones of Parker's voice were deceptively even, much as they had been that afternoon when he'd first thought they were being followed.

"Ashworth is intent on making sure you don't forget the

hold he has on you, Tess, and finding whatever else he can to tighten his grip. Unless you're willing to take away his power, you'll be at his mercy for the rest of your life."

As if he'd been touching her forever, he slipped his hand under the hair covering the back of her neck. The comforting feel of it seemed to offer reassurance. Or maybe it was support. Whatever it was, she wanted more of it. With him touching her again, she also desperately wanted to not think about Brad. She didn't want to talk about him or even acknowledge that he existed. She didn't want to do anything but savor the sweet escape she'd felt last night in Parker's arms.

"I already know that," she insisted. Before Ina had brought the envelope, she'd felt nothing but anticipation. What she began to feel now was the awful resignation she'd learned to live with and the draining helplessness that so often came with it. "Him hiring an investigator doesn't surprise me at all. Anything he does doesn't surprise me. I just have no idea what to do about any of it."

"I do."

Once Parker had truly considered it, the only effective solution had been pitifully obvious. That she now had copies of the photos was a bonus. Knowing Tess as he did, he knew she would fight him on his idea. But he had promised he wouldn't leave her to deal with her situation alone and he had no intention of going back on his word.

Clearly skeptical, she tipped her head. "How?"

"You're protecting your father along with the rest of your family. Right?"

Seeming unprepared for his approach, she hesitated, only to give him a nod when he eased his thumb toward her jaw.

"But your father is the one who should be protecting you. He has an obligation to you," he insisted, sounding affronted by the men she should have been able to count on—her husband, her father. It seemed both had failed her miserably. "You need to break Ashworth's hold. You want to clear your name. You can do both if you show your father the copies of those pictures and have him go public with them himself. Ashworth has nothing to hold over you once he does that."

Tess blinked up at the man whose touch calmed even as his words jerked at a whole new kind of distress. The thought of confronting her father about his affair had never entered her mind.

She totally dismissed the audacious idea now. "I'm not about to be the catalyst that ruins my parents' relationship. It wouldn't matter who released those pictures. Seeing evidence of Dad with another woman would devastate my mother. The public humiliation..." She cut herself off, hating the thought. "Mom would be victimized and Dad would be dragged through mud in the media and by their friends,..."

Still shaking her head, she stepped back, moving more from the idea than the man who'd proposed it but needing the space just the same.

"I'm furious with my father." Not to mention disillusioned and disappointed beyond belief. She'd always thought him a rock, the most principled man she knew. "But I'm not about to see his life destroyed."

Parker's eyes narrowed to slits of blue. "The way yours has been? Tess," he said flatly, "you're protecting everyone in your family but yourself."

It vaguely occurred to Parker that what she was doing shouldn't matter to him anywhere near as much as it did. But the consequences of his inability to keep from caring about her seemed less important just then than convincing her that her father was the key to her freedom.

"Your dad is the one who allowed you to be put in this position."

Defense shot to the surface. "It was Brad who did that."

"Your dad was the one who provided the material for you to be blackmailed with," he explained, his tone as reasonable as he could make it. "Ashworth didn't have anything else on you or he would have used it by now. He wouldn't be trying so hard to find something, if he did. You get rid of the ammunition he has with your dad and you'll get rid of the problem."

"I can't confront my father—"

"Other than wanting to protect everyone, why not?"

"For one thing, I'm his daughter and I'd be questioning his sex life."

"I didn't say it wouldn't be embarrassing." His eyes bored into hers. "But you can't *not* go to him with this. You'll never get your life back unless he takes responsibility for what his indiscretion has done to you."

As compliant as he suspected Tess had always been, it would take more guts than she probably thought she possessed for her to challenge the man many people saw as larger than life. William Kendrick was a legend of sorts, a man whose carpetbagger ancestors had passed on a small fortune that he'd parlayed into a bigger one by investing in everything from computers and commodities to a winery and sports teams. He was a modern-day Midas, a man whose touch turned everything golden, including his political career and his romance with a beautiful woman who'd given up her right to be queen to marry him.

But the problem wasn't William. It was Tess. In the past year, her world had narrowed to something that no longer allowed her to see beyond the restraining walls she'd been forced to hide behind. Confined in that limiting space, caught in survival mode, she clearly didn't feel she had any viable choices.

He would give her one.

"If you won't talk to him, I will."

The phenomenon was interesting, he thought. He hadn't changed his voice. Not in volume or tone. Despite that, in the sudden silence his ultimatum seemed to echo off the expensively papered walls.

Tess could only stare at him. Of all the things Parker could have just said, that was the absolute last thing she would have expected of him. He knew how badly she wanted calm in her life. He knew how she craved whatever anonymity she could find. And peace. That most of all. Yet he was actually pushing her into something that promised her even more upheaval.

She was falling hard for the man who would soon walk out of her life. She thought it odd that the realization should hit now. But that disturbing little reality wasn't what concerned her just then. What did was the thought of how monumentally unfair it was for the man she was falling in love with to threaten her with something that could destroy the very foundations of her family.

She hated that he was threatening her at all. It didn't matter that he seemed to be thinking only of her. It didn't matter that he had nothing at all to gain by her compliance. He was backing her into a corner, and that was not a place she wanted to be with anyone ever again.

"Under no circumstances are you to go to my father yourself. Do you understand?"

The flash of fire in her eyes was a good sign. But it wasn't enough for Parker. Suspecting she would continue to protect those she cared about at her own expense, he quietly strengthened his warning.

"I leave in four days, Tess. Take as much of that time as you need to talk to your dad, but I want to know before I leave that he's aware of what's going on with you."

The sense of being cornered compounded itself as she threw up her hands. "Why does this even matter to you?"

"Because I want to leave knowing you're not being jerked around anymore. I have the feeling you've been pushed around all your life. By the demands of your family, the public, your ex." She caved in to everyone's needs but her own. "I know you want to make it by yourself, but you never will unless you learn to push back."

"And you're not pushing?"

He knew he was. "I'm just showing you how it's done," he told her and felt as torn as she looked in the moments before her glance faltered and fell.

Tess didn't know which had the firmer grip just then—the desire to sink into his strength and hold on to him while she could or to run from the new set of anxieties he'd just raised. On some level she knew that what he insisted she do was probably her only way out. But she also knew that if she did it, she would be left to deal with the aftermath without him.

She had never expected him to be there for her beyond the time he'd agreed to stay. She knew he wasn't a man who thought in terms of permanence or commitment to much of anything but his job. His family was his mom, a few cousins and their kids, and he was content with that in ways she could never be. But he had become her friend, her confidant, her mentor. Her lover. And he was arming her to continue without him.

The thought had her pulling back and turning away. As easily as he could read her at times, it seemed wiser to keep her focus on something inanimate.

"We should look at the diagrams," she said, her voice nowhere near as strong as she would have wished. "I want to make sure the security is what it should be before you go."

She heard him move behind her. "I meant what I said, Tess."

He wasn't ready to drop the subject. She wasn't willing to discuss it anymore.

"I know you did." Papers rustled as she pulled them from her folder and set them in the space she'd cleared among the other papers on the table. "But I have my deadlines, too. Right now, I'd rather deal with this one."

They were at an impasse. When Parker felt her shoulders stiffen as he reached to turn her around, he realized that they were at a crossroads, too.

There was no mistaking her withdrawal from him. He could practically feel it in the tautness of the slender muscles beneath his hand. Hating the way she'd retreated inside herself, his own sense of self-preservation belatedly went to work, too.

He let his hand fall.

"Tell you what," he said. She could withdraw all she wanted. He would still go to her father if she didn't. "Why don't I look this over tonight? I can pull some specs off the computer for ancillary equipment if you need it. We can talk about it all in the morning."

For a moment she said nothing. She just stood with her back to him as if gathering her courage or her poise before she turned and tipped back her head.

"That would be good," she murmured. Her guarded glance fell to his chest. Lifting her hand, she touched her fingers to the soft cotton covering his heart. "Thank you."

She refused to meet his eyes as she let her fingers slide away. Curling them into her palm, she offered a quiet, "Good night," and stepped past him to head for the staircase.

Parker listened to her fading footsteps. The urge to go after her was strong. Realizing that his hand had just covered the spot she'd touched, the need to stay where he was felt stronger still. As out of hand as he'd let things get with her, it was probably better to start creating a little distance of his own. Heaven knew he'd done a lousy enough job of it so far.

## Chapter Ten

Tess spent the night dead certain she was about to tear her family apart. That awful conviction dogged every footstep the next morning as she paced the kitchen floor while Mikey finished his breakfast.

Four days. That was all the time she had to talk to her father about his affair, then watch Parker move on to the job he was working on even now.

She assumed it was the judicial conference they'd talked about during their drives that had him so preoccupied. She could see him on the cobblestone court between the house and garages, his head bent in concentration, his cell phone to one ear.

She didn't doubt for a moment that he would go to her father if she didn't do it herself. He wasn't the sort of man to make an idle promise or threat. The fact that she resented that threat made it difficult for her to appreciate that he was just doing what he'd been doing all along—helping her help herself. But even as upset as she was with him and his deadline, she couldn't deny that the problem with Brad was escalating.

He'd sent her the copies of the photos now hidden under her mattress to remind her of the damage he could do. If he had hired one private investigator, he would hire another. If she didn't do something to stop him, as Parker had insisted, his hold on her would never end. The lies would continue. Worst of all, the price of her continued silence to protect her family would be the damage that could ultimately be done to her son.

Leaving Mikey to his cereal and the cartoons on the television beneath the kitchen cabinet, she picked up the telephone from its charger on the desk in the alcove.

The longer she thought about making the call to the Hamptons, the more she dreaded it. The more she dreaded it, the more she paced. And the more she paced, the more agitated she became. Wanting only to break that pointless cycle and get the call over with before Parker showed up to remind her she needed to make it, she punched in the number and held her breath.

Rose, the housekeeper, answered on the third ring. Her tone as polite and reserved as always, the woman who'd run the Kendrick household for over twenty years told her that neither of her parents were there at the moment. Her mother was at a hair appointment and her father had spent the past few days in Washington, D.C., and Richmond in meetings. She believed he might be in Richmond even as they spoke.

After telling Rose that there was no message, she thanked her, hung up and glanced at her watch. If her father was in Richmond, he would be staying at what the family referred to as "the apartment." The residence on the top floor of the thirty-story Kendrick Building in downtown Richmond was actually a twelve-room penthouse with its own staff and its own private elevator. The Kendrick Corporation's corporate offices occupied several floors below it.

It was nearly nine o'clock, though. Being the early-morning sort, her father would be gone from there by now.

Intent on her mission, she called her father's office to speak to Edna Fordham, his personal secretary. The no-nonsense sixty-something woman who'd handled her father's daily business life for the past thirty years informed Tess that he was still in Washington but that he would arrive in Richmond tomorrow morning. She could clear a thirty-minute window between his meetings in the afternoon, unless she wanted to see him before he took his guests from Tokyo to dinner that evening. Or he would be in for a while the following morning, if she preferred something less rushed.

Her timing clearly wasn't optimal. But then, Tess figured there probably never was a perfect time to jerk the rug from under someone's world. Not wanting to confront her father in the middle of negotiations, she opted for the day after next and had just thanked the woman and hung up when Mikey announced that he was finished and ready to go outside.

Outside wasn't where Tess wanted to go just then. At least not with Parker out there. She checked the time again. She had two hours before he would drive her to her appointment with Ginny at Ginny's design studio in Camelot to start picking out furniture. Looking at the time in between as something of a reprieve from the man who seemed equally intent on avoiding her that morning, she washed off Mikey's milk mustache, grabbed some bread for the ducks and the two of them headed out the front door to take the long way around to the lake.

She could see Parker still on his phone as they crossed the side lawn by the tennis court. Though he seemed deep in concentration, his head came up as they moved to the path by the boxwood hedge. There was no doubt that he noticed them, but he seemed too preoccupied to give them much thought as Mikey ran along the path that led through the trees.

The dubious relief she felt having made her escape faded by the time the little weather-grayed boat dock, with its equally rustic boathouse came into view. As she handed Mikey the bread so he could feed the squawking ducks, she had the distinct feeling that she was being watched. The sensation didn't elicit the discomfort or distress it often did in public. It was something far more disturbing. It felt like a familiar knowing, some sixth sense that connected her to the man who'd become far too important to her and told her he was near.

In the still morning air, she turned from where her little boy crouched in front of two mallards by the mirrorlike water. Parker had followed them. He'd obviously kept his distance, because she had heard nothing as they'd moved along the walkways and paths. He kept that same discreet distance now as he stood watching her, as strong and silent as the massive oaks behind him.

She had the distinct feeling that he hadn't let them out of his sight. Now that she thought about it, she realized he wouldn't, either. Not after having found an intruder on the property yesterday.

The fact that he didn't approach brought a strange little ache. Even with no one else around, he'd reverted to his professional role.

The ache threatened to grow. She'd become accustomed to him being a part of her life rather than someone who watched from the periphery. He'd become the one person she could turn to about anything. Hating what he'd pushed her into, equally upset with what she was losing, she closed her eyes, took a deep breath and made herself do what he was doing: focus on what had to be done.

Beside her, Mikey tossed pieces of bread onto the ground

and scrambled back, grinning as the ducks eagerly attacked their treat. Warning him to stay back from the water, she did her best to hide the anxiety she didn't want Parker to see and started toward him.

With his hands in the pockets of his khakis and his dark glasses dangling by one stem from the short placket of his polo shirt, he walked toward her himself. His approach was almost casual. The look in his eyes when he met her halfway was not. She saw guardedness there and maybe a hint of the same caution that kept her from asking how he'd slept or if he'd been up most of the night as she had.

"I'll need to go into Richmond the day after tomorrow," she told him. "I have an appointment with my dad at ten."

One dark eyebrow slowly arched. "You called him already?" He sounded the same way he looked, as if he'd thought for certain she would fight the idea to the bitter end. "I'm impressed."

"Not him. His secretary. And don't be. I was making myself crazy. It was easier to just get the call over with."

Though caution still carved the masculine lines of his face, a smile entered the blue of his eyes. "You'll be glad you did this, Tess."

She couldn't make herself smile back. She couldn't think of anything to say, either, that didn't involve asking him how he thought she could ever be happy about something that would hurt so many people. But she didn't get a chance to say anything at all. Mikey had spotted his friend.

"Mr. Parker! Help me feed the ducks!"

With the bread wrapper dangling in one fist, he ran up to them and grabbed Parker's hand.

The innocence of the simple act squeezed at her heart.

"We have to leave in a few minutes. Ginny said she didn't mind if I was early."

She spoke to them both. But even as she did, she wasn't sure if she was deliberately limiting Parker's time with her son so Mikey wouldn't get even more attached to him than he already was or if she just needed to get them all out of there so she could focus on something that didn't put knots in her stomach.

Her meeting with Ginny that morning provided much of the diversion she was looking for. It also led to a trip to a furniture warehouse that afternoon, where her little entourage of four, including Mikey and Parker, was followed by no less than five employees bearing clipboards, tape measures and fabric swatches. She met Ginny again the following day to repeat the performance, accompanied by a few paparazzi this time, and spent both evenings in her bedroom, where she tried not to think about what Parker might be doing while she perused the specialty catalogues Ginny had loaned her for the things she needed to stock her kitchen and linen closets. She couldn't count the number of times she wanted to show him something she thought fun or interesting or exciting in some small way. Or to ask his opinion of the choices she'd already made. But she didn't ask what he thought or what he would have chosen instead because she didn't want his opinion to matter that much. She didn't want it to matter that she missed sharing with him, either. Mostly she didn't want it to matter that she missed him already.

He'd stopped offering to mentor her through meal preparation. He no longer joined them when they ate. As he had when they had first arrived at the estate, he kept as much physical distance between them as possible. It was as if he knew as well as she did that all it would take was for her to turn to him and they'd wind up back in his bed. But she had no desire to create more memories she'd just have to work to forget or to give him any more of her heart than he already had.

Still, she was grateful he was there. The paparazzi they had encountered on their furniture-buying excursions had started hanging around the front gate of the estate.

Jackson and Eddy had already been put on the alert for trespassers by Parker. He had also turned on the perimeter alarm system and notified the local police, who started doing drive-bys to clear the press away. Yet it wasn't just being exposed in her fishbowl once more that had Tess's nerves feeling so raw when the morning of her meeting with her father finally arrived. It wasn't even the meeting itself. It was seeing Parker come from the hall to the kitchen in his dark suit and tie, carrying his briefcase and travel bag.

"I thought you weren't leaving until tomorrow."

His glance skimmed the hair she'd knotted at her nape, the bronze beads at her throat, the cream silk suit that nipped her waist and skimmed her knees. Yet he barely met her eyes before he continued to the kitchen door.

"I think it's better I go now."

He didn't elaborate. As if he saw no need for further explanation, he opened the kitchen and utility room doors for her and the little boy with the stuffed dinosaur and motioned them ahead of him.

"The agent you originally wanted is back and on her way to Richmond," he continued, following them out to where he'd left the SUV by the back door. "She'll meet us at your father's office."

They were running late because each had been on phone calls—Tess with Ginny, who'd called about a problem with a sofa, and Parker apparently with his counterpart from Bennington's.

The unwanted distress she felt at his early departure suddenly met the anxiety of dealing with her dad.

"Are you leaving before or after I see my father?"

The tailgate of the vehicle closed on his luggage with a thud. Having opened the back passenger door herself, and with Mikey climbing into his car seat, she watched Parker's preoccupation fade as he walked toward her.

His glance shifted over her face, the look in his eyes as intimate as a caress. "I'm not going anywhere until I know you'll be okay, Tess."

The man didn't play fair. He'd held her at arm's length for the past two days. Now, with nothing more than the look in his eyes and the quiet sincerity in his deep voice, he was pulling her back.

Or so it seemed to her in the moments before she made herself break his visual hold and she climbed in beside her son. She told herself she shouldn't feel so relieved to know that he wasn't abandoning her at her father's doorstep. After all, she had handled most of the past year without him. She could handle this, too. But even that questionable relief had disappeared by the time they reached the gate at the end of the tree-lined driveway.

A dozen paparazzi surged in front of their black bull-nosed vehicle as the gates swung inward. Camera lenses, long, large, obtrusive things, were pushed toward its windows by photographers desperate to get a shot of her. As Parker had done yesterday, he gunned the engine once in warning, then sped up, turning onto the two-lane country road and leaving those who hadn't been bright enough to move jumping back to avoid getting run down.

Beside her, Mikey sat wide-eyed, holding her hand. Behind her, the gate had already closed and men were scrambling for the cars they'd parked on either side of the road.

"I'll lose them at the freeway."

Parker spoke with the calm assurance of a man who'd encountered nothing more than he'd expected and who knew how to do his job with a minimum of fuss. When they reached the freeway, instead of taking it west to Richmond, he took the entrance heading east. As more than a couple of their pursuers appeared behind them on the freeway, he took the next exit, crossed under the overpass and jumped back on the freeway heading east before the first car could reach the light and see which way they'd gone.

"It's going to be okay."

Tess looked up to see Parker looking at her in the rearview mirror. From the encouragement in his tone, she knew he wasn't talking about the trail of press they'd left behind. He was talking about the next little hurdle she was about to face.

Three days ago she would have hung on to his reassurance as if it were some sort of lifeline. Now, with him only hours from leaving, she steeled herself against the temptation to lean on him in any way—and let him know that things weren't as simple as he wanted them to be.

"There's something here I don't think you understand." With his focus on the road, she spoke to what she could see of his image in the mirror. "My relationship with my father was nothing like what you had with your dad. I know you had no respect for yours," she reminded him. She had no respect for his father herself, considering how he'd robbed his son of such an important bond. "But I idolized mine."

His glance caught hers. A heartbeat later, something like apology entered his expression. Before he could say anything she didn't want to hear or tell her again how badly she needed to do this, she looked out the window beside her, breathing deeply, gathering her courage around her like a cloak.

Her father had been her hero. He had been her knight in shining armor when she'd been a little girl and the man she'd measured others by when she'd grown up enough to realize that not all men were created equal. Over the years, she'd heard of how forceful and dauntless he'd been in politics and how aggressive, astute and ethical he was in business. She'd heard he was a force to be reckoned with in the boardroom, an uncompromising authority when the tough decisions had to be made.

Personally she'd known him only as the man who'd always had time for a phone call from one of his children no matter how busy his schedule or where in the world he might be. The man who was fair-minded and generous and dedicated to his family.

He wasn't supposed to be fallible. He wasn't supposed to be a hypocrite. And she shouldn't have had to let him think she'd grown up to be the spoiled, ungrateful and self-involved woman Brad and the press had portrayed her to be.

The unfairness in that thought was still with her nearly an hour later when Parker pulled into the private entrance beneath the gleaming modern structure of the Kendrick Building and silently escorted her and Mikey to her father's suite of offices on the twenty-ninth floor. The thought accompanied her into the lush private reception area where Edna, with her smart gray bob and silver-rimmed bifocals, immediately picked up the phone to announce her, then motioned her toward the closed double doors to his office. That empowering sense of injustice remained as she asked Parker to watch Mikey for her before she smoothed the jacket of her suit and, clutching the oversize purse on her shoulder, opened the door before she could let nerves ruin her edge.

Across an expanse of plush rust-colored carpet, huge windows allowed a view of sky, rooftops and river. In front of that panorama, her silver-haired father rose with athletic ease from behind his enormous mahogany desk.

She closed the door behind her and took a step forward. That was as far as she could seem to go.

She hadn't seen her father in nearly a year. But nothing about him had changed. At sixty-four, William Kendrick was still a tall, handsome and compelling presence. He wore his affluence, influence and power as easily as he wore his Italian designer suits. It also seemed that she could still detect disappointment in his sharp gray eyes as he walked up to her and wrapped her in a Polo-scented hug.

Disillusioned herself, with him, she couldn't make herself return the hug with much enthusiasm before he stepped away to look her over.

"It's been a while, Tess." Censure met concern. Or maybe what she saw was simply a father searching for something recognizable in the daughter he thought he'd once known. "Are you all right?"

"I've been better."

His mouth pinched, carving the deep lines bracketing it more deeply. "I'm sure you have." He stepped back, motioned her toward the leather sofa situated beneath a huge original oil painting that, to her, looked like something Mikey could have done with finger paint. "This business with you and Brad still isn't settled, I take it. I understand you're now fighting about whether or not he can see Mikey."

As with her mom when she'd phoned after Rose mentioned her call the other day, her first instinct was to change the subject. Before she'd left, she hadn't been able to answer their questions about her divorce, so she'd moved on to something else every time it had come up. Because she hadn't answered, they'd stopped asking, which left them only Mikey to talk about.

"Mom said she told you what Brad's mom was saying," he explained, letting her know how he'd come by the information. "I guess she heard it from Eleanor's hairdresser, though how she got it I have no idea," he muttered. "I thought Eleanor and

Bud," he continued, speaking of Brad's parents, "were in Cannes."

Shaking his head at the workings of the intercontinental grapevine, he lowered himself into one of the black leather barrel chairs in the seating arrangement. "But I doubt that you're here to talk about that. I understand you've bought a house. Real estate is an excellent investment," he informed her, sounding infinitely more comfortable with the subject. "I assume you're here for me to authorize an extra withdrawal from your trust."

His knowledge of her acquisition came as no surprise. He was a man with business advisors who kept him informed of everything he might possibly need to know about the Virginia real-estate market. The Kendrick name popping up in the public records of recorded sales would definitely be brought to his attention.

Then there was the fact that he paid for the lawyers she'd used.

"My finances are fine."

She'd made it as far as the end of the polished chrome coffee table between the sofa and chairs. She couldn't, however, seem to make herself sit. "I didn't come to see you about the house." Hoping her voice wasn't shaking as much as her hands, she opened the clasp on her large shoulder bag. "I came to see you about these."

She held out the manila envelope. Seeing it shake, she set it on the coffee table in front of him as if the thing might turn into a snake and bite her and stepped back.

The lines in his forehead deepened as he reached for it. Giving her a puzzled glance, he looked back to the envelope and pulled out the small stack of photographs.

Tess had never known her father to be caught off guard or to not know exactly what to say. He was, however, speechless as he slowly rose while flipping from one photo to another of him and the attractive brunette. When he reached the one with the woman looking upset and him obviously trying to calm her, he finally looked to Tess.

"How did you get these?"

"Brad took them with his cell phone. He was meeting someone for a drink at the James Hotel and saw the two of you in the bar. He said you were so involved you didn't even notice him."

She took a deep breath, plunged ahead. "He said he'd seen you check into a room and that he had others even more incriminating." She could only imagine what he'd caught on digital disk before that hotel room door had closed. "The only reason I'm showing them to you is because he's been using them to keep me quiet about the real reason I left him. He's using them now to keep me from defending myself against the lies he's telling his parents about me keeping him from Mikey."

The color that moved into her father's face would have alarmed her had it not been expected. She imagined embarrassment to be the least of what he was feeling at the moment. A little humiliation and panic were probably in order. Or so she was thinking when she saw his jaw lock an instant before something deadly flashed in his eyes.

The forbidding expression almost reminded her of the lethal look she'd seen on Parker's face when she'd first told him about her ex.

"Brad is blackmailing you?" His tone incredulous, he all but ignored the evidence of infidelity in his hands. "With these?"

She'd barely given him a quick nod when his paternal instincts spiked even higher.

"What in heaven's name does he want to keep you quiet about?"

She didn't care to think about the details, much less go into them with a man who already looked as if he were about to pop a vein. The basics were all that was necessary anyway. "Brad was an abusive husband," she said, wondering at how much easier it had been to admit the mistake of her marriage to the man waiting on the other side of the wall. "Mentally and physically. No one ever saw that side of him but me," she hurried on. "I left because of what he'd done to me and because I was afraid he'd turn on Mikey, too. He'd never wanted his son and he'd get so angry whenever Mikey would start to cry...."

She cut herself off, took a deep breath. Details weren't necessary.

She nodded to the pictures in her father's hand. "He told me he would give those and others even more condemning to the press if I ever made any allegations against him."

Her father's color was marginally better as he dropped the photos to the table. His anger, however, remained. "So that's why you never defended yourself."

"That's why."

"You were protecting me."

"And Mom."

Comprehension, disbelief, astonishment, sorrow. The emotions all clouded his face as the enormity of her admissions erased the displeasure and frustration he'd felt with her over the past year. For a moment he looked as if he wanted to reach for her and let his hug say all the things he apparently couldn't just then. Seeming to remember how stiffly she'd received his fatherly embrace moments ago, he settled for looking truly torn instead. She just couldn't tell which had the stronger grip just then—fury with his ex-son-in-law for all that he'd done to his daughter, regret for what she'd been put through or guilt over the affair she had confronted him with.

"Brad lied about having seen anything more, Tess. He doesn't have anything else on me, either. Those pictures aren't what they seem. I did have an affair," he admitted, the necessity for the truth outweighing any reluctance he might have felt offering it, "but it was over thirty years ago. That woman isn't my lover. She's my daughter."

Tess opened her mouth, closed it. Blinked. "Your what?"

"My daughter. She's a few months older than Ashley."

Tess stared at the man whose once-dark hair had gone silver-white over the years. He'd passed that deep shade on to her and Cord. With a glance at the striking brunette in the photograph, it seemed he'd passed it on to her, too.

She had another sister. Half sister, actually.

Now she needed to sit.

The end of the leather sofa was the closest. Sinking onto it, she found it was her turn to go speechless.

Apparently realizing more explanation was necessary, her father hitched the knees of his slacks and lowered himself back into the chair across from her.

"Your mom knew about the affair, Tess. It was a rough time, but we worked through it, and there hasn't been anyone but your mom since. I didn't know about Jillian, though. Not until she showed up a couple of years ago." He clasped his hands between his knees, looked from her to the woman looking so hurt and upset in the photograph. "She discovered I was her father just before her mother died. Those pictures are of the only time she and I have met."

Still stunned, Tess scrambled to keep up. He wasn't having an affair. But he had had one. A lifetime ago.

"Does Mom know about her?" she finally asked.

"She does. I don't keep anything from her. Not anymore," he qualified. "She said she'd handle the relationship any way I wished. But Jillian doesn't want anything to do with me."

"Then why did she seek you out?"

"I think she came to me mostly to let me know how much

I'd hurt her mother." The confession came quietly. "Whatever her reasons, she made it clear that she likes her life the way it is. She's a schoolteacher. Like you would have been if our lives had been less public," he explained, smiling a little at the connection. "She seems to be a very private person," he continued, the smile fading. "She knows her life would change if people discover she's a Kendrick. She doesn't want that, and frankly your mom and I have been all too happy to honor her wishes. There are things our friends and the public simply don't need to know about our personal lives."

"But what about Brad? If I don't keep going along with him, he'll leak those photos. Parker said the only way to take away his power is for you to come forward with the photos yourself."

Parker had been thinking, as she had at the time, that her dad would be confessing to an affair. And he would. Just not a current one. And with the bonus of a love child. "You'd have to explain what they are," she said quietly, trying to imagine if either man could come up with another alternative. "You know the press won't let it go until they find out who she is. Then her privacy will be gone, too."

A hint of consternation moved through her father's distinguished features.

"Let me worry about that." With his enviable ability to compartmentalize, he moved from the choice he had to make between two daughters back to the matter at hand. "Who's Parker?"

"My bodyguard."

"From Bennington's?" he asked, though why she had no idea. They never used any other firm.

Sensing that he was just aiming for more comfortable ground, she gave a nod. "Cord recommended him."

"Parker," he repeated. "Is he the one they call 'Bull'?"

She'd forgotten about that. "He is. He's who talked me into coming to see you. I don't think I would have if he hadn't…pushed."

"Pushed?"

"He said he'd come to you if I didn't."

From the way her father's eyebrow rose, it was apparent that there were any number of questions he could have asked just then—starting with how her bodyguard had come to know something she'd kept hidden from the rest of the world and what their relationship was that he would have gone to her father himself. From there he could have moved on to ask about Brad and why she hadn't gone to her mother or her sister about her problems during her marriage. About why she hadn't come to him sooner with the pictures.

Her reasons for confiding in a relative stranger undoubtedly had him curious. But she knew he knew the answer to every other question boiled down to the same thing: a sense of duty to her family. He and her mother had instilled it in all their children.

His telephone buzzed.

Ignoring the summons from his secretary, he rose, walked over to where she sat and kissed the top of her head. "I'm so sorry, Tess. About all of this. I had no idea…" His words trailed off. "None of it should ever have happened to you."

The simple, healing words came with the squeeze of his hand on her shoulder and a grim sort of smile as he straightened.

Relief waited to be felt. The responsibility for the photographs and whatever Brad might do with them was no longer hers but her father's. Her dad now knew the truth about her and, soon, so would her mom and her siblings. But even with the enormity of that weight lifted, she couldn't feel the sense of reprieve that should have filled her just then.

When she left there, she had to say goodbye to the man who'd returned her to her family.

The phone buzzed again.

With a nod toward the insistent instrument, he stepped back. "I have people waiting for me in the boardroom," he explained. "Is Parker here now?"

"He's outside with Mikey."

"Then come on. I'll walk you out. I want to thank him for getting you here. And, Tess," he said, "don't worry any more about Brad. I'll take care of him," he promised in a voice tinged with steel. "I just need to decide the best way to go about it so we're all ready for the fallout. In the meantime, it's good to know you're going to be with Parker. He obviously knows how to watch out for you."

## Chapter Eleven

Tess had the feeling that her father didn't look up to too many men. Yet that was what he'd had to do when she'd introduced him to Parker, who'd bested his six feet two by at least another inch. As the two powerful-looking males had sized each other up the way men did by the grip of their handshake and the directness of their eye contact, she'd also suspected that her father felt more grateful than he'd let on when he'd thanked Parker for bringing her to him.

Parker, on the other hand, gave her the distinct feeling that he was less impressed than others might have been meeting one of the more recognized men in the world. Though his manner had been completely professional, she knew he believed her dad to be something less than honorable.

She needed to disabuse him of that thought. Which she did the moment they stepped into the cherrywood-paneled private elevator outside her father's office and the doors closed behind them. With Mikey between them, they turned to face the doors.

"The woman in the photos is his daughter."

Parker's head jerked toward her.

"You're kidding."

"He had an affair, but it was thirty years ago. Mom knows about it." It seemed odd to feel relieved by such news. It felt stranger still to have another sister. "Brad lied about having more incriminating photos."

"So that's what your was dad talking about. When he said you would fill me in about the pictures," he clarified. "You'd told him I knew what was going on."

"Actually, I told him you would have come to him yourself if I hadn't. He figured it out from there."

That threat was what had initially pushed her from him. The need to protect what he hadn't already claimed of her heart had made her keep that distance. From his hesitation before he glanced away, he seemed fully aware of those details.

"How did he react to that?"

"It's probably one of the reasons he liked you."

She glanced at his strong profile. His curiosity had suddenly turned to something that looked suspiciously like guilt. Not guilt for the way things had turned out between them. She'd known all along that he wouldn't stay. She just hadn't counted on the hope that had somehow emerged that he might not want to end it so soon. Or at all.

There was no sense in wanting the impossible, he'd once told her.

She wanted it anyway. But none of that had anything to do with his silence now.

After her dad had told him how grateful he was for talking her into seeing him, he had candidly admitted how pleased he was that Parker would be with her. The Kendricks had always done their best to avoid sensational publicity, but as Parker had already known, it would be necessary now. With the press intrusions that would surely follow after he came forward to expose Brad in the next couple of weeks, he was glad to know that his daughter would be in Parker's care.

Fully aware that he wouldn't be around for two more hours, much less two weeks, Parker's glance had faltered a moment before he had rather ambiguously assured him that Bennington's would be sure all the Kendricks were taken care of. Tess had simply looked away, much as she did now, and tried for the poise she desperately needed to hide how badly she did not want their relationship to be over.

With her focus on the descending numerals above the rich wood on the door, she waited for Parker to say something, anything, that might let her think this wasn't their final goodbye.

Five floors later, she couldn't take his silence any longer. Still watching the numbers, her heart seeming to sink right along with them, she murmured, "I'm not going to see you again, am I."

There was no question in her tone, only the flatness of conclusion.

From the corner of her eye she saw his broad shoulders rise beneath his dark gray suit jacket as he drew a deep breath.

"Let's not do this, Tess." He knew he had done what he could to help her. All that he could do, he insisted to himself. With not a single unmet promise between them, the last thing he should feel was that he was abandoning her somehow. There was no denying that feeling, though. It sat like a knot of lead behind his breastbone. "I've always been pretty lousy at goodbyes."

"That's okay." Her focus still on the panel, her fingers tightened around her little boy's warm hand. "I'm not good at them either. I know you only signed on temporarily…and I'm sure when you did that you didn't expect to take on a rehabilitation project."

She glanced over at him then, her smile feeling terribly brave. "But, for the record," she said, echoing the phrasing he'd used on occasion with her, "I'm really glad you did. I'm grateful for all you did for me, Parker. Everything," she insisted, because even as painful as it was to know he would no longer be with her, she was somehow stronger for knowing she could handle that loss on her own. Somehow. "Especially for not leaving me to live my life in exile."

"Tess…"

His too-blue eyes held hers. It was just impossible to read the expression in those guarded depths before a small voice came from below them.

"Won't I see you, too?"

It wasn't until she saw Mikey's worried expression that she realized she and Parker were both holding his hands. But there was no time for her to consider just how much her son would miss him or for Parker to respond to his concern. The elevator doors had just opened to expose the fluorescent lights and gray concrete pillars of the parking garage.

Ten yards away, a silver SUV much like the black one Parker had rented for her sat on the yellow stripes delineating a restricted area. In front of it, Stephanie Wyckowski straightened from where she'd leaned against the driver's door. Looking more like an older friend picking her up to go shopping than a woman with a black belt in karate, the bodyguard she'd had through most of college still wore her light brown hair in a sleek bob and apparently preferred tailored pantsuits to anything else.

As they stepped from the elevator, Parker swung Mikey up in his arms to carry him to his waiting colleague.

From behind him, she heard his easy, "Hey, Wyckowski."

"Hey, Bull."

"This is Mikey." He smiled at the towheaded child soberly watching him. "How about we get you into the car, sport?"

Pulling her smile from Tess to her child, Stephanie opened the back door. "We have a car seat right here."

Since Mikey didn't know Stephanie yet, Parker had thought he'd strap him in himself. He'd no sooner felt the little boy's hand on his cheek, however, when he found himself stopped cold.

With his back to Tess, he pulled Mikey's small hand away and folded it carefully in his. "You be good for your mom. Okay?"

"'Kay," came the quiet reply.

Reluctance tugged hard as he turned to his counterpart.

"Why don't you take care of him," he said and handed him over. The odd pang he'd felt knowing he wouldn't see the child again had caught him completely off guard. With his self-protective instincts jerking into place, he masked the urge he felt to hug the boy by ruffling his pale hair instead.

"Give me a minute," he said to the woman now responsible for the child and turned to the one standing ten feet away.

The reluctant sensation in his chest turned into something less definable.

He honestly hadn't thought about what he would say to Tess when they parted. He hadn't let himself think about it, actually. He'd just done what he always did when something got messy or complicated in his life and gone about his business, focusing on his team and the next task, booking himself for a fishing trip with a couple of buddies between upcoming projects to make sure he had no spare time on his hands and generally doing what Tess was doing so admirably. Moving on.

Now, with his back blocking her from Stephanie's view

as he walked over to where she cautiously watched him, he didn't know what he could say that would matter, anyway.

Tipping her head, she gave him a curious little smile.

"Doesn't anyone ever call you Jeff or Jeffrey?"

He smiled back, shook his head. She was going to make it easy. "Jeff. And only my family."

Tess saw his smile fade.

"We never got you a car," he reminded her. They'd run out of time. "When does Cord get back?"

"A week or so, I think."

"Have him help you. It's really just a matter of deciding what you want and picking up the phone."

"It's okay," she assured him. If she let herself think about it, there would suddenly be a dozen things they needed to say, to do, to ask. But they'd run out of time on them all. "I'll take care of it."

Of course she would, he thought. He didn't need to worry about her anymore. He especially didn't need to worry about what her ex was doing to her now that her dad was on board. She would have her life back soon. Her freedom. Her reputation. That was everything he'd wanted for her.

Behind him, he could hear her new bodyguard moving about. The closing of a door echoed in the low-ceilinged space. A moment later came a metallic click as another opened. The fluorescent lights buzzed overhead.

The harsh sounds seemed to fade as his glance skimmed over the fragile contours of Tess's face, the soft lashes lining her lovely eyes, the lush fullness of her mouth....

It was time to go.

"Take care of yourself, Tess."

He couldn't bear to leave without one last touch of her softness. The temptation to kiss her jerked hard. But he knew kissing her would be a really bad idea with his colleague right there and the ever-present possibility of paparazzi, so he told himself he'd have to settle for just touching her instead.

He'd barely lifted his hand toward her cheek when Tess stepped out of reach.

"Don't forget to call your mom. And your cousins," she reminded him, clutching the big bag hanging from her shoulder. "You'll get busy and forget, so make yourself a note."

She didn't wait for him to respond before he found himself listening to the tap of her heels on the concrete as she slipped past him and into the vehicle beside her son.

Wyckowski gave him a look of pure speculation.

"Take care of them," he said to her and turned away.

Ignoring the oddly hollow sensation in his chest, he strode with pure purpose to the black SUV parked a few cars away to head for the airport.

Another assignment complete, he insisted to himself. He would write his report on the plane, file it, get it out of his head and never take another individual-client assignment again. Not even as a favor to Cord. His heart was in the challenge of the big projects anyway, and those challenges were all he needed. Or so he told himself as he deliberately blocked the thought that absolutely nothing about his relationship with Tess Kendrick felt finished.

That feeling of incompleteness didn't budge. It lay in wait beneath the preoccupations of the day, rising when he least expected it: when he had coffee, because it reminded him of the morning she made her first pot; when he would see a young mother with her child; when someone had handed him a note in a meeting on pale green paper, because the notes she would leave for him on the kitchen island had always been on paper that color. And always the feeling emerged when the day was over and the physical craving he felt for her drove him from his bed to pace restlessly or to hit the treadmill in his condo the few nights he'd been home or the gym of whatever hotel he was in.

That unwanted feeling was there now as yet another meeting ended in a conference room of the pricey two-hundred-room hotel that had been wired from subbasement to satellite dish with surveillance equipment for the judicial conference beginning in two days. Final security checks had been run on both hotel personnel and the building. Half of the hotel staff had just been briefed with the security team. The other half would be briefed in the morning. He would then leave for meetings on projects in New York and Boston and catch a red-eye back if he was needed for anything there before returning to headquarters in Baltimore.

"Would you like to come to dinner later, Parker? Maybe go over anything we didn't cover here." Amber Chapman gave him a charming smile. "The food in our Terrace Room is exceptional."

Amber was the hotel manager. Unquestionably attractive in a corporate-businesswoman sort of way, she was sharp, savvy and single. He'd figured her to be a few years older than he was, close to but not quite forty, though she could give women ten years younger a run for their money. Her seriously short blond hair framed an ageless face, and her toned body had definite appeal. She'd also quietly made it known over the past couple of weeks that she was available if he was interested.

At one time he might have been, too, just for the recreational aspects of it. But that was before his mind had been invaded by a certain leggy brunette ten years his junior.

He smiled back. "We've covered everything my team can think of. But, thanks, I already have plans."

"Anything exciting?"

"Another meeting." He and his counterpart from the Marshal's service had a few things they needed to go over themselves, but that wouldn't be until later. In the meantime, there was something on television he needed to watch. It was that need that made him anxious to leave now. "How about we all celebrate with dinner when this is over?"

There was no mistaking the disappointment in Amber's expression. A group thing definitely wasn't what she'd had in mind. But she recovered in an instant, telling him she imagined a celebration would definitely be in order, and left him to head for the nearest place he could think of that had a television. He would have gone to his room if he'd had time. As it was, it was two minutes to six and the evening news was about to start.

He took the stairs rather than wait for an elevator and cut across the expansive lobby to the establishment's busy upscale lounge.

Weaving his way through the mostly occupied tables, aware of heads turning as they tended to do at the sight of a tall bald guy when he entered a room, he sat down on a stool in easy view of the television that hung from the wall at the end of the long bar. The bartender, who knew him from all the security drills, nodded to him from where he visited with the customers who'd crowded at the other end of the shiny wood surface.

Though he would have much preferred something in the eighty-proof range, Parker ordered a cola because he still had to work and turned his attention to the news anchor on the screen.

Edna, William Kendrick's secretary, had called him that morning to tell him Mr. Kendrick had called his press conference. Parker had called her himself last week to have her ask Mr. Kendrick if someone could let him know when the

conference was to take place. Apparently Tess's father felt
notifying him was the least he could do.

The television was on mute, but closed-captioning ran in
a continual line across the bottom of the screen. There was
another gasoline price hike. Another politician had caused
an uproar over yet another politically incorrect statement.
William Kendrick shocked the nation with revelations of
another child and allegations against his former son-in-law.

"Can you turn that up?"

Parker motioned to the television. Without a word, the bartender picked up a remote control and aimed it at the set. Over
the quiet conversations taking place around him, the volume
came up.

"...who'd married his daughter, Tess, four years ago. Our
cameras were there as the family stood united with him."

William Kendrick was on the screen. Beside him at a
bank of microphones stood his wife, the still-beautiful blonde
whose blood ran as blue as the Danube of old. Caught in a
wide shot, right behind them in a show of true family soli-
darity, stood his four children and their spouses. Gabe, the
governor of the state, and his pretty, petite wife, Addie, the
family's former groundskeeper. Cord, tanned, with Madison,
the caterer Parker had kept an eye on when the paparazzi had
realized how serious Cord was about her. Ashley, as blond
and regal-looking as her mother, with Matt Callaway, Cord's
friend and the man who'd requested Parker's services to
guard her when her security had been threatened after he'd
won her at a charity auction. Right behind her dad, flanked
by her brothers and, Parker suspected, not feeling anywhere
near as poised as she looked, stood Tess.

"...taken pictures of me with a young woman," William
was saying as the shot narrowed on him and his wife. "That
woman is my daughter. I had a relationship early in my mar-

riage but had no idea she existed until a year and a half ago. Bradley Ashworth misconstrued the situation, took the pictures and used them to keep Tess quiet about the mental and physical abuse he subjected her to during their marriage. That was the reason she left him. His abuse. Not," he emphasized, his anger checked but dangerously apparent, "because she was bored and wished to have relationships with other men.

"He is continuing to tarnish her reputation," he went on as the lights from cameras flashed in front of him, "by alleging that she refused to let him visit his son. The fact is, he never asked to see him. Had I any idea of his duplicity—"

A shot of the announcer replaced the videotape.

"The family took no questions," claimed the talking head, "so there is wide-range speculation about the identity of Kendrick's alleged third daughter. There is also speculation about whether or not Tess Kendrick will press charges against her former husband for defamation of character. No comment was immediately forthcoming from Bradley Ashworth.

"In entertainment news…"

The voice droned on as Parker's glance fell to the glass the bartender had set in front of him. At the other end of the bar, the conversation changed as those who'd watched with him grasped the breaking news and ran with it. He had no idea what they were saying.

Staring at the ice cubes, he waited for the relief that should have come. He needed a sense of closure where Tess was concerned. If anything should have given him that, it was having seen for himself that her father had kept his word and in knowing that Ashworth was toast.

He lifted his glass, promised himself a martini later and tipped the dark contents toward the edge, watching the bubbles rise. Now he could forget her, he told himself. Now that the truth was out, the press wouldn't let any member of the Kendrick or Ashworth family rest, but at least people would know what kind of woman Tess really was.

Protective. And loyal to a fault.

She was also stubborn, nurturing and dynamite in bed, and he really missed her smile, her spirit and her son. But he tried not to think about that as he set the glass down, tossed a few bills on the bar and shoved the unwanted thought to the back of his mind.

The relief and sense of closure never came. He never felt it once in the entire two weeks it took him to admit that his life wasn't anywhere near as together as he'd thought it was—and that he needed to talk to the woman who'd known him well enough to know he needed reminders to stay in touch with his family.

The Kendricks had been besieged by the press. That had been evident to Parker from the headlines and photos on all the tabloids at every newsstand he encountered. Much of that coverage dealt with speculation about why William's newly disclosed daughter hadn't identified herself, William's statement that she did not wish to be identified and a couple of women coming forth claiming to be his offspring. As for Tess's ex-husband, stories had emerged from interviews with friends and acquaintances ranging from disbelief to allegations of him having cheated on college exams. Except for one "No comment at this time," the Ashworth camp had been profoundly silent.

It seemed the members of the Ashworth family had all holed up from the press. So had Tess. After an interview where she'd refused to comment about what action she might take against her ex-husband, she'd told the world she was just relieved that the truth was out and gone into seclusion at the family estate with her mother.

Hiding from the hounds was what she was actually doing, Parker thought, but he'd just been relieved to know she was there rather than avoiding reporters alone in her new home.

A pack of those reporters and photographers were lying in wait a short distance from the main gate of the estate. A security guard parked a few yards away kept them at bay. That guard stepped from his truck when Parker pulled up in his rental car to the stone pillar holding the intercom and keypad that allowed access. Parker knew the access code. He also knew that he no longer had the right to use it.

Aware of the press surging forward to see who'd just arrived, Parker fixed his focus on the uniformed sentry, gave him his name and asked if the guard wanted to call up to the house to get permission for him to enter or if he should use the phone in the call box himself.

The guard asked for identification, which made points with Parker, then checked it over, handed it back without comment and picked up the phone to call up to the mansion.

"The secret is not to overmix your dry ingredients with the butter and eggs, otherwise your cookies will be hard. Do you want to start with chocolate-chip?" Olivia asked over the ring of the telephone. "Or start with oatmeal? You can decide while I answer that."

Tess leaned against the island in the middle of the kitchen, her focus on the cookbook her mother's pleasantly plump cook had handed her. For as long as Tess could remember, the woman wearing a white blouse and apron, black slacks and athletic shoes had fed the Kendrick clan. Her marvelous food ranged from down-home to gourmet, and her presentations ranged from basic to art—which was why Tess asked a couple of weeks ago if she could help her prepare some of the meals.

Olivia's reaction to the request had been similar to Ina's when Tess had declined her help that first day back. Surprise, followed by curiosity. As much as Olivia loved to cook, she'd been more than happy to share her passion, and Tess's repertoire had grown under her tutelage. It wasn't the same as working with Parker. But then, nothing was.

She had spent the past three weeks and five days trying valiantly to not think about how badly she missed being with him, being held by him, talking with him. It didn't help that Mikey, who stood on a stool beside her preparing to help, had asked about him every single day for those first three weeks. Or that she couldn't think about the progress on her new home without wanting to share her excitement with him, then feeling that excitement ebb because he wouldn't be there with her. It didn't matter that he'd never, ever, given her reason to think he would be, as she kept reminding herself. But she couldn't deny that the unrealistic little hope had seeded itself the moment she'd realized he'd found the perfect place for her. Without him, things simply didn't feel…complete.

"Miss Tess?" The woman with the short, ruthlessly permed salt-and-pepper hair held her hand over the phone's mouthpiece. "There's a Mr. Parker at the gate. Do you know him?"

Tess's heart bumped her breastbone a scant second before her son exclaimed, "Mr. Parker? He's here?"

"Jeff Parker?" she asked, disbelieving. "From Bennington's?"

No one other than her family knew of the pivotal role Parker had played in the events of the past few weeks. Because of that, the name meant nothing to Olivia. Looking puzzled by Mikey's enthusiasm, she turned back to the phone.

"That's him," she said a moment later. "He wants to see

you." Her finger hovered above the button on the wall that would open the gate. "Shall I let him in?"

"Please."

Reaching behind her back, she untied the apron Olivia had loaned her, then bent to take Mikey's hands in hers.

"Honey, I need you to stay here. Olivia, will you keep him with you while I answer the door?"

"Of course I will." With the button pushed, she set the phone back on its port. Smiling at the child the entire staff doted on, she pulled a large ceramic bowl from a cupboard and set it on the island in front of him. "We'll just get our ingredients together and wait for you."

There was some discussion between Mikey and Olivia about which type of cookie to make, but none of it registered to Tess as she smoothed the cream-colored pullover she wore with matching capris and headed down the hall, through the butler's door and into the foyer. The route was more direct than going through the family breakfast and formal dining rooms, though she wasn't all that sure why she felt the need to hurry.

She had no idea why Parker was here. She wasn't sure, either, which desire was greater now that he was—the desire to see him or the need to protect herself from the feeling of loss that she'd yet to escape and that would undoubtedly feel raw all over again when he left. Rising through that confusion was the need to deny the hope that lingered despite all logic and sat waiting to either be crushed or set free.

Through the leaded-glass windows flanking the double doors she saw a dark sedan come up the drive and pull under the portico. With the need to protect herself winning out, she waited a full fifteen seconds after he knocked to open the door.

It seemed he hadn't expected her to open the door herself. Wearing an open-collared blue shirt that did incredible things for his eyes, he looked big, commanding and impossibly handsome, which he always had to her, and decidedly hesitant, which wasn't like him at all.

"Did Stephanie tell you I was coming?"

Confusion joined caution. "Was she supposed to?"

"I called this morning to see if you'd be here. I thought maybe she'd mentioned it."

"I haven't seen her since breakfast," she said. "She's on an errand for me."

A muscle in his jaw jerked.

They hadn't budged from the doorway.

Stepping back as much to escape the tension surrounding him as to allow him entry, she motioned him inside.

She hadn't moved far enough. That tension grazed her nerves as he walked past her, seeming to become her own as she closed the door and watched him stop near the middle of the foyer. Turning to face her, his guarded glance swept her face, the length of her body, then moved around the high-ceilinged space with its enormous spray of gladiolus in the urn on the center table. His focus had no sooner settled back on her than Mikey came racing through the butler's door.

Yelling "Mr. Parker!" he launched himself into the man's suddenly outstretched arms.

Mikey grinned from ear to ear as Parker scooped him up. "Did you come to see me?"

The normally unflappable man seemed totally disarmed. With his arm across the little boy's bottom to support him and looking up because Mikey's head was above his own, Parker chuckled. "I sure did. I came to see your mom, too."

"Do you want to see my new trike?"

Tess stepped forward. "Mikey," she murmured, preparing to take him.

"How about I come see it in a while? If it's okay with your

mom," he qualified, lowering the child's feet to the floor. "I need to talk to her first."

Crouched in front of her son, Tess took him by his little shoulders and gently turned him to face her. She had never seen him so delighted to see anyone. Clearly his silence the past five days about the man towering beside them didn't mean he'd forgotten his friend.

"You're supposed to help Miss Olivia while Parker and I talk," she reminded him. "Stay in the kitchen. Okay?"

"I'm sorry, Miss Tess." Olivia bustled through the butler's door, the soft soles of her shoes chattering like mice on the marble. "I turned to get the eggs and he was gone." She held out her hand to the boy as Tess rose. Only then, with her glance already in the vicinity of Parker's powerful thighs, did she lift it to his wide chest, wider shoulders and up to his face. She seemed to get stuck on his arresting features a moment before she jerked her glance to his shaved head.

Tess could easily imagine the older woman mentally muttering, *Now there's a big one* as she gave him a polite smile and hurried off with her budding little baker in tow.

The butler's door closed.

"Is anyone else here?" he asked, sounding as if he might be hoping for a little privacy.

"The chauffeur just took Mom into Richmond to meet Dad."

"What about Ina?"

"Stephanie took her to the new house to clean it. I'd have done it myself, but every time I leave, I get followed."

Parker's brow lowered. "Why did Stephanie take her?"

"Because I asked her to. Ina would have driven herself, but anyone who leaves here gets followed by a reporter looking for any quote they can get about all that's going on. I don't want her hassled."

They took care of those who took care of them. That had

always been her mother's motto. If she could ever trust anyone outside this house to work for her, it would again be hers, too.

Having just assured himself that the potential for interruption was minimal, Parker shifted his concentration to his concerns about her. Those concerns had been there ever since her father's press conference.

"How bad has the press been here?"

One slender shoulder lifted in a philosophical shrug. "Things have quieted down in the past few days. But they'll probably get crazy again tomorrow. Brad is to issue the statement his lawyers worked out with ours."

"Are you okay with whatever it is they've come up with?"

"I am," she quietly confirmed. "Dad's not. He would rather see him prosecuted. All I really care about is that he's out of my life."

She crossed her arms over the design beaded into her top, turned away to pace. It was surprisingly easy to confide such details to him. But then, talking to him had always felt right. Aside from that little phenomenon, none of what was happening now would be happening at all had it not been for him. He deserved to know how everything had worked out.

"He's to make a public apology in exchange for me not pressing charges in a civil suit. I'm not sure what the district attorney came up with as far as a criminal action, but I'm not sure it matters. The rumors around here are that he's already somewhere in South America."

"So he might not make the apology at all."

"I'm not counting on it. But that doesn't matter either. If he doesn't show up, he's as good as admitted his guilt."

Parker watched her move to the table centered in the entry, touch a bloom, walk back toward him. He'd hoped for something a little more spectacular for Ashworth. Public flogging had come to mind. But since that particular form of punishment had been abandoned by the courts, he'd had to scale his fantasy to the current justice system.

From what Tess had told him, it sounded as if Ashworth might have thwarted that, too. But if he had left the country, he really hadn't gotten away with much. There was even a certain poetic justice in Tess's ex-husband's fate. Not only had his reputation and golden-boy image already been shot to hell, he was the one now living his life in exile.

Knowing how badly Tess wanted to get past the last few years, he took a certain satisfaction in that knowledge.

With that satisfaction came an even greater relief for her.

"Either way, you get your life back."

"Exactly," she murmured.

"I hope it won't be long before that happens."

He'd seen how the reactions of others had affected her. He knew how much pain they had caused. But now, beneath her guardedness came a small smile.

"It's already started," she told him. In big ways and small, she'd noticed the changes in people's attitudes toward her. Her family had simply been alternately relieved and outraged, but when she'd finally explained about her marriage and the blackmail, they had collectively understood her silence.

Her mother had also apologized profusely for dismissing the unhappiness she and her sister had sensed early in her marriage. She'd said she honestly thought every marriage had an adjustment period. Heaven knew—along with the rest of the world now—that hers had. The world just didn't know those details. Believing that marriage and its dynamics were the business only of the partners in it, she'd figured Tess's marital difficulties were none of her business either. She had, however, made her and Ashley both promise that if there was ever again a serious problem they needed help with, they would confide in her or in each other—and pride be damned. A woman alone was a warrior. Two women were an army.

Then there were the changes in Tess's friends and associates. Ginny had apologized outright for believing the worst about her—and immediately told everyone that she'd been working with Tess all along. A few old friends had called to express their regret for what she'd been through. During her only shopping trip into Camelot the other day, a shop owner and his staff had done as other locals had occasionally done in the past for her and her family when the press was being particularly pesky and banded around her to block a reporter who'd followed her inside. But what mattered to her most was how her acceptance by others affected her son.

"Pamela Whiting called the day after the press conference." And nearly tripped over herself apologizing, too. "Mikey is now on the admissions list for La Petite Academie." Near the top, Tess suspected, though she'd made it apparent to Pamela that she didn't expect special treatment. *Fair* was all she wanted.

Parker smiled at that news, the kind of smile that told her he was genuinely pleased with what he heard. She didn't doubt that he was pleased, either, for Mikey's sake. A bond had clearly grown there. Yet she felt herself grow even more self-protective.

"Is that why you're here?" she finally asked, needing to know. "To check up on us?"

The unfamiliar hesitation she'd seen in him when she'd opened the door moved into his expression once more. Along with it came a certain self-protectiveness of his own.

"That's part of it," he admitted.

"And the other part?"

He hated the distance between them. Only a few feet of

marble separated them. As badly as he needed to touch her, even that felt like a mile.

He took a step closer. That need felt as essential to him as his next breath. But he had no idea if his touch would be welcome. The last time he'd reached for her, she'd pulled away.

Jamming his hands into the pockets of his khakis, he quietly searched her face.

"I wanted to know if you still want a normal life for yourself and your son. Normal in the relative sense," he qualified, since they both knew certain restrictions would always exist with wealth and recognition.

Feeling as cautious as he looked, Tess tightened her arms around herself. "That's exactly what I want." He knew that. He was probably the only person on the planet who did know how badly she wanted that, too.

"Even now that you're back in the good graces with your family and friends?"

"That's something I wanted even before all this started. I've never been good at the public stuff. Not the way Mom and Ashley are." Which was one of the reasons she'd been such a huge disappointment to her ex, she'd long since realized. She was more a behind-the-scenes type. That was why she'd had such a passion for her preschool project. But Parker knew that, too.

"Why?" she asked, searching him back.

Parker was accustomed to feeling in control, in charge. He definitely didn't feel that way now. He thought he had prepared himself. He thought he knew what he was going to say. But he'd never laid himself on the line before, and the reality was infinitely more stress-inducing than planning the strategy. This woman held his heart in her hands.

She had once asked if he ever wished he could go back to a particular point in his life and choose a different direction.

He'd thought then about the void he sometimes felt deep inside. That void had opened as wide as the Pacific when he'd left her. The last thing he wanted was to someday look back at this point in time and regret not asking her to stay in his life.

He just wished she would give him something, anything, to let him know he wasn't about to make a fool of himself.

"Because I thought we might be able to find that life together," he finally admitted, going for broke. "If you think what we had has anywhere to go."

He knew he had given her no reason to expect anything at all from him, so he had no idea what to expect from her now. As it was, all he saw in the delicate lines of her face was a faintly shell-shocked look that allowed him the time he needed to either back down or strengthen his case.

"You can stop me anytime here," he told her.

Her response was the definite negative shake of her head.

Encouraged by the fact that she hadn't stopped him cold, he took a step closer.

"You'd thanked me for all I taught you." Caving in to the need for contact, he pulled his hand from his pocket and skimmed his fingers over her cheek. "But whatever you learned from me was nothing compared to what I learned from you."

Almost instinctively her head moved toward his touch.

That telling reaction was all the sign he'd needed. Feeling more relieved than he thought possible that she hadn't moved away, he drew the first full breath he'd taken since she'd opened the door and traced the shape of her jaw with his fingers. "I saw everything differently when I was with you, Tess. Things I took for granted."

When she'd needed a house, instead of looking for a building that could be wired to protect those inside, he'd found himself searching out a home. When he'd been with her and Mikey, he hadn't simply seen an incredible woman and a great little kid, he'd seen them as a man might see a wife and a son. He'd thought, too, that he'd known all there was to know about loyalty and commitment, until she'd made him see that he was avoiding the most important commitment of all.

"I hadn't realized how badly I wanted a family until I met you," he admitted. He might well have gone forever denying that if it hadn't been for her, too. He hadn't wanted to make the same mistakes his father had made, but he'd never made it past the idea that he had to choose between his profession and family. Not until he'd met the woman who'd shown him how much he was missing from his life— and that he could care deeply about both. That was the key: the caring. It had been there with her almost from the day they'd met.

"I'm not pushing for anything right now," he insisted, remembering what had happened the last time he had pressed her. "Honest. I just need to know if we have a chance."

Ten minutes ago, Tess couldn't have imagined anything that would take away the sense of loss she'd felt when he'd walked away. Now that empty sensation was filled with something that felt suspiciously like the hope she had tried so uselessly to suppress.

"Oh, Parker," she murmured, too stunned to know what else to say.

It seemed that was enough. Something darted through his eyes as his hands slipped to her waist—relief, she thought, but he turned his head toward the butler's door just then, stealing the possibility of her knowing for sure as Mikey came running in again.

"Mr. Parker? Can you see my tricycle now?"

Tess felt Parker's hands reluctantly move from her waist.

"Give me five minutes," he said.

"Not now?"

"Not now," he replied, smiling as Mikey came closer.

"Why?" he wanted to know.

What Parker had heard in Tess's voice more than made up for her child's lousy timing. Crouching in front of the little boy he'd missed almost as much as he had the child's mother, he clasped his hands between his knees. "Because I want to tell your mom something first."

"What is it?"

He pulled him closer, bent his head to his little ear. "That I love her," he whispered, smiling at the scents of bath soap and orange juice. "Now go play."

Mikey clearly hadn't a clue why his friend was whispering. Pulling back, looking utterly puzzled, he tipped his head.

"Do you love me, too?"

Parker's hand covered the top of Mikey's head. "Yeah, sport," he muttered, ruffling the child's cornsilk hair. "I do. Now give me a minute. Okay?"

Appeased, at least momentarily, Mikey grinned and wandered back to the door just as Olivia appeared once more.

"I'm so sorry, Miss Tess." Pure speculation danced in her eyes as Parker rose. "I don't understand why he won't stay with me," she murmured and coaxed him back into the kitchen with her.

Tess understood completely. The child was excited that his friend was back. There were things he wanted to show him. Things he wanted to share.

Parker turned to find Tess staring at him. The hope he'd seen in her eyes had just merged with a caution.

"Did you mean that?" she asked.

He didn't blame her for her wariness. Her son meant the

world to her. She was as protective of him as he felt about them both.

"Yeah," he murmured, lifting his hand to trace the line of her jaw once more. He felt better when he was touching her. He felt even better when she was touching him back. "I've never meant anything more in my life, Tess. I love him. I love you," he admitted, wondering at how easily the words came. "I want to marry you." He needed her to know that up front. "And I promise," he said, aware of her quick breath at his admission, "that you're both safe with me in every way that matters."

Tess's hand fisted the fabric of his shirt as her eyes searched his. He knew exactly what she needed to hear. Yet, with him, the words really weren't necessary. She had trusted him from the very beginning.

"So," he coaxed, lifting his hand to smooth back her hair. "That chance I asked about. How is it looking so far?"

Her heart felt as if it might pound right out of her chest as she rose on tiptoe and curved her arms around his neck. He wanted to marry her. He wanted them to be a family. Heaven knew how very much she wanted that, too.

"Not bad," she murmured, her smile breaking free. Sighing inside when his strong arms finally closed around her, that smile turned as warm as sunshine. "Since I love you, too."

Something primitive flashed in his eyes. It might have been possession. It might have simply been need. When his hand slowly framed her face and his mouth covered hers, she felt both in the kiss that altered her heart rate and her breathing, and was left with no doubt that with this man was exactly where she was supposed to be.

With her body stretched the length of his, she smiled as he lifted his head. "If this is what I get," she murmured, curving her hand to the side of his face, "I'll have to tell you that more often."

Parker turned his head, kissed her palm. Fitting her against him, wondering at how incredible she felt in his arms, he drew her closer. This was the closure he'd been looking for. Only it wasn't an end. It was the continuation of something that felt very much as if it had been meant to be all along.

"Promise?" he asked.

"Promise," she whispered back—and heard him chuckle against her mouth when the persistent little boy he loved as his own came back in wanting a hug, too.

\* \* \* \* \*

*Look for the next book in Christine Flynn's miniseries*
*THE KENDRICKS OF CAMELOT*
*In June 2007.*
*Available wherever Silhouette Books are sold.*

*Turn the page for a sneak preview of*
*IF I'D NEVER KNOWN YOUR LOVE*
*by*
*Georgia Bockoven*

*From the brand-new series*
*Harlequin Everlasting Love*
*Every great love has a story to tell.* ™

*One year, five months and four days missing*

There's no way for you to know this, Evan, but I haven't written to you for a few months. Actually, it's been almost a year. I had a hard time picking up a pen once more after we paid the second ransom and then received a letter saying it wasn't enough. I was so sure you were coming home that I took the kids along to Bogotá so they could fly home with you and me, something I swore I'd never do. I've fallen in love with Colombia and the people who've opened their hearts to me. But fear is a constant companion when I'm there. I won't ever expose our children to that kind of danger again.

I'm at a loss over what to do anymore, Evan. I've begged and pleaded and thrown temper tantrums with

every official I can corner both here and at home.
They've been incredibly tolerant and understanding, but
in the end as ineffectual as the rest of us.

I try to imagine what your life is like now, what you
do every day, what you're wearing, what you eat. I want
to believe that the people who have you are misguided
yet kind, that they treat you well. It's how I survive day
to day. To think of you being mistreated hurts too much.
If I picture you locked away somewhere and suffering,
a weight descends on me that makes it almost impossible to get out of bed in the morning.

Your captors surely know you by now. They have
to recognize what a good man you are. I imagine you
working with their children, telling them that you have
children, too, showing them the pictures you carry in
your wallet. Can't the men who have you understand
how much your children miss you? How can it not
matter to them?

How can they keep you away from us all this time?
Over and over, we've done what they asked. Are they
oblivious to the depth of their cruelty? What kind of
people are they that they don't care?

I used to keep a calendar beside our bed next to the
peach rose you picked for me before you left. Every
night I marked another day, counting how many you'd
been gone. I don't do that any longer. I don't want to
be reminded of all the days we'll never get back.

When I can't sleep at night, I tell you about my day.
I imagine you hearing me and smiling over the details
that make up my life now. I never tell you how defeated
I feel at moments or how hard I work to hide it from
everyone for fear they will see it as a reason to stop believing you are coming home to us.

And I couldn't tell you about the lump I found in my breast and how difficult it was going through all the tests without you here to lean on. The lump was benign—the process reaching that diagnosis utterly terrifying. I couldn't stop thinking about what would happen to Shelly and Jason if something happened to me.

We need you to come home.

I'm worn down with missing you.

I'm going to read this tomorrow and will probably tear it up or burn it in the fireplace. I don't want you to get the idea I ever doubted what I was doing to free you or thought the work a burden. I would gladly spend the rest of my life at it, even if, in the end, we only had one day together.

You are my life, Evan.

I will love you forever.

\* \* \* \* \*

*Don't miss this deeply moving Harlequin Everlasting Love story about a woman's struggle to bring back her kidnapped husband from Colombia and her turmoil over whether to let go, finally, and welcome another man into her life.*
*IF I'D NEVER KNOWN YOUR LOVE*
*by Georgia Bockoven*
*is available March 27, 2007.*

*And also look for*
*THE NIGHT WE MET*
*by Tara Taylor Quinn,*
*a story about finding love*
*when you least expect it.*

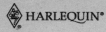

**HARLEQUIN® Romance®**

presents a brand-new trilogy by

# PATRICIA THAYER

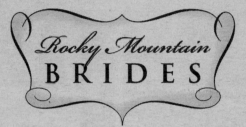

*Rocky Mountain*
# B R I D E S

**Three sisters come home to wed.**

*In April don't miss*
## Raising the Rancher's Family,

*followed by*

### The Sheriff's Pregnant Wife,
*on sale May 2007,*

**and**

### A Mother for the Tycoon's Child,
*on sale June 2007.*

# From *New York Times* bestselling author
# SHERRYL WOODS

## *The Sweet Magnolias*

**February 2007**

**March 2007**

April 2007

# SAVE
# $1.⁰⁰ off the purchase price of any book
in *The Sweet Magnolias* trilogy.

Offer valid from February 1, 2007 to April 30, 2007. Redeemable
at participating retail outlets. Limit one coupon per purchase.

5 2 6 0 7 6 0 2

5 65373 00076 2    (8100) 0 11383

MSWSMT07

# REQUEST YOUR FREE BOOKS!
## 2 FREE NOVELS PLUS 2 FREE GIFTS!

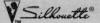

# SPECIAL EDITION®
## Life, Love and Family!

**YES!** Please send me 2 FREE Silhouette Special Edition® novels and my 2 FREE gifts. After receiving them, if I don't wish to receive any more books, I can return the shipping statement marked "cancel." If I don't cancel, I will receive 6 brand-new novels every month and be billed just $4.24 per book in the U.S., or $4.99 per book in Canada, plus 25¢ shipping and handling per book and applicable taxes, if any*. That's a savings of at least 15% off the cover price! I understand that accepting the 2 free books and gifts places me under no obligation to buy anything. I can always return a shipment and cancel at any time. Even if I never buy another book from Silhouette, the two free books and gifts are mine to keep forever.

235 SDN EEYU   335 SDN EEY6

| | | |
|---|---|---|
| Name | (PLEASE PRINT) | |
| Address | | Apt. |
| City | State/Prov. | Zip/Postal Code |

Signature (if under 18, a parent or guardian must sign)

Mail to the **Silhouette Reader Service™**:
**IN U.S.A.**: P.O. Box 1867, Buffalo, NY 14240-1867
**IN CANADA**: P.O. Box 609, Fort Erie, Ontario L2A 5X3

Not valid to current Silhouette Special Edition subscribers.

**Want to try two free books from another line?**
**Call 1-800-873-8635 or visit www.morefreebooks.com.**

* Terms and prices subject to change without notice. NY residents add applicable sales tax. Canadian residents will be charged applicable provincial taxes and GST. This offer is limited to one order per household. All orders subject to approval. Credit or debit balances in a customer's account(s) may be offset by any other outstanding balance owed by or to the customer. Please allow 4 to 6 weeks for delivery.

**Your Privacy:** Silhouette is committed to protecting your privacy. Our Privacy Policy is available online at www.eHarlequin.com or upon request from the Reader Service. From time to time we make our lists of customers available to reputable firms who may have a product or service of interest to you. If you would prefer we not share your name and address, please check here. ☐

# Silhouette®

## Romantic
# SUSPENSE

### Excitement, danger and passion guaranteed!

*USA TODAY* bestselling author
## Marie Ferrarella
is back with the second installment
in her popular miniseries,
*The Doctors Pulaski: Medicine
just got more interesting...*
DIAGNOSIS: DANGER is on sale
April 2007 from Silhouette®
Romantic Suspense (formerly
Silhouette Intimate Moments).

*Look for it wherever
you buy books!*